KT-474-379

f Words

(2008), *Vis ... ... of Days* (2014, winner of the Independent Foreign Fiction Prize), and *Go, Went, Gone* (2017), all published by
Portobello. Her fiction is published in twenty-six languages.

SUSAN BERNOFSKY has translated works by Robert Walser, Hermann
Hesse, Gregor von Rezzori, Yoko Tawada, Ludwig Harig and Franz
Kafka. Her translation of Jenny Erpenbeck's *The Old Child and Other Stories*
was awarded the 2006 Helen and Kurt Wolff Translator's Prize.

From the reviews of *Go, Went, Gone*:

'A highly sophisticated work about how blatant injustice exists together
with forces that lurk beneath the surface . . . With extraordinary emotional
power, [Erpenbeck's] analytical skills are now matched by a tenderness to
human beings that remains utterly unsentimental' *Spectator*

'Susan Bernofsky's finely crafted translation . . . reaches Anglophone
readers at an opportune moment . . . Erpenbeck binds the upheavals of
past and present, Europe and Africa. Lyrical and satirical by turns, she
shows that fearful isolation, emotional or political, hurts wall-builders
and wall-jumpers alike' *Economist*

'[In] this wise, moving novel . . . Erpenbeck demands that her fellow
countrymen show compassion to those whose lives have been "cut off, as
if with a knife"' *Metro*

'Acclaimed novelist Jenny Erpenbeck has gone further than most in
examining the ephemeral nature of human life . . . Ultimately Erpenbeck
– wise, caring and profound – triumphs in this heart-rending plea for
universal tolerance and respect' *Big Issue*

'[It] takes us, with immense storytelling skills and quiet, effective restraint
into the depths of the lives of others' 'Best Books of the Year', selected
by Marina Warner, *TLS*

'A deeply thoughtful and involving novel about migrancy now . . .
grippingly interrogatory fiction' 'Best Books of 2017' chosen by Helen
Simpson, *Observer*

'A remarkable novel which questions our understanding of borders and
identity and which calls above all for compassion' *Skinny*

'Superb . . . told in sparsely lyrical prose [this] book is a powerful and
compassionate response to the ongoing crisis' *Literary Review*

JENNY ERPENBECK

Go, Went, Gone

Translated from the German by Susan Bernofsky

Portobello
Books

First published in Great Britain by Portobello Books in 2017
This paperback edition published by Portobello Books in 2018

Portobello Books
12 Addison Avenue
London W11 4QR

 The translation of this work was supported by a grant from the Goethe-Institut, which is funded by the German Ministry of Foreign Affairs.

This book has been selected to receive financial assistance from English PEN's "PEN Translates" programme, supported by Arts Council England. English PEN exists to promote literature and our understanding of it, to uphold writers' freedoms around the world, to campaign against the persecution and imprisonment of writers for stating their views, and to promote the friendly co-operation of writers and the free exchange of ideas. www.englishpen.org

A CIP catalogue record for this book is available from the British Library.

1 3 5 7 9 10 8 6 4 2

ISBN 978 1 84627 622 4
eISBN 978 1 84627 621 7

Offset by Avon DataSet Ltd, Bidford on Avon, Warwickshire
Printed and bound by CPI Group (UK) Ltd, Croydon, CR0 4YY

www.portobellobooks.com

For Wolfgang
For Franz
For my friends

God made the bulk; surfaces were invented by the devil.

–WOLFGANG PAULI

Even if it's driving me crazy, I have to really force myself to kill an insect. I don't know if it's out of pity. I don't think so. Maybe it's just a matter of getting used to certain states of affairs and then attempting to find one's place among these existing states, an acquiescence.

–HEINER MÜLLER

Go, Went, Gone

1

Perhaps many more years still lie before him, or perhaps only a few. In any case, from now on Richard will no longer have to get up early to appear at the Institute. As of today, he has time—plain and simple. Time to travel, people say. To read books. Proust. Dostoevsky. Time to listen to music. He doesn't know how long it'll take him to get used to having time. In any case, his head still works just the same as before. What's he going to do with the thoughts still thinking away inside his head? He's had his share of success. And now? At least what passes for success. He's published books and been invited to conferences, his lectures always filled up. Students were assigned his books to read, highlighting passages to learn by heart for their exams. Where are his students now? Some hold junior faculty positions, two or three are even tenured. Others he hasn't heard about in years.

There's one he's still friendly with, and a few others drop him a line periodically. That's how it is.

From his desk, he sees the lake.

Richard makes coffee.

Cup in hand, he goes out to the backyard to check for new molehills.

The lake lies placid before him, as it has all summer long.

Richard is waiting but he doesn't know for what. Time is now completely different. Suddenly different. He thinks. And then he thinks that, obviously, he can't stop thinking. The thinking is what he is, and at the same time it's the machine that governs him. Even if he's all alone with his head now, he can't just stop thinking, obviously. Even if no one gives a hoot what he thinks.

For a brief moment he imagines an owl using its beak to flip the pages of his study, *The Concept of the World in the Work of Lucretius*.

He goes back in.

He asks himself whether it's too warm to be wearing a blazer. Does he even need a blazer if he's just puttering around the house alone?

Years ago, when he learned by chance that his lover was cheating on him, the only thing that helped him get over his disappointment was turning this disappointment into work. For months, he made her behavior his object of inquiry. He wrote almost a hundred pages, investigating all the factors that led up to the betrayal, as well as the way in which the young woman had carried it out. His work had no particular impact on their relationship, as she left him for good not long after. But still these labors got him through the first few months after his discovery, months in which he'd felt truly miserable. The best cure for love—as Ovid knew centuries ago—is work.

But now he's being tormented, not by time filled with pointless love but by time itself. Time is supposed to pass, but also not pass. For an instant he has a vision of a furious owl tearing apart a book entitled *On Waiting* with its beak and talons.

Maybe a cardigan is more appropriate to his new condition. More comfortable, at any rate. And seeing that he no longer goes out in human society on a daily basis, it's surely no longer necessary for him to shave every single morning. Let grow what will. Just stop putting up resistance—or is that how dying begins? Could dying begin with this kind of growth? No, that can't be right, he thinks.

They still haven't found the man at the bottom of the lake. It wasn't suicide. He died in a swimming accident. Ever since that day in June, the lake has been placid. Day after day, it's been perfectly calm. Calm in June. Calm in July. And even now, with autumn on the way, it remains calm. No rowboats, no shrieking children, no fishermen. This summer, anyone diving headfirst off the dock at the public beach could only be an outsider who hasn't heard yet. While this bather is drying off after his swim, a local might address him who's out walking her dog, or a bicyclist who dismounts for a moment to ask: So you don't know? Richard has never mentioned the accident to an unsuspecting visitor: what would be the point? Why ruin things for someone who's just trying to enjoy the day? Strangers who walk past his garden gate on their outings return just as happy as they came.

But he can't avoid seeing the lake when he sits at his desk.

On the day it happened, he was in the city—at the Institute, even though it was Sunday. That was back when he still had the master key that he's meanwhile turned in. It was one of those weekends he'd spent trying to gradually empty out his office. All the drawers, the cabinets. At around one forty-five p.m., he had just been taking books from the shelves, the floor, the sofa, the armchair, the small table, and packing them into boxes. Twenty, twenty-five books at the bottom of each box, and on top of them things that weighed less: manuscripts, letters, paper clips, folders, old newspaper clippings. Pencils, pens, erasers, the letter scale. There'd been two rowboats nearby, but none of the people seated in them had the impression there was anything amiss. They saw the man waving his arm and thought it was a joke, they rowed off, leaving him behind—or so he's heard. But no one knows who was in the rowboats. A few strong young men, apparently, who might have saved the day. But no one knows who they are. Or maybe they were afraid the man would pull them down with him, who knows.

His secretary had offered to help him pack. Thanks so much, but . . . Somehow it seemed that all these people—even, or maybe especially, the ones who liked him—were intent on ejecting him from their field of vision as quickly as possible. For this reason, he preferred to do the packing on his own, on Saturdays and Sundays, when the Institute was quiet. It took a great deal of time to pull out all these things, some of which had stood for years on shelves or lain in drawers unseen, and to decide whether to put them in a big, blue garbage bag or one of the boxes he planned to take home. Despite himself, he kept flipping through this or that manuscript, reading for fifteen or even thirty minutes at a time. One student's term paper on *The Odyssey*, book 11. Another—by a student he'd been a bit in love with—on "Levels of Meaning in Ovid's *Metamorphoses*."

Then one day in early August there'd been a reception with several speeches on the occasion of his retirement. The secretary, some of his colleagues, and even he himself had tears in their eyes, but no one—not even he—had actually cried. After all, everyone got old sooner or later. *Was* old sooner or later. In previous years, it had often fallen to him to give the speeches marking these departures, often he'd been the one to discuss with the secretary how many hors d'oeuvres, and whether there should be wine or champagne, orange juice or sparkling water. Now someone else had taken care of these arrangements. Everything would still function without him. That too was his doing. During the past several months, he'd frequently been forced to hear what a worthy successor would be replacing him, such an excellent choice (one he'd helped make); he too would praise the young man whenever the subject came up, as if he himself were among those looking forward to the man's arrival, unflinchingly uttering the name that would soon replace his own on the departmental letterhead. Starting in the fall, this successor would take over his lectures, using the lesson plans that he himself—now a professor emeritus—had set down in the weeks before his departure, preparing for this time that would have to get along without him.

The one departing must arrange his own departure, that's how it's always been, but only now does he realize that he never fully understood what that meant. He doesn't really understand it now either. He can't even comprehend that his departure is just a part of everyday life for all the others—only for him is it an ending. Every time someone's said to him during these past few months how sad it is, what a shame, how unimaginable that he'll be leaving soon, he's found it difficult to respond with the expected emotion, since the laments uttered by this person ostensibly devastated by his imminent departure only demonstrate clearly that the sad, unimaginable fact of this departure—a crying shame!—has already been accepted as inevitable.

All that remained of the appetizer trays served at the Institute on the occasion of his departure were the parsley sprigs and a few rolls with salmon—in this heat, people were no doubt wary of the fish. The lake that now lies gleaming before him always knew more than he did, it seems to him, even though it's his profession to ponder things. *Was* his profession? It makes no difference to the lake whether it's a fish decomposing beneath its surface or a human being.

The day after the reception was the start of the summer holiday, one person was traveling here, another there—he alone had no travel plans, since the process of gutting his office, with its many years of growth, was now entering its final phase.

Two weeks later, the boards from the bookshelves stood against the wall, tied together with twine, the packed boxes were stacked behind the door, and the few pieces of furniture he planned to have delivered to his home were piled in a small, awkward heap in the middle of the floor. A broom with warped bristles leaned against it, a pair of scissors lay on the windowsill beside a dusty envelope, four and a half large trash bags of detritus stood in a corner, a roll of tape lay on the floor, there were still a few nails sticking out of the wall, bereft of their pictures. Finally, he turned in his key to the Institute.

Now all he has to do is find the right spot in the house for each piece of furniture, open the boxes, and incorporate their contents into his private realm. *Bone to bone, blood to blood, as if bonded together.* That's right, the Merseburg Incantations. This too—what's known as learning: all he knows, everything he's ever studied—is now his own private property and nothing more. Since yesterday, everything's been down in the basement, waiting. But what would a day well-suited for unpacking look like? Definitely not like today. Maybe tomorrow? Or later. Some day when he doesn't have anything else to do. Is it even worth it to unpack? If he had children. Or at least nephews and nieces. As it is, everything his wife always referred to as his *stuff* now exists for his pleasure alone. And will exist for no one's pleasure when he's gone. Sure, some used book dealer will probably take his library, and a few volumes—a first edition, a signed copy—might wind up on the shelf of a bibliophile. Someone who, like him, is permitted to accumulate *stuff* during his lifetime. And so the cycle will continue. But everything else? All these objects surrounding him form a system and have meaning only as long as he makes his way among them with his habitual gestures, remembering this, remembering that—and once he's gone, they'll drift apart and be lost. That's another thing he could write about sometime: the gravitational force that unites lifeless objects and living creatures to form a world. Is he a sun? He'll have to be careful not to lose his marbles now that he's going to be spending entire days alone without anyone to talk to.

But even so.

The old farmhouse cupboard missing a piece of its crown molding surely won't share a household after his death with the cup in which he always makes his Turkish coffee in the afternoon; the armchair he sits in to watch TV will be repositioned every evening by hands other than those pulling out the drawers of his desk; his telephone won't have the same owner as the sharp knife he uses to slice onions, nor will his electric razor. Many things he cares about, things that still work or that he just likes, will be thrown away. Then an invisible link will connect the garbage dump, where, for instance, his old alarm clock will end up, to the household of the man who can afford his blue onion pattern china, and the link will be that they both once belonged to him. After his death, of course, no one will know about that link. But doesn't a link like that go on existing in perpetuity? Objectively, as it were? And if so, what unit of measure might apply to it? If the meaning imparted by his presence is truly what transforms his household—from the toothbrush all the way to the Gothic crucifix hanging on the wall—into a universe, the next fundamental question to ask is: does meaning have mass?

Richard really will have to be careful not to lose his marbles. Perhaps he'll start feeling better once the dead man's been accounted for. They say the ill-fated swimmer was wearing goggles. A detail like that might provoke laughter, but summer's almost over, and he has yet to see a single person laugh about it. At the town festival recently (which took place despite the accident, but no one was dancing), he heard the president of the Anglers' Club say several times over: He was wearing swim goggles! Swim goggles! As if this were the hardest thing to endure about the swimmer's death, and indeed, all the other men standing there holding their mugs of beer said nothing for a long while, just silently peered into the foam in their glasses, nodding.

He, too, will go on doing what gives him pleasure until the end, following his head's desires all the way to the tomb. He wants to ponder. Read. And eventually when his head stops working, there'll be no head left to know what's wrong. It might take a while for the body to float to the surface, they say. It's already been almost three months now. It's also possible, someone said, that the body won't ever turn up, that it's ~~gotten~~ caught in the sea grass or has sunk forever into the muck at the bottom of the lake (it's said to be a good meter thick). The lake is deep, eighteen meters. It's lovely near the top, but in truth an abyss. All the local residents, including him, now gaze with a certain hesitation at the reeds, at the lake's mirrorlike surface on windless days. He can see the lake when he sits at his desk. The lake is as beautiful this summer as in any other, but this year there's more to it. As long as the body of the dead man hasn't been recovered, the lake belongs to him. All summer long— and now it's almost autumn—the lake has belonged to a dead man.

2

One Thursday in late August, ten men gather in front of Berlin's Town Hall. According to news reports, they've decided to stop eating. Three days later they decide to stop drinking too. Their skin is black. They speak English, French, Italian, as well as other languages that no one here understands. What do these men want? They are asking for work. They want to support themselves by working. They want to remain in Germany. Who are you, they're asked by police officers and various city employees who've been called in. We won't say, the men reply. But you have to say, they're told, otherwise how do we know whether the law applies to you and you're allowed to stay here and work? We won't say who we are, the men say. If you were in our shoes, the others respond, would you take in a guest you don't know? The men say nothing. We have to verify that you're truly in need of assistance. The men say nothing. You might be criminals, we have to check. They say nothing. Or just freeloaders. The men are silent. We're running short ourselves, the others say, there are rules here, and you have to abide by them if you want to stay. And finally they say: You can't blackmail us. But the men with dark skin don't say who they are. They don't eat, they don't drink, they don't say who they are. They simply are. The silence of these men who would rather die than reveal their identity unites with the waiting of all these others who want their questions answered to produce a great silence in the middle of the square called Alexanderplatz in Berlin. Despite the fact that Alexanderplatz is always very loud because of the traffic noise and the excavation site beside the new subway station.

Why is it that Richard, walking past all these black and white people sitting and standing that afternoon, doesn't hear this silence?

He's thinking of Rzeszów.

A friend of his, an archaeologist, told him about discoveries made during the tunneling operation at Alexanderplatz and invited him to visit the excavation site. He has time enough on his hands, and swimming in the lake isn't an option, because of this man. His friend explained that there used to be an extensive system of cellars all around Town Hall. Subterranean vaults that housed a marketplace during the Middle Ages. While people waited for a hearing, an appointment, a ruling, they would go shopping, much as they do today. Fish, cheese, wine—everything that keeps better chilled—was sold in these catacombs.

Just like in Rzeszów.

11

As a student in the 1960s, Richard would sometimes sit on the edge of the Neptune Fountain between two lectures, his trouser legs rolled up, his feet in the water, book in his lap. Even then, unbeknownst to him, these hollow spaces were there beneath him, only a few yards of earth separating them from his feet.

Several years ago, back when his wife was still alive, the two of them had visited the Polish town of Rzeszów on one of their vacations—a town with an elaborate system of tunnels running beneath it, dating from the Middle Ages. Like a second town, invisible to the casual observer, this labyrinth had grown beneath the earth, a mirror image of the houses visible aboveground. The cellar of every house gave access to this public marketplace that was lit only by torches. And when there was a war up above, the residents of the town would retreat underground. Later, in the time of fascism, Jews took refuge here until the Nazis hit on the idea of filling the subterranean passageways with smoke.

Rzeszów.

But the rubble-filled vaults beneath Berlin's Town Hall escaped detection even by the Nazis, who contented themselves with flooding the subway tunnels in the final days of the war. Probably to drown their own people who had fled underground, taking refuge from the Allies' air raids. *There you go again, cutting off your nose to spite your face.*

Have any of the men collapsed yet? asks a young woman holding a microphone, behind her a colossus has a camera on his shoulder. No, one of the policemen says. Are they being force-fed? So far, no, the policeman says, see for yourself. Have any of them been sent to the hospital? I think one was yesterday before my shift, another man in uniform says. Could you tell me which hospital? No, we're not allowed to say. But then I can't place my story. That's too bad, the first policeman says, I'm afraid there's nothing we can do about that. The young woman says: If nothing special happens, I can't

12

make a story out of it. Sure, makes sense, the policeman says. No one will want to run it. The other officer says: There might be some action later today, maybe in the evening. The young woman: All I have left is an hour, tops. There has to be time for editing. Makes sense, the man in uniform says and grins.

Richard doesn't glance over at Town Hall two hours later either when he's walking again past the train station, he's looking at the big fountain on the left, its various terraces arranged like a staircase leading up to the base of the TV tower. Built during Socialist times and bubbling over with water summer after summer, it was the perfect spot for happy children to test their mettle, balancing their way across the stone rows separating the fountain's pools as their laughing, proud parents looked on, and both children and parents alike would now and then gaze up at the tower's silvery sphere, enjoying the vertigo: It's falling! It's falling right on top of us! Three hundred sixty-five meters to its tip, measuring out the days of an entire year, a father says, and: No, it's not falling, it just looks that way, a mother says to her dripping children. A father tells his children—but only if they really want to hear it—the story of the construction worker who fell from the very top of the tower as it was being built, but because it's so tall, it took the man a very long time to fall to the bottom, and meanwhile the people who lived in the buildings down below were able to drag mattresses outside while the worker was still falling, an entire huge pile of mattresses while he fell and fell, and the pile was finished just in time for the worker to arrive at the end of his fall, and he landed as softly as the princess and the pea in the fairy tale and got right back to his feet without a scratch on him. The children delight in this miracle that saved the worker, and now they're ready to go back to playing. At the Alexanderplatz fountain, summer after summer, humankind appeared to be in fine fettle and content—the sort of condition generally promised only for the future, for that distant age of utter

13

contentment known as *Communism* that mankind would eventually make its way to via a sort of staircase of progress leading into dazzling, astonishing heights, a state to be achieved in the next hundred, two hundred, or at the very most three hundred years.

But then, defying all expectations, the East German government that had commissioned this fountain suddenly disappeared after a mere forty years of existence along with all its promises for the future, leaving behind the staircase-shaped fountain to bubble away on its own, and bubble it did, summer after summer, reaching to dazzling, astonishing heights while adventurous children continued to balance their way across, admired by their laughing, proud parents. What can a picture like this that's lost its story tell us? What vision are these happy people advertising now? Has time come to a standstill? Is there anything left to wish for?

The men who would rather die than say who they are have been joined by sympathizers. A young girl has sat down cross-legged on the ground next to one of the dark-skinned men and is conversing with him in a low voice, nodding now and then, rolling herself a cigarette. A young man is arguing with the policemen: It's not as if they're living here, he says, and the policeman replies: Well, that wouldn't be permitted. Exactly, the young man says. The black men are crouching or lying on the ground, some of them have spread out sleeping bags to lie on, others a blanket, others nothing at all. They're using a camping table to prop up a sign. The sign leaning against it is a large piece of cardboard painted white, on which black letters spell out in English: *We become visible*. Beneath this, in smaller green letters, someone has written the German translation with a marker. Was it the young man or the girl? If the dark-skinned men were to glance in Richard's direction at just this moment, all they would see is his back making a beeline for the train station, he is dressed in a blazer despite the heat, and now he vanishes among all the other people, some of whom are in a hurry and know exactly where they're going, while others meander, holding maps, they're here to see "Alex," the center of that part of Berlin long known as the "Russian zone" and still often referred to as the "Eastern zone" in jest. If these silent men were then to raise their eyes, they would behold—as a backdrop to the bustle of the square and elevated one floor above—the windows of the Fitness Center, located beside the tower's plinth under an extravagantly pleated canopy. Behind the windows they would see people on bicycles and people running, bicycling and running toward the enormous windows hour after hour, as if trying to ride or run across to Town Hall as quickly as possible, either to join them, the men with dark skin, or to approach the policemen to declare their solidarity with one or the other side, even if it would mean bursting through the windows to fly or leap the last bit of the way. But obviously both the bicycles and the treadmills are firmly mounted in place, and those exercising on them exert themselves without any forward progress. It's quite possible that these fitness-minded individuals can observe everything happening on Alexanderplatz in front of them, but they probably wouldn't be able to read, say, the words on the sign—for that, they're too far away.

3

For dinner, Richard makes open-face sandwiches with cheese and ham, with a salad on the side. The cheese was on sale today (at the store now invariably referred to by the West German designation *Supermarkt*—it was a *Kaufhalle* back in Socialist times). It was almost past its sell-by date. He doesn't have to scrimp, his pension covers all his needs, but why pay more than necessary? He slices onions for the salad—he's been slicing onions all his life, but just recently he saw in a cookbook the best way to hold the onion to keep it from sliding out from under the knife, there's an ideal form for everything, not just in matters of work and art, but also for the most mundane, ordinary things. When it comes down to it, he thinks, we probably spend our entire lives just trying to attain this form. And when you've finally achieved it in a few different areas, you get wiped off the planet. In any case, he no longer feels the need to prove anything to anyone with the skills he's mastered, not that there's anyone left to prove anything to. His wife no longer sees what he does. His lover wouldn't have been the least bit interested in the art of slicing onions. He's the only one left who can feel pleased when he masters or understands something. He is pleased. And this pleasure has no objective. This is the first advantage of living alone: vanity proves to be superfluous baggage. And the second: there's no one to disrupt your routine. Frying cubes of stale bread to make croutons for salad, wrapping the string around the teabag to squeeze out the liquid when you remove it from the pot, bending the long stems of the rosebushes down to the ground in winter and covering them with earth—and so forth. The pleasure he takes in having everything in its proper place, accounted for, well-husbanded so that nothing is wasted, the pleasure he takes in achievements that don't hinder others in their own attempts to achieve: all this, as he sees it, boils down to pleasure taken in a routine, a sense of order that he doesn't have to establish but only find, an order that lies outside him and for this reason connects him to everything that grows, flies, and glides, while at the same time it separates him from certain people—but this he doesn't mind.

Back when his lover started to make fun of him and got more frequently annoyed when he corrected her, he still hadn't been able to let go of certain fixed ways of doing things that seemed to him absolutely appropriate. He and his wife had almost always been in agreement, at least about things like this. At the end of the war, she'd been shot in the legs, a German girl strafed by German planes as she fled the Russian tanks. If her brother hadn't dragged her out of the street, she certainly wouldn't have survived. So his wife had learned at the age of three that everything you can't size up properly is potentially lethal. He himself had been an infant when his family left Silesia and resettled in Germany. In the tumult of their departure, he almost got separated from his mother; he would have been left behind outright if it hadn't been for a Russian soldier, who, amid the press of people on the station platform, handed him to his mother through the train's window over the heads of many other resettlers. This was a story his mother told him so many times that eventually it seemed to him he remembered it himself. The *mayhem of war* was what she called it. His father had no doubt engendered mayhem of his own as a soldier on the front lines in Norway and Russia. How many children did his father—himself little more than a child in those days—separate from their parents? Or hand to their parents at the last possible moment? Two years passed before the former soldier found his family again—they'd meanwhile settled in Berlin—and saw his son for the first time. The Red Cross missing-persons announcements kept coming over the radio for another few years, but meanwhile his father sat once more beside his mother on the sofa, enjoying a piece of "bee sting" cake with coffee made from real coffee beans, and the infant who'd almost gone astray amid the mayhem was now a schoolboy. The boy could never ask his father about the war. Leave him be, his mother said, shaking her head, waving him away, leave your father alone. His father would just sit there in silence. What would have become of the infant if the train had pulled out of the station two minutes earlier? What would have become of the girl—later Richard's wife—if her brother hadn't pulled her out of the street? In any case, there never would have been a wedding joining an orphan boy to a dead girl. *Do not disturb my circles*, Archimedes (tracing geometric figures in the sand with a finger) is said to have exhorted the Roman soldier who then fatally stabbed him. You can never count on freedom from mayhem—Richard and his wife had always agreed on this. No doubt that's why she understood so much better than his young lover what he was after in his constant search for what was right and proper. (She'd also had a drinking problem. But that was another story.)

He sits down and turns on the TV, the evening news has various local and regional items to report on: a bank robbery, the airport workers' strike, gas prices rising again, and at Alexanderplatz a group of ten men—refugees apparently—have begun a hunger strike, one of them collapsed and was taken to a hospital. At Alexanderplatz? The cameras show a man on a stretcher being slid into an ambulance. Right where Richard passed by this afternoon? A young journalist speaks into a microphone as several figures crouch or lie on the ground behind her, the camera picks up a camping table with a cardboard sign on top: *We become visible*, with the German translation written in smaller, green letters. Why didn't he see the demonstration? His first slice of bread had cheese on top, now comes the second slice, with ham. This isn't the first time he's felt ashamed to be eating dinner in front of a TV screen displaying the bodies of people felled by gunfire or killed by earthquakes or plane crashes, someone's shoe left behind after a suicide bombing, or plastic-wrapped corpses lying side by side in a mass grave during an epidemic. Today, too, he feels ashamed, but goes on eating as usual. As a child he learned the meaning of adversity. But that doesn't mean he has to starve himself just because a desperate man has begun a hunger strike. Or so he tells himself. His going hungry would do nothing to help one of these striking men. And if that man were living in circumstances as favorable as Richard's, he would surely be sitting down to dinner now, just like him. Even today, at his advanced age, Richard is still working to cast off his mother's Protestant inheritance: remorse as a default position. But she hadn't known about the camps. At least that's what she said. He

18

wonders what once, before the age of Luther, filled that region of the soul now colonized by the guilty conscience. A certain numbness has become indispensible since Luther nailed his theses to the door of the church—a form of self-defense, probably. He sticks his fork in the amply filled salad bowl, telling himself it would be a logical fallacy to just stop eating one day out of solidarity with this or that poor, desperate person somewhere in the world. He'd still be trapped in his cage of free agency, imprisoned by the luxury of free choice. For him, refusing to eat would be just as capricious as gluttony.... The onions in the salad taste good. Fresh onions. And the men still refuse to give their names, the young woman is just saying. She appears concerned about the hunger strikers, she is convincing in her concern. Is this concerned tone of voice something journalists now formally study? And who's to say if the footage of that man on the stretcher is really from Alexanderplatz? *Summa* was the name given in the Middle Ages to the universal reference books in which a map of Madrid looked exactly like a map of Nuremberg or Paris—the map simply bore witness to the fact that the names Madrid and Paris belonged to different cities. Today, things were perhaps not terribly different. Hadn't he seen figures being carried off on stretchers in countless news reports in all sorts of different catastrophes around the world? Did it even matter whether these images flashing past, in tenths of seconds, really shared a time and place with the horrors that gave rise to the reports? Could an image stand as proof? And should it? What stories lay behind all the random images constantly placed before us? Or was it no longer a matter of storytelling? Today alone, six people died in swimming accidents in the greater Berlin area, the newscaster says in conclusion, a *tragic record*, and now it's time for the weather. Six people just like that man still at the bottom of the lake. *We become visible*. Why didn't Richard see these men at Alexanderplatz?

4

At night Richard gets up to pee and then can't fall back asleep again, as has started to happen these past few months. He lies there in the dark, watching his thoughts as they stray around. He thinks of the man lying at the bottom of the lake, down where the lake is cold, even in summer. He thinks of his empty office. The young woman with the microphone. Back when he was able to sleep through the night, a night had felt like a reprieve, but it hasn't felt like that in a long time now. Everything keeps going on and on, not even stopping in the dark.

The next day he mows the lawn, then opens a can of pea soup for lunch, then he rinses out the can and makes coffee. His head hurts, so he takes an aspirin. Headache. Stomachache. *Umach steak*. He and his lover liked to jokingly mix up words. Or else pronounce typographical errors. In this way, *old* became *odl*, *short* became *shotr*, and so on. Why didn't he see the men? *We become visible*. Ha.

Richard takes the prose translation of the *Odyssey* from the bookshelf and reads his favorite part, chapter 11.

Later he drives to the garden supply center to have his lawnmower blade sharpened.

In the evening, he makes open-face sandwiches and salad and calls his friend Peter, the archaeologist, who tells him about the bulldozer at the edge of the pit at Alexanderplatz that suddenly wound up with a modernist statue in its bucket. From the Nazi exhibition *Degenerate Art*, he says. Just imagine. Maybe the offices of the Third Reich's Chamber of Culture took a hit in an air raid, and their cache of forbidden treasures tumbled down into the Middle Ages, as it were. Absolutely incredible, Richard says, and his friend replies: the earth is full of wonders. Richard thinks—but doesn't say—that the earth is more like a garbage heap containing all the ages of history, age after age there in the dark, and all the people of

all these ages, their mouths stopped up with dirt, an endless copula-
tion but no womb fertile, and progress is only when the creatures
walking the earth know nothing of all these things.

The next day it rains, so Richard stays home and finally clears away
that pile of old newspapers.

He pays a few bills by telephone, then writes out a shopping list
for later.

2 lb. onions
2x lettuce
½ loaf white bread
½ loaf dark rye
1 butter
cheese, cold cuts?
3x soup (pea or lentil)
noodles
tomatoes

16mm screws
varnish
2 hooks

After lunch he lies down for twenty minutes. The blanket he covers
himself with—genuine camelhair—was a Christmas present from
his wife many years ago.

He decides to wait for a sunnier day to start unpacking the boxes
in the basement.

The student whose manuscript, "Levels of Meaning in Ovid's
Metamorphoses," he'd packed in one of the boxes sometimes dozed
through his seminar, hiding her face behind her hands. But the paper she'd submitted had been perfectly fine.

By afternoon, the rain is down to a slight drizzle, so he gets in his car and drives to the supermarket—the one that used to be a *Kauf-halle*. Tomorrow is Sunday, he mustn't forget anything. Then he drives to the garden center for the last few items. The store smells of fertilizer, wood shavings, and paint; they also have maggots to use as fishing bait, diving masks, and eggs fresh from the village.

Diving masks.

The local and regional news hour that evening includes a brief report: the refugees on hunger strike have been removed from Alexanderplatz. The demonstration is over.

What a shame, he thinks. He'd liked the notion of making oneself visible by publicly refusing to say who one is. Odysseus had called himself Nobody to escape from the Cyclops's cave. Who put out your eye, the other giants ask the blind Cyclops from outside. Nobody, the Cyclops bellows. Who's hurting you? Nobody! Odysseus, whose false name—one that cancels him out—the Cyclops keeps shrieking, clings to the belly of a ram and in this way slips out of the man-eating monster's cave undetected.

The placard with the inscription *We become visible* is probably in some trash can now, or—if it's too big to fit—lying on the ground, sodden with rain.

5

During the next two weeks, Richard sees to the new door for the shed, he has the flue in the fireplace repaired, he transplants the peonies, varnishes the boat's oars, deals with all the unopened mail that's piled up over the course of the summer; he goes once to physical therapy and three times to the movies. Every morning, he reads the newspaper over breakfast as always. Every morning he drinks tea—Earl Grey with milk and sugar—and eats one piece of bread with honey and one with cheese (sometimes with a slice of cucumber) but only on Sundays does he add a soft-boiled egg. He can take his time every day now, but he still only wants an egg on Sundays. The way he's used to it. It's a novelty to be able to linger over his tea as long as he likes, and so he now reads certain articles all the way through that he might once have skimmed. He'd really like to know what's become of the ten men from Alexanderplatz, but he doesn't see anything about that. He reads that off the coast of the Italian island of Lampedusa, sixty-four of three hundred twenty-nine refugees drowned when their boat capsized, including some from Ghana, Sierra Leone, and Niger. He reads that somewhere over Nigeria a man from Burkina Faso fell from a height of ten thousand feet after stowing away in an aircraft's landing gear, he reads about a school in Kreuzberg that's been occupied by a group of black Africans for months, reads about Oranienplatz, where refugees have apparently been living in tents for a year now. Where exactly is Burkina Faso? The American vice president recently referred to Africa as a country, even though—as the article about this faux pas pointed out—there are fifty-four African countries. Fifty-four? He had no idea. What is the capital of Ghana? Of Sierra Leone? Or Niger? Some of his first-year students had been unable to recite even the first four lines of the *Odyssey* in Greek. During his own studies, that would have been unthinkable. He gets up and takes out his atlas. The capital of Ghana is Accra, the capital of Sierra Leone is Freetown, the capital of Niger Niamey. Had he ever known the names of these cities? Burkina Faso is a country to the west of Niger. And Niger? In the Department of German, just a few doors down the hall from him at the university, there had often been students from Mozambique and Angola in the 1970s, mechanical engineering or agriculture majors who were also learning German from his colleagues. Cooperation with these partner nations ceased when German Socialism came to an end. Was it because of these students that he'd purchased the book *Negerliteratur*? He can't remember, but he still knows exactly where to find it on his bookshelf, books are willing to wait, he says whenever visitors ask if he's read all the books on his shelves. . . . The capital of Mozambique is Maputo, the capital of Angola is Luanda. He shuts the atlas and goes to the other room, to the shelf with *Negerliteratur*. "Negro" is a word no one would say now, but back then people printed it on book jackets. When was that? During Richard's postwar childhood, his mother had often read to him at his request from the book *Hatschi Bratschi's Hot-Air Balloon* that she'd found in a suitcase in the rubble of Berlin.

> *Cannibal mama's in a rush,*
> *Supper will bring such joy.*
> *Grab him, won't you, hurry up!*
> *Shouts the cannibal boy.*

He'd particularly liked the pictures of the little cannibal boy with the bones from his last meal stuck crosswise into his hair. His mother must have given the book away at some point, and later, when he asked a bookseller about it as an adult, he learned that while the book still existed, it had been reprinted in a new politically correct edition featuring an Africa devoid of cannibals, and the original version could be found only in rare book shops at astronomical prices. Here too the prohibition had served only to make the prohibited item more desirable. The workings of causality are indirect, not direct, he thinks, as he's had occasion to think so many times in recent years. But the book *Negerliteratur* is still exactly where it's always been on the shelf, waiting for him. Indeed, the title dates from 1951. He opens the book and reads a few lines. *The earth is round and completely surrounded by swamp. Behind the swamp lies the land of the bush spirits. Under the earth there is only more earth. What comes after that, no one knows.*

6

By the time Richard finally finds the former school in Berlin's Kreuzberg district, it's already dusk. There are no lights illuminating the old schoolyard, so the black figures walking toward him can scarcely be distinguished from the night air. The stairwell stinks. The walls are covered with graffiti. On the second floor, he looks through an open doorway right into the men's bathroom, he goes inside to see what a men's bathroom looks like here: three of the four booths have been sealed up with red-and-white tape. The other side of the room is empty, maybe that's where the showers used to be. The pipes have been removed, all that's left are the tiles and a hideous stench. He goes out again. Not a person to be seen, black or white. There's only a handwritten note on the wall reading *Auditorium*, with an arrow pointing up. Now he can hear voices, too, coming from upstairs. Probably everyone's at the assembly already. He's a bit late. He got lost on the way from the S-Bahn station because he still doesn't know his way around West Berlin. *The Berlin Senate invites local residents and refugees to participate in a general discussion of recent events in the auditorium of the occupied school in Kreuzberg*, he read in the newspaper. So what's he doing here? He doesn't live in the neighborhood, and he's not a refugee either. Is the only freedom the fall of the Berlin wall brought him the freedom to go places he's afraid of?

The auditorium is full of people, they stand and sit on the floor, on chairs and tables. The refugees' mattresses have been pushed to the sides of the room, a few tents have been set up in the middle, firmly anchored on the herringbone parquet. What counts as outside, as inside? The former stage of the auditorium is also covered with mattresses, squeezed in tightly side by side, the theater curtain hangs between white Corinthian columns, it's been raised, revealing pallets, blankets, sheets, bags, and shoes. Richard thinks he sees isolated figures lying under the blankets asleep, but he isn't sure.

I've studied now . . .

People are just taking turns introducing themselves, saying their names, and all of this is being translated twice. Richard has attended many assemblies in the course of his lifetime, but never one like this.

Ich heiße, ich komme aus, ich bin hier, weil.

My name is, I'm from, I'm here because.

Je m'appelle, je suis de, je suis ici.

A good seventy people say who they are. *I've studied now Philosophy and Jurisprudence, Medicine—and even, alas! Theology—from end to end with labor keen.* The auditorium has an ornamental plaster ceiling with a chandelier in the middle, and dark paneling on the walls. Not so long ago, this was a high school.

Aus Mali, Äthiopien, Senegal. Aus Berlin.

From Mali, Ethiopia, Senegal. From Berlin.

Du Mali, de l'Éthiopie, du Sénégal. De Berlin.

A few jackets and t-shirts hang from the crossbars of the windows. Have they been hung up to dry? Where do they do laundry in this former school? Not so long ago, speeches were being made on this stage, and pieces played on the piano, newly admitted students were welcomed, and valedictorians honored. Plays were performed, the curtain was drawn aside to reveal Goethe's Faust seated at his desk. *And see that nothing can be known! That knowledge cuts me to the bone.* It's really true—even during this meeting, there are people lying under some of the blankets, asleep.

Aus Niger. Aus Ghana. Aus Serbien. Aus Berlin.

From Niger. From Ghana. From Serbia. From Berlin.

Du Niger. Du Ghana. De la Serbie. De Berlin.

Will they send him away for not being a local resident? He doesn't want to say who he is, or why he's here. Especially since he isn't sure himself. The few white people present include Kreuzberg neighbors, members of refugee-aid organizations, relief workers, and members of an initiative to turn the school into a cultural center, there are representatives from the district office, and the youth-services staff. There's a journalist, but she's asked to leave because the meeting isn't meant to be open to the general public. Among the many black people in attendance are some who have been living here in the school for eight months. Some have been living here for six months, and some have been living here for two. The refugees here state their names and say where they're from, unlike those at Alexanderplatz, but despite their willingness to do so, this doesn't seem to solve the problem. The capital of Ghana is Accra, the capital of Sierra Leone is Freetown, the capital of Niger Niamey.

No, Richard doesn't want to say his name.

Just as he's thinking this, an earsplitting bang is heard suddenly coming from the stairwell, something like an explosion that immediately eradicates all thinking, leaving behind only instinct. Instinctually, the relief worker knows: they are on the third floor. The man from Ghana knows the door to the other stairwell is locked. The neighbor: Don't they know there are white people here? Another neighbor asks herself, what'll happen to my son? Many of the refugees think: So in the end I just came here to die. Even Richard knows something: This is it.

But then all who've been covering their ears, including Richard, take their hands down, and they're still breathing, and now they start thinking again, and they think: So it wasn't a bomb. And they think again: But it could have easily been one.

But just at this moment when they're about to quickly sweep away all the fears they had—or that had them — just at this moment, the lights suddenly go out, and for a few seconds all the people in the room are black. What's going on? What's the idea? several people murmur in the room. Good Lord, someone says. Then the light comes back on.

As if the past two minutes hadn't yet produced a sufficient quantity of unforeseen occurrences, the moment it's light again one of the Africans suddenly starts screaming and waving his arms around, cursing and hurling a pillow across the room, followed by a blanket. What's wrong? What's gotten into him? Is he in shock? No, someone says. What's happened is that during the explosion or the darkness that followed, someone stole his laptop from under his pillow. What's a refugee doing with a laptop? the neighbor thinks. He must be one of the men who sell drugs in the park around the corner, thinks the woman from down the block. The idea of private property doesn't work if all a person possesses is a blanket and pillow, thinks Richard, who for reasons unclear even to himself has made his way here from the suburbs. He walks past the screaming man, past the others who are trying to calm him down, he leaves behind the tumult and the auditorium in which the meeting hasn't really even started yet, and goes into the stairwell, which is still filled with swirling clouds from the firecrackers set off by some Berlin provocateur wanting to take a stand against the administration of the district office, or some youngster with dark skin who has nothing better to do than scare people to death, or a neo-fascist who hates the refugees and their sympathizers, or else some poor refugee who wanted to steal a laptop from some other poor refugee in a moment of panic.

Richard goes down the stairs, which are difficult to see because of all the smoke, and walks past the brightly lit but empty men's bathroom, down to the ground floor. If he weren't walking so slowly, for fear of missing his footing on the stairs, one might think he was fleeing.

7

It's lovely when everything smells of leaves in autumn, wet leaves that press into the earth and stick to the soles of your shoes. Unlocking the garden gate, filling his lungs with the dark air—this is what Richard's late-night homecomings have looked like for twenty years now. It's been autumn in this garden for twenty years. For twenty years it's smelled like this, and he's unlocked the garden gate in just this way and locked it again behind him. Time here is like a vast country to which one can return home season after season. Unlike many of his neighbors, Richard hasn't placed motion detectors in the trees to light his way when he passes among the trunks to go inside. Sometimes the moon is shining, but he doesn't mind when it's pitch black like tonight; then each step he takes belongs more to the forest than to him, and a state of wakefulness replaces seeing. Darkness—even the domesticated darkness of a garden—briefly turns a human being into a vulnerable animal. Then he remembers the man who even now, gently swaying, floats somewhere out there at the bottom of the lake.

Was he cowardly just now in Kreuzberg? Probably. Here in the garden it always seemed to him that his faint sense of fear bound him more closely to this place. Here in the garden, he was never afraid of the fear he felt. In the city, things are different.... His friends make fun of him because he still refuses to drive into the city center. Now that the Wall is gone, he no longer knows his way around. Now that the Wall is gone, the city is twice as big and has changed so much that he often doesn't recognize the intersections. Once he'd known all the city's bombed-out gaps, first with rubble, then without. Later still there might be a sausage stand, or Christmas trees for sale, or often nothing at all. But recently all these gaps have been filled with buildings, corner lots built up again, firewalls no longer visible. As a child, before the Wall went up, he sold blueberries (having picked them himself) at the West Berlin train station Gesundbrunnen so he could buy his first glossy ball. Glossy rubber balls existed only in the West. When he saw the Gesundbrunnen station for the first time after the fall of the Wall, the tracks leading east were completely overgrown with tall grass, the platforms covered with birch trees swaying in the wind. If he'd been a city planner, he'd have left it just like that in memory of the divided city, and to symbolize the ephemeral nature of all things built by human hands, and maybe just because a stand of birch trees on a train-station platform is beautiful.

Richard pours himself a glass of whiskey and turns on the TV. There are several talk shows, an old Western, news programs, a film with an Alpine setting, animal films, action films, quiz shows, science fiction, and crime dramas. He turns off the sound and goes over to his desk. While behind him a female police detective rattles a basement doorknob, he glances through some papers lying on his desk: insurance policies, telephone contracts, the invoice from the auto-repair workshop. He didn't want to say his name at the assembly just now, but why not? An assembly at which seventy people introduce themselves one after the other—how utterly absurd. Even now, at his desk, he shakes his head at the thought, while the detective behind him speaks with a teenage girl crouching in a corner in tears. Saying his name, it appeared to him, would have been a sort of confession—at the very least he'd have been confessing his presence at that gathering. But how is it anyone's business he was there? He isn't trying to help anyone, he doesn't live near the school, and he wasn't sent by the Senate. He just wants to watch and be left in peace while he's watching. He isn't a part of a group, his interest is his own, it belongs only to him and he is completely dispassionate. If he hadn't been so cool-headed all his professional life, he wouldn't have understood so much. Probably the attempt to

30

find out who was there in the auditorium had something to do with the state of war that had overtaken the building. But what does a name tell you? A person who wants to lie can always lie. You have to know a lot more than just the name, otherwise there's no point. Richard gets up, goes over to the sofa, and sits in front of the silent TV for a moment with his last sip of whiskey. A young man has grabbed an older one by the collar and is shoving him against a wall, both are screaming at each other, then the young man lets go again, the other one leaves, and the young man shouts something after him. Then he sees the detective's office with its glass walls, blinds, coffee cups, papers …

8

At breakfast, Richard has Earl Grey with milk and sugar, accompanied by a slice of bread with honey and another with cheese. On the radio, Bach's *Goldberg Variations* are playing. Years ago, Richard gave a lecture on the topic "Language as a System of Signs." Words as signs for things. Language as a skin. But words remained words all the same. They were never the thing itself. You had to know a lot more than just the name, otherwise there was no point. What makes a surface a surface? What separates a surface from what lies below it, what separates it from the air? As a child, Richard used to push the skin around on his hot milk—a repulsive skin that had been milk just a moment before. What's a name made of? Sound? But not even that if it's written and not spoken. Maybe that's why he loves to listen to Bach: there are no surfaces, just crisscrossing storylines. Crossing here, crossing there, moment after moment, and all these crossings join together to make something that in Bach's world is called music. Each moment is like slicing into a piece of meat, into the thing itself. This year he'll reserve himself a ticket for the *Christmas Oratorio* in the cathedral again. For the first time since his wife's death. He clears his plate, shakes the crumbs into the garbage can, then takes his coat and slips into the brown shoes that are his most comfortable pair—never brown in town, they say, but no matter. If you fall off a galloping horse, they say, you should get right back in the saddle and keep going, otherwise the fear creeps into your bones forever. Fear is what he felt yesterday in the occupied school. So: stove off, lights off, keys, subway pass.

Walking across Oranienplatz in broad daylight is easier than paying a nocturnal visit to a godforsaken school. Not long after the fall of the Wall, Richard went to Kreuzberg with his wife for the first time. They'd gotten into the habit of walking in one of the city's Western districts every Sunday. (The evening before, they'd read up on the neighborhood in a guidebook, and then on Sunday morning they'd take their stroll.) Huguenot refugees were the original settlers in the streets surrounding Oranienplatz—lots of gardeners among them, apparently—long before Kreuzberg was part of the city proper. And then Lenné planned out the shape of the square the century before last, back when there'd still been a canal here, the square forming its banks, with a bridge where the street is now. Later Richard showed his lover this square, explaining to her who Lenné was, there was a good bookstore around the corner, a repertory cinema, and a lovely café.

Now the square looks like a construction site: a landscape of tents, wooden shacks, and tarps: white, blue, and green. He sits down on a park bench, looks around, and listens to what's being said. No one here asks his name. What does he see? What does he hear? He sees banners and propped-up signs with hand-painted slogans. He sees black men and white sympathizers, the refugees are wearing freshly laundered pants, colorful jackets, and striped shirts, light-colored sweatshirts with vivid lettering—where do you do laun-

32

dry on an occupied square? One of them is wearing gold-colored sneakers. Could he be Hermes? The sympathizers have white skin, but their clothing is black and torn, their pants, their t-shirts, and sweaters. The sympathizers are young and pale, they dye their hair with henna, they refuse to believe that the world is an idyllic place and want everything to change, for which reason they put rings through their lips, ears, and noses. The refugees, on the other hand, are trying to gain admittance to this world that appears to them convincingly idyllic. Here on the square, these two forms of wishing and hoping cross paths, there's an overlap between them, but this silent observer doubts that the overlap is large.

Before Richard moved to the outskirts with his wife, they'd lived in an apartment, a mere two hundred yards as the crow flies from West Berlin. And they lived there almost as peacefully as they later lived in the countryside. The Wall had turned their street into a cul-de-sac where children roller-skated. Then in 1990 the Wall was cleared away piece by piece, and each time a new crossing point was opened, a crowd of emotional West Berliners punctually gathered, eager to bid a warm welcome to their brothers and sisters from the East. One morning, he himself became the object of these tearful welcomes: the East Berliner who'd lived on this street that had been cut in half for twenty-nine years, crossing over on his way to freedom. But he hadn't been on his way to freedom that morning, he was only trying to get to the University, punctually taking advantage of the S-Bahn station at the western end of his newly opened street. Unemotional and in a hurry, he'd used his elbows to fight his way through this weeping crowd—one of the disappointed liberators shouted an insult at his back—but for the very first time, Richard got to school in under twenty minutes.

Just a year ago, the park bench he's now sitting on was just a perfectly normal bench in a Kreuzberg park. People out for walks

33

would sit down here to rest their legs and relax. In the 1920s, the canal that had existed here in Lenné's time was filled in by the city government because it stank so badly. Is the water still flowing down there somewhere among the grains of sand?

In any case, no one sits here these days out of a desire to relax. If Richard doesn't get right back up again, it's only because he isn't here for recreational purposes. The ordinary activity of sitting on a park bench has lost its ordinariness because of the refugees camping on the grass behind the benches. Berliners who've known since Lenné's time how to comport themselves in this park while seated on a bench are no longer certain: there's no old lady feeding the sparrows, no mother rocking her baby carriage gently back and forth, no student reading, no trio of drinkers conducting their morning meeting, no office worker eating his midday snack, no lovers holding hands. "The Transformation of Sitting" might be a good title for an essay. Richard remains seated, remaining in spite of. Whenever an "in spite of" occurs, in his experience, things get interesting. "The Birth of In Spite Of" would make a good title for an essay too.

The only person with white skin who seems to be just as much at home in this square as the refugees is a rawboned woman in her early forties. She's just showing a Turkish man where he can leave the flatbreads he's brought as a contribution. Somewhat later she accepts a bicycle from a man with a beard, passing it on to one of the refugees, and both watch the refugee as he happily pedals off. He's got shrapnel in his lung, by the way, she says, and the bearded man nods. Libya, she says, he nods, then both are silent for a moment. The man says, I guess I'll be on my way. A young woman with a microphone in her hand approaches.

I'm not doing any interviews just now, the rawboned woman says.

But it's important that the Berliners—

Maybe you've heard that negotiations are underway for winter lodgings.

That's why I'm here, the interviewer says.

Has he already started looking like a bum, is that why the two women seem unfazed that he's sitting here just a few feet away from them, listening?

Then you might also know that the Senate's only offering eighteen euros a night per man from now until April.

Yes, I've—

Well, the rawboned woman says, the only one who's willing to offer housing to these men is already asking for twice as much. So if you write in your newspaper that there are rats here and only four toilets left, and sometimes nothing warm to eat for three days, and if you write that last winter tents collapsed under the weight of the snow, then I promise you: the only person who'll be happy about your article is this investor.

Oh, the young woman says, I see. She lowers her microphone.

Once again Richard thinks—as so often in recent years—that the effects of a person's actions are almost always impossible to predict and often prove to be the exact opposite of what the person originally intended. And if the same principle holds true in this case, he thinks, it's possibly because the Berlin Senate's negotiations with the refugees all have to do with borders, and a border is a place where, at least in mathematics, signs often change their value. No wonder, he thinks, the word *dealings* refers not just to actions but also business and trade.

Now not switching on her microphone, the young interviewer asks the rawboned woman:

What do the men do here all day long if they're not allowed to work?

Nothing, the woman says. And as she turns away, she adds: When doing nothing gets to be too much for them, we organize a demonstration.

I understand, the interviewer says, nodding, and now the raw-boned woman walks away.

Then she packs up her microphone again, still standing in front of the bench he's sitting on with her back to him, not noticing that all this time she's had a silent observer. Meanwhile the rawboned woman walks over to the open tent that appears to be the kitchen, pausing on the way to pick up a wooden signboard that's fallen over and ripped a hole in a tent nearby.

Richard sees one black man walking over to another and shaking his hand in greeting. He sees a group of five men standing together talking, one of them is on the phone. He sees the man who was given the bicycle riding in a circle around the square, sometimes even weaving riskily among others on the gravel paths. He sees three of the refugees in an open tent sitting behind a table, in front of them a cardboard box labeled "Donations." He sees an older man sitting alone on the back of a bench—there's something wrong with his eye — and a man with a blue tattoo on his face thumping another on the shoulder in parting. He sees one man chatting with a female sympathizer, and another in a tent with an open flap, he's sitting on a cot, typing something into a phone. There's someone lying on the next cot, but only the feet are visible. He sees two men having an argument in a language incomprehensible to him, when one of them raises his voice and shoves the other away with a hand to his chest, making him stumble backward, the man on the bicycle has to swerve to avoid them. He sees the rawboned woman speaking with a man in the kitchen holding a cooking pot, and he sees the elegant corner building that furnishes the backdrop for all of this, probably dating back to around the period when there was still a canal where he is sitting. It looks like a former department store, but now there's a bank on the ground floor. Back when there was a canal here, Germany still had colonies. The word *Kolonialwaren* was still visible in weathered script on some East Berlin facades as recently as twenty years ago, until the West started renovating everything, including the last vestiges of these ancient grocer's shops with their imported wares. *Kolonialwaren* and WWII bullet holes might adorn the very same storefront. (The dusty shop window of such a building — its tenants evicted to prepare for renovation — might also display a Socialist cardboard sign reading *Obst Gemüse Speisekartoffeln* (*OGS*) to advertise the "fruit, vegetables, and potatoes" that gave East German greengrocers their acronym.) You can still find "German East Africa" on the globe in his study. The paper covering the sphere is peeling a little over the Mariana Trench, but the globe is still nice to look at. Richard has no idea what German East Africa is called today. He wonders whether, back when there was still a canal right where he's sitting now, slaves were sold at that department store. Might black servants have carried the sacks of coal up to the fifth-floor apartments of Lenné's contemporaries? The idea makes him grin. An old man sitting alone on a park bench grinning to himself might raise eyebrows. Anyhow, what's he waiting for? Does he really think that after a year of these men camping out on this square, something unforeseen might happen today of all days, just when he's decided to come visiting from the suburbs? Nothing happens, and after two and a half hours he starts to feel chilly, so he gets up from the bench and goes home.

Often when he was starting a new project, he didn't know what was driving him, as if his thoughts had developed an independent life and a will of their own, as if they were merely waiting for him to finally think them, as if an investigation he was about to begin already existed before he had started working on it, and the path leading through everything he knew and saw, everything he encountered and experienced, already lay there waiting for him to venture down it. And probably that's just how it was, given that you could only ever find what was already there. Because everything is always already there. In the afternoon, he rakes leaves for the first time. In the evening, the newscaster says it's just a matter of time before a solution is found for the untenable situation of the refugees on Oranienplatz. Richard's heard sentences like this many instances before, referring to all sorts of untenable situations. Other things too—the leaves becoming earth again, the drowned man washing up on shore or dissolving in the lake—are basically just a matter of time. But what does that mean? He doesn't even know yet if time exists for the purpose of making various layers and paths overlap, or if it's to keep things separate—maybe the newscaster knows. Richard feels irritated without knowing why. Later, already lying in bed, he remembers something the rawboned woman said: When doing nothing gets to be too much for them, we organize a demonstration. And suddenly he knows why he spent two hours today sitting on Oranienplatz. It's something he already knew back in August when he first heard about the hunger strikers—the men who refused to give their names—and he knew it when he walked into the black schoolyard yesterday, but only now, in this moment, does he know it fully. Speaking about the actual nature of time is something he can probably do best in conversation with those who have fallen out of it. Or been locked up in it, if you prefer. Next to him, on the half of the bed still covered with the bedspread—the half where his wife used to sleep—lie a few of his sweaters, slacks, and shirts that he's worn over the last few days and hasn't yet cleared away.

9

Richard spends the next two weeks reading several books on the subject of the refugees and drawing up a catalog of questions for the conversations he wants to have with them. After breakfast he goes to work, at one p.m. he has lunch and naps for an hour, then he sits down at his desk again or reads until eight or nine p.m. It's important he ask the right questions. And the right questions aren't always the ones you put into words.

To investigate how one makes the transition from a full, readily comprehensible existence to the life of a refugee, which is open in all directions—drafty, as it were—he has to know what was at the beginning, what was in the middle, and what is now. At the border between a person's life and the other life lived by that same person, the transition has to be visible—a transition that, if you look closely enough, is nothing at all.

Where did you grow up? What's your native language? What's your religious affiliation? How many people are in your family? What did the apartment or house you grew up in look like? How did your parents meet? Was there a TV? Where did you sleep? What did you eat? What was your favorite hiding place when you were a child? Did you go to school? What sort of clothing did you wear? Did you have pets? Did you learn a trade? Do you have a family of your own? When did you leave the country of your birth? Why? Are you still in contact with your family? What was your goal when you left home? How did you say your goodbyes? What did you take with you when you left? What did you think Europe would be like? What's different? How do you spend your days? What do you miss most? What do you wish for? If you had children who were growing up here, what would you tell them about your homeland? Can you imagine growing old here? Where do you want to be buried?

10

On one of the days Richard spends at his desk and in his reading chair, the tents and shacks on Oranienplatz are torn down and the refugees divided among facilities run by various charitable organizations throughout the city and on the outskirts, facilities that have declared themselves willing—now that the temperatures have started to drop below fifty degrees at night—to take in refugees. Richard doesn't hear about this, since he's spending the day reading about the acquisition of territory on the southwest coast of Africa by a trader named Lüderitz. Herr von Lüderitz, after going bankrupt in Mexico, had made an advantageous marriage and then, acting on advice from the son of a missionary who'd been proselytizing up and down the western coast of Africa, purchased two tracts of land. One for a hundred pounds in gold and two hundred rifles, the other for five hundred pounds and sixty rifles. Calculated in German miles, which are longer than the English miles the chieftain was using. Wouldn't it be splendid to forge a path clear across to the Indian Ocean? The German Reich showed some initial reluctance to guard Herr von Lüderitz's picket fence, but after the British—seeing how easy it was—occupied a few harbors themselves, Bismarck sent two battle-worthy ships. From that point on, the lands belonging to the merchant Lüderitz were designated colonies and enjoyed the protection of the German state. Sitting at the dinner table, Richard is still shaking his head over this course of action. Can headshaking be considered a sign? But for whom, if he's the only one sitting here? *There sits my mother upon a stone—I feel an icy shiver! There sits my mother upon a stone, and her head is wagging ever.* Tomorrow he'll go visit the refugees for the first time with his catalog of questions.

The next day he arrives at Oranienplatz to find the square cordoned off and surrounded by police; he's just in time to see the last of the boards, tarps, mattresses, and cardboard signs being shoved into a heap by a bulldozer, loaded onto trucks and carted away. Only a lone African woman remains, sitting in a tree, apparently she's refusing to leave, but neither the cleaning crew nor the police show any interest in the woman or the tree. None of the other refugees is anywhere to be seen. Where the earth has been laid bare again by the removal of the tents and huts, the system of tunnels dug by rats is clearly visible; they appear to have profited from the refugees' poorly shielded provisions. Richard thinks of Rzeszów. One of the police officers tells him that the refugees helped dismantle their own shacks, that was part of their agreement with the Berlin Senate. What sort of agreement? he asks. The police officer is afraid he can't say. And where are the refugees now? They've been split among three different facilities. Oh, and one is in the suburbs not far from Richard—he knows right away what place the officer means, a red-brick building with dusty windowpanes that belongs to the nursing home and has stood empty for nearly two years.

As he rides home on the S-Bahn, the automatic voice warns passengers at every station about the gap between train and platform, just the same as always, and just the same as always Richard thinks that this announcement is being broadcast not out of safety concerns but so the insurance will pay if someone really does get hurt.

So now the Africans are being housed in the nursing home.

And why not? The building was standing empty.

He gets off the S-Bahn and walks home.

11

The next day is October 3—the members of the Anglers' Club are celebrating German unity at the top of their lungs—and Richard finally takes on the cardboard boxes from the Institute that have been sitting unopened in the basement all this time, unpacking the books and finding spots for them on the shelves. It takes him all of the next day too, and the one after that. Over the weekend he cuts the boxes into pieces and finally, on the eve of the *Day of the*

Republic (the East German national holiday formerly celebrated on October 7), he places the tidily stacked pieces of cardboard in the blue recycling bin.

On Monday he goes shopping, and returns home with his groceries. Since there's no room left in the crisper drawer for the head of lettuce, he lays it on the cool tiles in the vestibule. For years now he's wondered every time he's driven past this nursing home whether he'll spend his so-called "twilight years" there. There's no such thing as "nighttime years."

Not until Tuesday morning does he take his coat and slip into the brown shoes that are his most comfortable pair. Stove off, light off, keys. It's twenty minutes by foot.

In the lobby of the home, he tells the receptionist he wants to speak with the refugees.

Where are you coming from?

I just came from home.

No, I mean, from what institution?

No institution. I'm just here out of interest.

Do you want to make a donation?

No.

It's not so simple, the woman at the reception desk says. Through a large plate-glass window, he can see into the breakfast room of the senior residence, as the nursing home is called these days. The elderly residents are sitting at four-person tables, some wearing bibs, some in wheelchairs.

I'm a professor at Humboldt University, Department of Classical Philology.

This is a sentence he's used many times before. Technically he's now *professor emeritus*, but he's still getting used to this new status. Back in the East he earned distinctions that are now recognized in the West. But even so, his pension—as with every professor whose career started in Eastern times—is smaller than that of his West

42

German colleagues. ("Eastern times" is such an interesting construction, with time being assigned a point of the compass. Now it's the West for all time and in every cardinal direction in this city and land.)

You still need an appointment.

With the refugees? he asks.

No, first off with the director of the home.

The birth of questions is something that always delights him. The appearance of the refugees in this suburb is just such a moment. Fear produces order, he thinks, as do uncertainty and caution. During the hour and a half he has to wait before his appointment, he goes for a walk in the park behind the castle. Leaves are scattered on the pond, and among them swim ducks and swans.

The director of the home receives him in his office, saying:

What exactly do you want from them?

I'm working on a research project.

I see, the director says. He thanks the professor emeritus for the business card he has just handed him across the desk.

The director now mentions *Dublin II*, he speaks of *repatriation*, of *detention pending deportation*, of the *Asylum Procedure Act*. He asks his visitor if he knows what a *title of residence* is.

Title? The professor almost never invokes his own title, really only in cases when he needs to lend weight to some request, as with the receptionist just now. And Dublin? He and his wife were there once on a hiking trip four or five years after the fall of the Wall. There was heather, sheep, lots of rain. At breakfast in the small B&Bs they stayed at, they often found themselves sitting with fellow East Germans, searching like them for that familiar sense of isolation that could no longer be found at home, a sense of refuge, as if sheltering from the wind behind a wall....

Then the director offers a few more sentences that go more or less like this:

43

The men are quartered here only provisionally. The rooms aren't up to the standards that would be required for a long-term solution. In fact, this building should have been a construction site by now. We're overdue for renovation. There aren't enough kitchens, enough washrooms for this many people, and the number of men per room is far from ideal, there are cots everywhere.

That's not why I'm here, the visitor says.

I just don't want you to get the wrong idea. We jumped in to lend a hand because no one else wanted to.

I'm not a journalist, the visitor says.

No, of course not.

Both of them are silent for a moment.

Did the men want to leave Oranienplatz?

That's a difficult question.

I understand.

After another brief moment during which no words are spoken, the director nods and says:

So let's go up.

12

The red-brick building where the refugees are now housed is locked. From the inside. A man in a blue uniform unlocks the door for them, and a second uniformed officer sits inside behind an old office desk.

Whenever you enter the building, you'll need to show your ID to the security guard.

All right.

It's a fire-safety measure. We need to know how many people are in the building at all times.

Vse v poriadke is how you say "all right" in Russian, Richard thinks, but he just nods and slides his ID across the desk. The ma-

terial this fake wood veneer is made of used to be called *Sprelacart*.
The desk was probably salvaged from the *Volkssolidarität* bureau or
maybe the offices of the Party's sectional directorate.

Now they are permitted to continue on past the security guards,
taking a right down the corridor that leads to the stairs. They pass
a room whose door has been removed from its hinges, the room
contains a pool table and a few armchairs in which three young
men are sitting, each holding a cue, but they aren't playing pool,
none of them speaks, and Richard doesn't see any balls on the table.

There is fluorescent light, frosted glass, a sage-green banister
leading up the stairs with hand-forged tendrils, the paint flaking
off in spots.

The second floor is empty; there's no water, the director explains.

They turn down a corridor on the third floor, a row of doors on
either side. At the height where the handles of wheelchairs might
scrape the wall, a wide wooden rail has been mounted between the
doors.

Are the men even here at this hour?

There's always someone here.

The doors still bear the names of the rooms' elderly former residents. Are they all dead now? Or have they been transferred to
other facilities?

One more thing, the men are allowed to leave the building, but
it's still probably best if you hold your conversations here.

That isn't a problem.

Just thought I'd mention it. What languages can you speak?

English, Russian—but that's probably not much use here (the
director shakes his head)—and also Italian.

Good, then let's start here.

The director knocks on one of the doors and opens it without waiting for a response, like a doctor or nurse in a hospital ward. The
visitor now sees a number of cots with blankets and pillows. On

45

some of the cots, men lie asleep; other cots are empty, and at the back of the room a man leans against the wall, listening to music through his earbuds. In the front of the room is a TV set with a cot placed lengthwise before it, where a massive figure sits with three others beside him. If truth be told, Richard wouldn't mind beating a retreat. But the director is already introducing him: A professor wants to do interviews for a project, he has a few questions. The TV is showing a program about fisheries. Richard sees nets full of fish, men wearing orange waterproof clothing, boats in storms, and lots of water. Do the men here even know what that is: a professor? Richard sees duffle bags stowed under the cots, shoes lined up in pairs beneath a windowsill; some of the sleepers are so tightly wrapped in their blankets, so motionless and silent they look like mummies. The massive man sitting on the cot in front of the TV nods to him: No problem, he says.

So I'll leave you to it, the director says, departing.

The large man wears a red t-shirt with illegible script on it. The refugees aren't all doing so badly, Richard thinks, otherwise how could this fellow be so burly? The burly fellow nods to him, straightens the sheet on the cot next to his and offers him a seat. *Never sit on a bed in your street trousers*. But there aren't any chairs. What would happen if he looked up *Strassenhose* in the Grimms' German dictionary? Fishing is a tough business, especially in winter. The voluminous man, who appears to be the decision-maker here, introduces himself: My name's Rashid. And this is Zair, this is Abdusalam, and the tall guy is Ithemba. And you? Richard says his name and thanks them for their willingness to speak with him. Then he pulls out his list of questions.

Soon afterward, his notebook contains these lines: The north of Nigeria is Muslim, the south Christian. The Christians fled from Kaduna when Sharia law was introduced. Kaduna? The languages in northern Nigeria include Yoruba and Hausa. Yoruba? Hausa? The Yoruba are mostly Christians. Rashid is Yoruba and Muslim. Most Hausa, on the other hand, are Muslims, but not everyone, of course. Hausa is spoken and understood in Ghana, Sudan, Niger, and Mali too. Most understand Arabic as well. The men in this room all come from Nigeria, but different regions. Rashid is from the north. Abdusalam is from the coast. Nigeria has a coast? Zair was born near Abuja, the capital. There's also a Ghana room, a Niger room, and so on. That's how the tents were organized on Oranienplatz, you could find your way better, Rashid says. So here in Room 2017, we are, so to speak, in Nigeria. One of the sleepers has begun to snore quite loudly, but none of the others laughs at this or even seems to notice. The burly fellow, Rashid, and Zair, the one sitting next to him, were in the same boat. What vegetation is there in your country? Do people have pets? Did you learn a trade? When the Italian coast guard tried to take the refugees aboard, all of them rushed to one side of the boat, and that's why the boat capsized. (The door opens, a black man looks in, says something in a language the visitor doesn't understand—Hausa, perhaps?—he receives an answer and disappears.) Did you go to school? Rashid couldn't swim. He grabbed onto a cable, and this is how he remained above water. Zair can't swim either, but as the boat began to tip upside down, he climbed over the edge of the boat sticking up in the air to its underside, and from there he was rescued. What kind of place did you like to hide when you were a child? But 550 out of 800 drowned. The TV now shows a large number of fish on a conveyor belt, women's hands in rubber gloves pick up each fish and in just a few seconds slice it into filets with a large knife. In Hamburg they ran into each other again, Rashid and Zair, and recognized each other at once. The sleeper snores on. They were on the same boat. 550 out of 800 drowned. Richard no longer desires any more information on fish processing. So he asks: Does one of you maybe remember a song? A song? No. One doesn't, the other doesn't, and a third doesn't either. But Abdusalam does. For

47

the first time he looks up briefly, it's the first time he's said a word, maybe he's ashamed because he's slightly cross-eyed. Just as Richard hoped, someone turns down the volume on the TV, and Abdusalam looks down again, at his hands, and begins to sing.

Everyone in Nigeria knows this song from the Eyo festival on the island of Lagos. Lagos? Tall Ithemba holds out the cracked display of his phone to show Richard a photo. Richard sees white hats, white robes down to the ground; white beards and netting obscure the faces, that's how the ghosts accompany their departed king to his grave. Some leap high into the air, in the photo they appear to be squatting half a meter above the ground, as if they've just arrived from midair and are about to land. On Sunday, ghosts with black hats announce the following week's procession; on Monday the announcers wear red hats, on Tuesday yellow, on Wednesday green, and on Thursday purple.

What do you do here all day long, Richard asks in the middle of nodding at the cracked display, and he's glad that in English there's only one way to say "you." It's possible that he's actually already addressing the men as intimates, thinking "du" in German in his head, but why would he? He wouldn't use "du" even with his students. We want to work, big Rashid says now, but we can't get working papers. It is hard, Zair says, very hard. One day is just the same as another, says tall Ithemba. We think and think, because we don't know what will happen, Abdusalam says and looks down. Richard would like to respond but he can't think how. After less than an hour of listening he is more exhausted than after one of his lectures at the university. When an entire world you don't know crashes down on you, how do you start sorting it all out? He says he must leave but will be back again. He has plenty of time for listening, he'll listen to everything. He has time.

After he closes the door behind him, he turns around to look at the room number again so he'll remember: the number 2017, written

48

on the sage-green door, the third from the left. After this come six or seven more sage-green doors, and on the other side of the hall, the same. At the end of the corridor, where the hallway turns to the right, is a window with a view of a brown-plastered wall. Three pairs of shoes lined up neatly on the sill. Only now does he notice the fluorescent light in the hallway intermittently flickering.

13

When Richard returns the next day, the security guard tells him that a staff member will be right there to take him upstairs; he isn't allowed to enter the building unaccompanied. *Vse v poriadke.* All right. For a year and a half, anyone who wanted to could speak with the refugees in the middle of the city, he himself could have done so a couple of weeks ago on his park bench. But the moment they signed an *agreement*, it became necessary to administer them. Bureaucratic geometry—he read this term a few days ago in a book by a historian on the consequences of colonialism. The colonized are smothered in bureaucracy, which is a pretty clever way to keep them from taking political action. Or was it just a matter of protecting the good Germans from the bad Germans, sparing the Land of Poets the indignity of being dubbed the Land of Killers once more? A propane stove in a tent on Oranienplatz might easily tip over, someone wrote anonymously in the comments section beneath a newspaper article back when the square was still occupied by the Africans. So had the Berlin Senate acted to preserve the Africans' safety or its own? In the latter case, the action that had been taken—installing the refugees in better quarters—was just a mask. And what lay behind it? What actual action lay behind this action you could see? Who was putting on a show for whom? Of course there was no way of knowing Richard wasn't the one talking about the propane stove. The Africans probably had no idea who Hitler was, but even so: only if they survived Germany now would Hitler truly have lost the war.

The staff member who comes to get him and bring him upstairs is an elegant older woman. Passing the billiard room (now deserted), they climb the stairs with the tendril-shaped railings; there is milky light from the fluorescent ceiling lamps flickering in the hallway, and on the sage-green doors. The woman knocks and opens the door to 2017 without waiting for a response, the same as the director of the home the day of his first visit. In 2017 there are once again several figures lying in their beds asleep, possibly Rashid, Zair, Ithemba, Abdusalam—Richard can't tell. The TV is off, and no one reacts to the open door.

The woman closes the door and continues on to 2018, knocking and pressing down on the door handle, but the door is locked. At 2019 she knocks and opens, and against the left-hand wall is a bed on which someone sits writing. Isn't that the fellow Richard saw with the bicycle on Oranienplatz? The man is very young, with unruly curls. When the staff member asks if he'd like to speak with the professor, he signals his assent by throwing his head back like a restive horse. He lays the sheet of paper, already covered from top to bottom with German vocabulary words, on the bed beside him; above his head, a list of irregular verbs hangs on the wall, *Gehen, ging, gegangen*: go, went, gone. Only now, as Richard pulls up the only chair in the room to sit down, does he see that the other two beds have people lying in them, asleep under the blankets. That doesn't matter, the staff member says when she sees his hesitation. So it doesn't matter. For a moment it horrifies him that these young men are suddenly being forced to be so old here: Waiting and sleeping. Taking meals for as long as the money holds out, and besides that: waiting and sleeping.

What country are you from?
Here it is again, that "you" that sounds like a "du." But perhaps

it's just because of the boy's age. He could be Richard's grandson. He looks exactly the way Richard always imagined the Greek god Apollo would look.

Del deserto, the boy says in Italian.

Richard and his wife took several language courses in Tuscany, the first of them on their summer holidays the year after the Wall fell, because they loved Dante.

How do you know Italian?

We had a year of lessons in the camp. But instead of saying "camp," the boy uses the German word *Lager*.

In Lampedusa?

No, after that, in Sicily.

Richard recalls the Greek temples in Agrigento and the man on the motorcycle who snatched his wife's handbag. They'd stepped simultaneously into the worlds of antiquity and capitalism, as if entering a diorama encompassing 2500 years.

Now he repeats his question:

What country are you from?

I come from the desert.

If Richard only knew how large the Sahara was exactly. Was he from Algeria? Sudan? Niger? Egypt?

For the first time in his life, the thought occurs to him that the borders drawn by Europeans may have no relevance at all for Africans. Recently, opening the atlas to look up the capital cities, he was struck by all the perfectly straight lines, but only now does he grasp the arbitrariness made visible by such lines.

From the desert. All right.

But now the boy smiles—at his expense, no doubt—and says: I come from Niger.

So this must be the Niger room. But what people has its home in Niger? Richard asks:

Are you also a Yoruba?

No, Tuareg.

And again he's at a loss. There's a model of car called Touareg.

He remembers hearing something once about blue veils worn by men. But what else?

Father? Mother?

No, no parents.

No parents?

The young man tosses his head back, which might mean *yes*, or else *no*.

Don't you have any family?

The boy is silent. Why should he tell a stranger that he doesn't know why he never had any parents? In the desert there's a lot of space. If you know the way the dunes wander, you can recognize the sand among all the sand. Why should he tell him that he doesn't know if his parents are still alive? There was fighting going on at the time when he was born. Maybe his mother or his father was among the people buried alive beneath the sand by the Nigerien soldiers, or hacked to pieces, or burnt alive. Here and there, they told stories like this, perhaps he was stolen from his parents. In any case, he'd worked as a slave for as long as he could remember. Worked with the camels, donkeys, and goats from morning to night. Why should he show a stranger the scars left on his head and arms by beatings given him by his so-called family? They tried to beat him to death.... His only friends were the animals.

When your mother or father has to work, you stay with your aunt, the boy says.

I understand, Richard says.

One of the sleepers turns over and wraps himself more tightly in his blanket.

What language did you speak there?

Tamasheq.

Is that the Tuareg language?

Yes.

And you also understand Hausa?

Yes.

And Arabic?

Yes.

And French?

Yes.

And now you're learning German?

Yes.

You write well, Richard says, pointing at the sheet of paper on the blanket beside the boy.

But only German letters.

Should he tell the stranger that the children of the herders would sit beside their mothers in front of the tent, learning to write Tifinagh—the Tuareg script—in the sand while he had to go milk the camels one last time before nightfall? He would see the written characters in the sand before the wind wiped them away overnight, would see them on swords, skins, and rocks in the middle of the desert—the cross, the circle, the triangles and dots—and would have liked to know their meaning. *See, saw, seen.* But he was an *akli*, a slave. All he could read was the stars. The seven sisters of night, the warrior of the desert, the mother camel and her child.

Had his parents simply forgotten him?

Or sold him?

Only now does Richard see that the boy has four lines inscribed in the skin of each cheek.

What does that symbol mean?

It's a mark of the Tuareg people.

Richard asks his questions and hears the answers, but he is still at a loss.

Can you tell me how you lived?

The young man takes his phone, looks for something, and finally shows Richard a photograph of a large round hut with a domed roof.

So Apollo has a phone with internet access.

Three men can build a hut like this in one day, he explains, using reeds, palm leaves, skins, woven mats, and sticks. When you depart a place, he says, you take the hut apart and go. The leaves, the reeds, the ashes from the fire—all that disappears quickly in the desert.

But you take the skins and the mats with you?

Yes, and the poles. Trees are rare.

And the dishes, the household objects, the clothing—you take all your possessions with you?

Yes.

And everything you own is carried by a few camels?

Yes.

When Richard and his wife moved into their house twenty years ago, they'd filled eighty boxes just with books, not to mention other boxes with dishes, linens, and clothes, the furniture, rugs, and pictures, the lamps, the piano, the washing machine, the refrigerator. They'd stuffed every last inch of a large moving van with their possessions.

And food, of course, the boy says.

For how long?

Sometimes two months, sometimes three, depending on the route.

Two or three months?

Yes. You load up the camels, the boy repeats, take down the huts and go. With his hands, he makes a gesture intended to show the flatness of what is left behind, and says: like on Oranienplatz.

The professor emeritus, who's hearing so many things for the first time that it's as if he's become a child again, now suddenly understands that Oranienplatz is not only the square designed in the nineteenth century by the famous landscape architect Lenné, not only the square where an elderly woman walks her dog every day, or where a girl on a park bench kissed her boyfriend for the first time. For a boy who has grown up among the nomads, Oranienplatz— where he made his home for a year and a half—is one station on a long journey, a temporary place, leading to the next temporary place. When they tore down the shacks—purely a political issue for Berlin's interior minister—this boy was thinking of his life in the desert.

All at once Richard remembers the time a Viennese colleague of his, strolling through a vineyard during a symposium in the south of Austria, suddenly stopped short, drew in a lungful of air, and asked if he could smell it too: the Sirocco, his colleague said, came from Africa and across the Alps, sometimes even bringing a bit of desert sand along with it. And indeed: on the leaves of the grape-vines you could see the fine, ruddy dust that had made its way from Africa. Richard had run his finger across one of the leaves and observed how this small gesture produced a sudden shift in his perspective and sense of scale. Now, too, he is experiencing such a moment; he is reminded that one person's vantage point is just as valid as another's, and in seeing, there is no right, no wrong.

At just this moment someone knocks on the door and opens it a crack—here is a face he doesn't know yet.

Awad is his name, the new arrival says. He's heard there's some-one here who wants to hear his story. He lives right next door, in Room 2020. He gives Richard's hand a quick shake, nods, and is already gone.

And now? Richard asks the boy.

Nothing, he says.

Do they actually give you money here? he asks.

Yes, for two weeks now, the boy says, but that isn't good, I want instead to have work.

Work.

Work.

He has to go now, these conversations exhaust him more than he expected.

I'll be back, Richard says, the way one might speak to a sick person who may or may not last the night. Or is the sick person him? In his head, he conjugates the verb "to perish." The two other men on their cots are still asleep. He says goodbye to this boy who looks exactly the way he always imagined Apollo.

In the supermarket that used to be a *Kaufhalle*, the crates of mineral water, soda, and beer are stacked just inside the entrance. Then comes the bread, then the fruit and vegetables—cucumbers, iceberg lettuce. The refrigerator shelves hold sausages and cheese. Don't forget the horseradish, toothpaste, paper towels, and socks; just before the cash register he takes a lighter from the rack and batteries for his radio in the bathroom, that'll be 32.90 euros, just a moment, I have change, or should I pay by card, no, you don't have to, all right, fine. This is his world, it's become the world in which he knows his way around. He's never bought groceries for two or three months at a time, not even during the bird-flu panic. He always writes out his shopping lists at home in the order of the supermarket shelves he now passes as he walks through the store. Lying on his deathbed some day, he'll still remember which pallet holds the crates of beer.

14

On Thursday Richard assembles the paperwork for his taxes, calls the health insurance company, and has his mechanic put the winter tires on his car. Not until Friday does he return to the red-brick building with his ID, *vse v poriadke*. Here again are the green pool table without balls and the black men gathered around it just like the other day. Black men, green table—black and green are the official colors of Hannover's soccer team, which confusingly is called "the Reds," as if Germany's national soccer league had a Communist faction. The older woman staff member silently accompanies him upstairs and leaves him, at his request, in front of the door to Room 2020, a sage-green door like all the others.

He knocks and waits, and Awad opens the door.

How are you? Awad asks.

Probably he's doing well, what else should he say?

How are you?

Awad's doing well too.

Empty phrases signify politeness in a language in which neither of them is at home.

Awad opens the door wider to invite him in, he'd like to tell him his story, he says after shutting the door again behind his visitor. Because if you want to arrive somewhere, you can't hide anything.

Is that really true? Richard asks.

Awad says: Of course! and offers him a chair.

Richard thanks him, sits down, and thinks of that nobody Odysseus. He thinks of the silent men in front of Berlin's Town Hall that summer. He also thinks of how he hid his lover from his wife and at the same time hid the everyday life he shared with his wife from his lover. Does Awad mean that *he* has never arrived in his own life?

But Awad's "of course" refers only to the fact that his offer was meant in earnest, for—as he says now—he's already told the psychologist everything too.

The psychologist?

If Richard prefers, Awad says, he can just call the psychologist, just a moment, he has her card with the telephone number, but really that's not, Richard says, no, really, I'm happy to, no problem, just a moment, it's got to be here somewhere. Awad hunts for the business card of the psychologist to whom he's already told his

57

whole story, looking first on the table, then on the windowsill, then the shelf, then the cupboard, and finally in his bag, which is under the bed. Really, it isn't necessary, Richard says, it's not at all important, he says, turning this way and that depending on where Awad is looking for the card at a given moment, and if Awad can't find the card now, then maybe later, that's perfectly fine, but Awad doesn't stop looking: it's got to be here somewhere, he just had it, where could he have put it?

Richard sees that a blue plaid curtain has been drawn halfway across the window. Could that have been left behind by the previous elderly inhabitants of this room?

Just a moment, Awad says, the psychologist knows everything about me. Richard will never call the psychologist, but he can't say so to this man who's working himself into more and more of a frenzy, digging around on the shelf and in his duffle bag over and over, lifting up the papers on the windowsill for the fourth time, even looking under the blankets, and opening and shutting the door to the cupboard after every circuit he makes of the room with searching eyes.

Instructions for the use of the dishwasher in the common kitchen hang on the wall. The three other beds in the room are empty and have been neatly made up.

Where are the others? Richard asks.

Playing pool, Awad replies, and now finally he abandons his search, looking drained as he turns back to his visitor, I'm sorry, he says, unfortunately I can't find the card.

My name is Richard, Richard says.

Awad was born in Ghana. His mother died giving birth to him. *Just like Blanchefleur*, Richard thinks, *just like the mother of Tristan*. The first day of my life, Awad says, is also the day I lost my mother. And your father? Awad doesn't answer. Until the age of seven, he says, he lived with his Nana, his grandmother. Is your grandmother still alive? Have you seen her since then? Do you remember what she looks like? No. When Awad was seven years old, his father brought him to live in Libya. This grandmother—whose daughter died giving birth to her first child, whose grandson learned to speak from her and was washed by her every evening before going to bed, standing on a board so the hot earth wouldn't burn his feet—this now very old and possibly even deceased woman tries to fight her way out of the memory-free zone surrounding her grandson, fight her way into the world of all that can be told, but she doesn't succeed, her grandson calls her *Nana*, as all Ghanaian grandmothers are called, and beyond that she has no name, she remains trapped in this lower stratum and silently sinks back down again. What will the man in the lake do when the lake freezes over soon?

Did you ever go back to Ghana?

No, never.

His father worked in Tripoli as a driver for an oil company. Awad was sent to school, they lived alone in an eight-room house. Often there were guests and when his father got home from work, he cooked for everyone. His father played soccer with him and bought him toys. Gave him pocket money, quite a lot actually. He flew with him to Egypt on vacation—the flight to Cairo only took thirty minutes—I know my way around Cairo really well, Awad says, we went over there a lot. "Over there" is what West Germany was called back in GDR times. Awad's father waited until evening to raise the blinds on the southern side of the house, where the sun shone all day long. His father taught him how to dry his back after a shower, with a towel stretched diagonally across it. His father taught him to cook, and gave him his first electric razor.

My father told me who I am, Awad says.

And then Awad just sits silently for a moment, gazing at the fake-wood veneer on the table's surface. This table, too, may have stood twenty-five years ago in a *Volkssolidarität* office, or in the House of

German-Soviet Friendship, but Awad has no way of knowing this, and he certainly has no way of knowing what *Volkssolidarität* or German-Soviet friendship was.

And then?

I started to work as an auto mechanic. I had friends. It was a good life.

And then?

On the street outside, a truck is backing up, you can hear the warning signal, a high-pitched beeping sound, over and over. In Morse code, it would be zero. Every odd week in the calendar, the plastic recycling is picked up. Or maybe it's a furniture delivery truck trying to turn around in the driveway.

Then my father was shot.

Richard would like to say something at this point, but he can't think of anything.

A small yellow label is affixed to the table leg, Inventory # 360/87.

Richard had seen his father one last time in the hospital after his death, the nurses had bound the dead man's jaw to his skull with a bandage to keep his mouth from hanging open for all eternity. The bandage made his father look like a nun, Richard had barely recognized him.

Awad sits bent over, propping himself on his arms and gazing ever deeper into the table's surface as he goes on speaking.

A friend of my father's called me. They were here in the office! he shouted. Your father! That's all. I said I didn't understand what he meant. Then he started shouting again. This man who never shouted, who was always friendly to me. Now he was shouting at me and said I should run home as fast as I could and lock the door. Then the connection was broken off, and I started running. But when I got home, the front door was already ripped off its hinges, the windows were shattered. Inside everything was destroyed in the hallway, the rooms, the kitchen. There were shards everywhere, the furniture was upside-down, the TV was smashed, everything. I climbed out one of the back windows and tried to call my father's friend again. I tried again and again. But I couldn't get through. Once I also dialed my father's number.

Nothing.

That's how the end was.

Until night came, I waited on the street. Where was I supposed to go? It was the same street I walked to go to school and later to work. Then a military patrol came. They forced me to get in the back of a truck and brought me to a barracks camp. I saw dead people lying on the street, some of them shot, others stabbed. On this day, I saw the war. On this day, I saw the war.

There were already hundreds of people in the barracks. Most of them were black Africans, but there were also some Arabs, from Tunisia, Morocco, Egypt. Not only men, but also women, children, babies, old people. They took everything away from us: money, watches, phones, even our socks, he says and starts laughing. He laughs and laughs. It's not easy, he says, and stops laughing. It's not easy, he says again, shaking his head, it's not easy, as if this were the end of his story.

And then?

When I tried to complain, he says, they hit me in the head with a rifle butt. You can still see the scar: Awad parts his hair with his fingers and shows the scar to the professor emeritus with whom he's speaking today for the first time in his life. If you want to arrive somewhere, you can't hide anything, he had said to Richard at the beginning of their conversation.

If you're lucky, you get beaten, if you're unlucky, you get shot, someone said to console me. Then they took the SIM cards out of our phones and destroyed them before our eyes. They broke the memory, Awad says. None of us had anything left except a t-shirt and pants or a skirt. For two days we sat there in the barracks while the European bombs fell on Tripoli. We were afraid one of the bombs would hit us, since it was a military camp. On the third day they brought us to the harbor and made us get on a boat. Who among you knows how to steer a boat like this? Two or three Arabs said they did. They raised a Gaddafi flag on our boat, Awad says laughing: a Gaddafi flag!

So were they Gaddafi people? Or rebels?

We didn't know. They all had the same uniforms.

Before this moment, Richard had never really thought that members of the military who turned against the government would still be wearing their country's uniform.

In any case, no one was on our side. Even though I grew up in Libya. Libya was my country. Awad nods to himself and for a while he says nothing more.

And then?

Then they shot a salvo in the air and said to us: Anyone who tries to swim back will be shot. We didn't know where the boat was going. Maybe to Malta? Or Tunisia? Only later did we understand it was going to Italy. We were squeezed in so tight, you could only get up for a few minutes, then you sat down again right where you were sitting before. The woman behind me peed without getting up. When I tried to prop myself up, everything was wet. We were in the boat for four days. There were only a few bottles of water, and we gave them to the children. When things got too bad, we adults drank salt water. It's not easy, Richard, it's not easy. We made a bigger hole in an empty plastic bottle with our teeth, and then we tied together a couple of shoelaces, attached the bottle, and let it over the side to scoop up the seawater. You have to drink. A few people died. They were sitting right there next to us, and then one would say, very quietly: my head, my head, and then bend his head like this; and then the next moment he was dead. When people died, we threw them in the water.

Richard thinks about all the airplanes from which he's looked out the oval window at some sea or other. How the waves, seen from above, appear not to be moving at all, and the white foam looks like stone. In the middle of the previous century, the Libyan coast briefly belonged to Italy. Now Libya is a different country, and to refugees who leave by boat, Italy appears first in the form of a small rocky elevation surrounded by a great deal of water. If it appears to them at all.

War destroys everything, Awad says: your family, your friends, the place where you lived, your work, your life. When you become foreign, Awad says, you don't have a choice. You don't know where to go. You don't know anything. I can't see myself anymore, can't see the child I used to be. I don't have a picture of myself anymore.

My father is dead, he says.

And me—I don't know who I am anymore.

Becoming foreign. To yourself and others. So that's what a transition looks like.

What's the sense of all of this? he asks, looking back at Richard again.

Now Richard is the one who's supposed to answer, but he doesn't know how.

Isn't it like this, Awad says: every adult human being—man or woman, rich or poor, if he has work or not, if he lives in a house or is homeless, it doesn't matter—every human being has his few years to live, and then he dies?

Yes, that's how it is, Richard says.

After this, Awad says a few more things, as if he wants to make it easier for Richard to remain silent. For three-quarters of a year, he was in a camp in Sicily, ten people to a room. Then he had to leave. The moment they sent you away, you had to find your own place to sleep, you were free! Without a job, a ticket, or food, and you couldn't rent a room. *Mi dispiace, poco lavoro*. There was no work. At the end of the day you're still on the street. If your parents didn't raise you well, you become a thief. If you had good parents, you fight to survive. *Poco lavoro. Poco lavoro.* But Richard, what can you eat? Richard has read Foucault and Baudrillard, and also Hegel and Nietzsche, but he doesn't know what you can eat when you have no money to buy food. You can't wash, so you start to smell bad. *Sempre poco lavoro.* That's how life was on the street for us. I slept in the train station. During the day I walked around, and at night, I came to the station to sleep. I can't remember anymore how I spent the days. Richard, you think I am looking at you, but I don't know where my mind is. I don't know where my mind is.

What a lovely but unfortunately untranslatable way of putting things, Richard thinks, despite the richness of the German language. In German you can say that your thoughts are elsewhere, or that you don't know where your spirit is, or your soul. Why does German have no word for "mind"? Maybe one has to say: this just isn't me.

Once Awad helped out in a kitchen for three days, cleaning up and washing the dishes, and they gave him eighty euros. With this money he went to a travel agent to book a flight to Germany. What was he supposed to say when the woman in the travel agency asked whether he wanted to fly to Cologne, to Hamburg, Munich, or Berlin? He didn't know Cologne, he didn't know Hamburg either, nor Munich, nor Berlin. Just a ticket to Germany, he said. The woman in the travel agency was losing her patience, but that didn't matter to him, his mind wasn't there. There it was again: that lovely untranslatability. Was he lost in thought, absent, had he taken leave of his senses, was he beyond it all?

War after war, since 1613 German children have sent cockchafers flying from the backs of their hands off into the beyond with this chanted ditty:

Cockchafer, fly!
Your father's off at war.
Your mother's in Pomerania,

Pomerania's burned to the ground.
Cockchafer, fly!

Goethe's Iphigenia, too, is present and absent, as an emigrant in Tauris, seeking the land of her childhood *with her soul*. Seen from this perspective, it's downright ridiculous to measure a transition by the presence of a body. Seen from this perspective, the uninhabitability of Europe for a refugee suddenly stands in direct relationship to the uninhabitability of the very flesh that is given to every human spirit to inhabit until the end of his days. So Awad chose Berlin. Unwashed, he caught his flight. After he arrived, everyone around him was speaking this new language he couldn't understand, all he could do was nod. He saw people getting into a bus: did it go to the center? Three nights at Alexanderplatz. A man said to him there was a square. *With Africans like me? Then surely I'll be able to wash there.* The man bought him a ticket from the machine. *A machine that spits out tickets? Deutschland is beautiful!*

Then he saw the tents.

I stood alone. The man went away. Never in my life had I slept in a tent.

That's where he was supposed to live?

In a tent?

He stood in the middle of the tents, crying.

But then he heard someone speaking Arabic, a Libyan dialect.

At Oranienplatz, they gave him something to eat and a place to sleep.

Oranienplatz provided for him, as his father had provided for him in Libya.

He will never forget his father, he will always revere his memory.

And in just this way he will never forget Oranienplatz. He will always revere its memory.

This is what Awad says in conclusion, and after that there is truly nothing left to say.

15

When was it that Richard had read Gottfried von Strassburg? Was it before that time he'd stood waiting in that back courtyard in the broiling heat for his wife to come down? Or in the years that followed? In any case, after his wife died, the lines about the love between Blanchefleur and Rivalin kept coming back to him: *He was she and she was he. / He was hers and she was his*. Blanchefleur loved Rivalin, Tristan's father, so much that after his death in battle she stayed alive only long enough to bear his child and then succumbed to *fatal heartache*. What name to give the child? *The marshal long was silent*, the epic reports. *He thought quite deeply*. Conceived in mourning and born in mourning, the child was finally given the name Tristan, since "triste" names this sadness. Richard is having difficulty remembering the foreign names of the Africans, so when he sits at his desk taking notes in the evening, he transforms Awad into *Tristan*, and the boy from the day before yesterday into *Apollo*. These are names he'll be able to keep straight later on.

At breakfast the next morning, his head is full of questions. Why in the world are the men being denied the right to hold a job in a country where even the right to a place in heaven is predicated on work? Why aren't they being asked about their histories and provided for as victims of war? He spends the day studying the regulation known as *Dublin II*, and it takes him until it is time to turn on the desk lamp again to understand that all this law regulates is jurisdiction.

It doesn't concern itself with the question of whether or not these men are victims of war.

The details of their histories are the sole legal responsibility of the country where they first set foot on European soil. Only there may they seek asylum, nowhere else. But the way their cases are handled varies from country to country.

Austria and Switzerland had the most coveted borders back

when there were wars in the Balkans. Now that things in Africa aren't going as they should, Greece and Italy are having to take in the most refugees. If there were a war someday in Iceland, causing the citizens of that country to flee—then Norway and Sweden would have to issue passports to these refugees who couldn't go home, and offer them jobs and the chance to settle down—or not.

Richard understands: Dublin II allows all the European countries without a Mediterranean coastline to purchase the right not to have to listen to the stories of arriving refugees. In other words, so-called "asylum fraud" is nothing more than telling a true story in a country where no one's legally obligated to listen, much less do anything in response. And the soon-to-be-implemented fingerprint scanning system, he reads, will preclude all misunderstandings as to whether an individual belongs to a group that must be listened to or not.

He remembers Tristan telling him the day before that he can't get the images of the dead lying on the streets of Tripoli out of his mind. When you become foreign, Awad says, you don't have a choice. Somewhere here is where the problem lies, Richard thinks: the things you've experienced become baggage you can't get rid of, while others—people with the freedom to choose—get to decide which stories to hold on to. On his way downstairs from Awad's room he runs into the older woman in the sage-green stairwell and asks her why Awad has been to a psychologist. He couldn't stop crying, she says, sometimes for hours at a time. No one here knew what to do.

While Richard sits at his desk reading, and his mirror image in the black windowpane displays its shock of gray hair, he understands another thing as well. The Italian laws have different borders in mind than the German laws do. What interests him is that as long as a border of the sort he's been familiar with for most of his life runs along a particular stretch of land and is permeable in either direction after border control procedures, the intentions of the two countries can be perceived by the use of barbed wire, the configuration of fortified barriers, and things of that sort. But the moment these borders are defined only by laws, ambiguity takes over, with each country responding, as it were, to questions its neighbor hasn't asked. The neighbor, meanwhile, has topics of its own to discuss, which may or may not include what that other country wants to know.

Indeed, the law has made a shift from physical reality to the realm of language.

The foreigner, who is at home in neither of these countries, is trapped between these now-invisible fronts in an intra-European discussion that has nothing at all to do with him or the actual war he's trying to escape from.

Italy, for example, allows refugees to depart for other countries, in fact it's happy to let them go, since it has more than enough of them. Italian law gives them the freedom to travel to France, Germany, indeed any European country, to look for work. Germany, however—for reasons still not clear to Richard—refuses to take them, so after a three-month stay as "tourists," they're required to return to Italy for at least a quarter of a year. They're only allowed to look for work in Germany after five uninterrupted years of asylum in Italy—and even then, only if they can produce a so-called *illimitata* issued by the Italians, a document granting them the same residency rights as Italian citizens. If they aren't in possession of an *illimitata*, they can still leave Italy so as not to starve there, but no one else will let them in.

For a moment, Richard imagines what it would be like to have someone explaining these laws to him in Arabic.

Then he gets up, does five squats to limber up again after the hours of sitting at his desk, and puts on a necktie. That evening he's been invited to a birthday party three gardens down for his friend Detlef. Detlef's wife Sylvia was sick for most of the past year, so they've

68

ordered a dinner just this once from a catering service. Stainless-steel warming trays will hold roast wild boar, fish, rice, and boiled potatoes with parsley, then there will be a tureen of Asiatic soup, and cold platters with chicken skewers and quiche Lorraine, bowls of green and black olives, sun-dried tomatoes, capers, and glazed onions, a pink-tinted mousse and a light-green one decorated with parsley, rice salad, sliced duck breast, white bread and dark rye, mustard, mayonnaise, ketchup and green salad. And for dessert an assortment of fruit, chocolate cake, and mascarpone with raspberries. He's not sure he's all that hungry.

Richard, what can you eat?

The doorbell rings again, a bouquet, his coat, no need to take your shoes off. A catering service really isn't a bad idea! That's what we thought, too. They even take the dirty plates away after. Fantastic!

He and his friends still aren't done exploring all the blessings of this other world that has become more and more tightly intertwined with theirs over the past almost twenty-five years. These residents of a street formerly called Ernst-Thälmann-Strasse after the leader of the German Communist Party are still surprised to discover that these tiny blue flames really can keep the food nice and warm for over two hours as if it were fresh from the kitchen.

It's delicious, really, and I was afraid it wouldn't be enough, well, the chocolate cake is slightly, oh, come on, not at all.

Of the twelve or fifteen friends Richard sees every year at this party, he's known most of them half his life, and some almost his entire life long. He's been friends with the host since elementary school. Detlef met his first wife, Marion (who's now gone out to the terrace to smoke in peace), at Richard's twenty-fifth birthday party. Marion was a cellist in the same orchestra in which Richard's wife Christel played the viola. During their university years, Richard and Christel sometimes looked after the couple's baby when they wanted a night out. Meanwhile it's been almost forty years since Detlef and Marion parted ways, but the two have remained friends, and their son builds bridges in China. After the disbanding of the orchestra, Marion opened a tea shop and now lives with her second husband outside of Potsdam. Anne, the photographer sitting on the sofa, was a wild creature. Richard spent two or three nights with her shortly after their high school graduation. After the fall of the Wall she lived for a while in France, but she's been back for two years now, taking care of her elderly mother. *That heap they've built down there is a real monstrosity, all they care about is the money.* And that fat man sitting on the bench studied economic history and then taught at the university, but in the West, Socialist economic history was the wrong subject to be an expert in, so now he repairs computers. His wife doles out his cigarette allowance, three packs a week—it's unclear whether this is out of thrift or concern for his health—in any case, he always comes to this party alone. *A burglar alarm isn't a bad idea. So listen, in December I'm going to a spa. What a great idea, which one?* Some of Detlef's friends now require reading glasses when they peruse the back covers of the books on the gift table. Monika, the professor of German literature, and her mustache-wearing husband Jörg, now leaning with her against the windowsill, often went on vacation with Richard and Christel, usually to the Baltic. *I'm not allowed to babysit my grandchild anymore, my daughter-in-law has become so incredibly . . . I was just over there until two weeks ago, in Chicago as a visiting professor. . . .*

Sylvia, his friend's second wife, is a quiet one. You can tell just by looking that she hasn't had an easy year. When she moved into Detlef's house, years before the Wall fell, she still wore a ponytail and had a girlish look about her. Christel sometimes helped her with the dishes at the end of this annual party after all the others guests had already left, while Richard and Detlef carried all the extra chairs back into the other rooms. *I'd love another glass. Yes, red wine, please. Do you have some of that mineral water that's not so fizzy? That would be perfect.* Some of these friends bought condominiums as an investment in the post-Wall years, because they thought that's what you did now, in the West. Sight unseen, they'd purchased mold-infested dumps in Cologne, Duisburg, or Frankfurt am Main, then they couldn't find renters and went broke. The graphic designer over there would have liked to have children, but she always picked the wrong men. *Lord knows I've traveled enough in my days. Anyone want another beer? Still, Merkel is a physicist, don't forget that.* Does Detlef have false teeth already? But that's something you don't ask even a close friend. *Krause died last week, did you hear?* Christel once had a fling with this Krause. Before him. A dentist. *This summer I saw the pyramids.* . . . That journalist he sees now sometimes brings him along to opera premieres, he gets press tickets, for example last spring they saw the opening night of *Carmen*. And Andreas, the serious-looking fellow leaning against the hutch, had a stroke two years ago and since then has been on disability and has started writing poems that he sometimes reads aloud to his friends. But look for a publisher? *There are already so many books on the market, what's the point?* At last year's party, he announced that he'd decided to read nothing but Hölderlin. *Nothing else is worth your time.* When the Wall stood, the capital city of the GDR was a system that could be apprehended as a whole—every person here knows so much about all the others that their lives are permanently interwoven. *The hedge is so tall already, how in the world did you manage that? It's the soil. The operation was in March, but no chemo, thank God, you'll see, it'll be all right.* Most of these friends were born, like him, at the very end of the war or already in peacetime. In his infancy, his mother had sat with him in the air-raid cellar, his father was still at the front. Later, in the GDR, that would have been unimaginable. It's perfectly clear what's happening in the Middle East: the formerly Socialist countries are being systematically eradicated, one after the other. Here in Europe, it's still peacetime, and now some of their circle have begun to die. *If it were summer, we could be grilling outside. Say, what's Joachim up to? He's having a rough time of it, he's drinking too, but that's understandable.*

71

16

On Monday Richard makes his way to the red-brick building almost as automatically as he'd commuted to the university during the first half of the year. He crosses the street's bumpy cobblestones, wondering what convicts cut and polished the granite. He walks past the vacant lot where until recently a large villa stood with bay windows, a glassed-in veranda, and carved wooden ornaments, but now there's nothing but pallid sand waiting for the new construction to begin—there's no better way to make history disappear than to unleash money, money roaming free has a worse bite than an attack dog, it can effortlessly bite an entire building out of existence, Richard thinks. Now he's reached the display board mounted on the side of the road in front of the nursing home, the speed limit here is twenty miles per hour, but 45, 35, 40 light up in digital numerals on the display whenever a car passes, after the sign they hit the brakes, the usual story, shame and remorse—the crooked pair that's made him cower, too, always when it's already too late, when his wife held up a letter from his lover that he'd done a bad job of hiding, holding it in her hand as she stood there screaming at him. From the nursing home—where he, too, perhaps will one day spend his twilight years—an elderly woman now emerges, holding tight to a walker, her shopping bag dangling from the walker's gray handle, and given the speed with which she is advancing toward him, going out for groceries is probably her plan for the entire morning.

When he goes into the red-brick building, Richard is informed by the security guard that the men have German class today: always Mondays and Thursdays. Why shouldn't he join them for German class, assuming, of course, that the teacher agrees. He walks down the hall, around the corner. The teacher defies his expectations: she's a young woman from Ethiopia who for whatever reason speaks excellent German. She gives her permission, and so it comes to pass that on this Monday a professor emeritus will sit in her classroom. He takes a seat in the penultimate row of the large room and squeezes his knees in under the desk, Apollo sits two rows in front of him, writing something at his desk—*write, wrote, written*—and further up he sees Tristan (Awad), who has spotted him and greets him with a nod. He nods back. He can't quite tell if the man bending far over his desk up in front is Abdusalam, who sang the song last week. Didn't this Abdusalam wear his hair in tiny braids? Richard is having a hard time remembering particular people, the hair and faces of the men who fill this room are all so dark. Rashid, the boat refugee, is the only one he'd recognize at once, because he's so large, but Rashid isn't there.

The Ethiopian woman and her adult pupils are practicing reading letters. Then they practice reading words. In alphabetical order, she mimes an *Auge* (eye), a *Buch* (book), a *Daumen* (thumb), omitting the trickier "C," then she turns to the vowels. *Hier*—she says, *hi-i-i-ier*, using her hand to accompany all the air that comes out of her mouth when she pronounces the German word for "here." While she is teaching, the doors remain open. From time to time a tardy pupil arrives, and from time to time a pupil packs up his things, excuses himself, and leaves. In the last half hour, the young teacher leads exercises for the more advanced students using the auxiliary verbs *haben* (to have) and *sein* (to be). *Ich gehe*, she says—I go—and walks a few steps from left to right, her arms akimbo, then she points back over her shoulder, indicating back where the past is, and says: *Gestern bin ich gegangen*—yesterday I went. She says: verbs of motion generally require the auxiliary verb *sein* to form their past tense. *Sein*, conjugated as follows: *ich bin, du bist, er ist*, and so on. Then she goes on to illustrate the usage in the first person, "I went, I flew, I swam": *ich bin gegangen, ich bin geflogen, ich bin geschwommen*.

She now marches back the way she came, arms akimbo again, she spreads her arms to fly, she swims past the blackboard. *Ich bin super*, Apollo says suddenly. Yes, she says, you are super, but now let's practice forming the past tense.

When the lesson is over, the men file out past Richard, and a couple of them nod to him: Zair? Tall Ithemba? Apollo shakes hands with him, Tristan too, how are you? I'm fine, and you? I'm okay, I'm a little bit fine, Tristan says.

You're a good teacher, he says to the Ethiopian woman after the men have left.

And pretty, too, he thinks.

My degree is actually in agriculture, she says, packing up her cardboard letters. No one knows when the formal instruction the Senate has promised to offer in a real school is going to start.

Very pretty.

At Oranienplatz when she smelled marijuana, she realized something had to be done before these men lost everything. Richard wonders whether she wants a husband and is teaching here for that reason.

You have to fill your time with something, she says.

Your time? For a moment he's confused, wondering whether she means him. But no, she's referring to the men.

I understand.

To understand what a person means or says, it's basically necessary to already know what that person means or is saying. So is every successful dialogue just an act of recognition? And is understanding not a path, but a condition?

The teacher shuts the windows, reaching high up, which makes her breasts flatten. From the wooden frames, dry bits of white paint trickle to the floor.

Discussions like these with his students always quickly led to different topics: the notion of progress, the question of what freedom truly is, and the "four-sides model" describing how every speech act is always also tactical and inherently carries hidden meaning, since it is always also speaking about itself, in other words, about whether it, the speech act, is there or not. In just the same way as the listener always understands more than just words, the act of listening always contains the questions: What should you understand? What do you want to understand? What will you never understand but want to have confirmed?

The heat can't be turned off, the teacher says.

How long have you been teaching?

I started this summer when the men were still at Oranienplatz. Studying gives them something to do even outside of class, that's the good thing. But sometimes they have trouble concentrating.

The teacher wipes the board clean of the words *Auge*, *Buch*, and *Daumen*.

The pronunciation probably seems strange to them, he says, and then all the irregular verbs.

That's not the reason. There are so many disruptions in their lives that there's no room in their heads for new vocabulary. They don't know what's going to happen to them. They're afraid. It's difficult to learn a language if you don't know what it's for.

How long has it been since he was last with a woman?

What these men urgently need to be able to calm down is some peace, she says.

That's something he's never thought of: since these men aren't being permitted to arrive, what looks to him like peacetime here is for them basically still war.

The teacher picks up her bag, he pushes his chair back to the table.

Would you please turn out the lights when you leave? Already she's said goodbye and is outside. She's quick, he likes that.

These eternally flickering fluorescent tubes that sap the daylight's strength.

He shuts them off.

When he glances over his shoulder, the room really does look empty now. *Virgin Astraea, last of all the immortals* has left him. These desks at which he and the refugees were just sitting are, as he realizes only now, far too small for full-grown students. They were no doubt discarded by some school, probably the former Johannes R. Becher Polytechnic, now known as Lakeshore Primary. (The poet Johannes R. Becher wrote the words to the GDR's national anthem and later served as minister of culture.) On the sides of the desks, Richard sees hooks mounted thirty years ago to hold the book bags of the pupils of yesteryear, members of the Young Pioneers who are now sales clerks, engineers, or unemployed, with one or two divorces, zero to four children. The chairs are mismatched, some with yellow seat cushions, others with burgundy, some made of wood, others metal. He knows these chairs well from the time of party assemblies, residential district clubs, office parties to celebrate the founding of the Republic. Wherever the West came marching in, chucking out this Socialist furniture was always a top priority. Even now, almost twenty-five years after so-called reunification, you can sometimes still see the interlinked legs of these now out-of-favor wooden or gray-legged chairs poking up out of dumpsters, always in large quantities. His mother would have said: *They're still perfectly good*. He hasn't heard this sentence in a long time. Maybe he should have put on his light-blue shirt today.

17

Richard's plan for the next day is finding Rashid and Ithemba again. The security guards know him now and let him go upstairs unaccompanied. Here are the pool table without balls, the gracefully curved banister, and still there's no water on the second floor.

On the third floor, just as he's reached the sage-green door numbered 2017 and is about to knock, it flies open right in front of him, and a frantic Rashid dashes out, followed by three or four others, making for the stairs. From the stairwell, Richard now hears incomprehensible shouting, several voices all at once, and rapid, heavy footsteps up and down. The door is still swinging on its hinges, and no one's left in the room, so Richard follows this wild hunt into the stairwell, first they ran upstairs and now they are on their way down. What's up there on the fourth floor, where Richard's never been, the top floor of the building? He just has time to step back into the hall before they storm past. *For a hard foe is the Olympian to meet in strife. Yea, once ere this, when I was fain to save thee, he caught me by my foot and hurled me from the heavenly threshold; all day I flew, and at the set of sun I fell in Lemnos, and little life was in me.* Without even noticing Richard, Rashid thunders down the stairs, he's now being followed by ten or twelve younger men, among them Apollo, whose curls are bouncing up and down due to the rapid motion, as if in anticipation of some delightful outing. The fluorescent light in the stairwell has started flickering again, illuminating the sage-green twilight with intermittent lightning flashes. Richard goes upstairs (where he's never been) and finds, at the point where the stairs come to an end, another open door flapping on its hinges and a large room with three or four figures sitting around a circular table. Except for the gurgling of the coffeemaker, everything is quiet. When Richard comes closer, he sees that one of the people sitting at the table is the older woman who escorted him upstairs on his first few visits. Apparently this is the office used by the staff members who've been sent by the Berlin Senate. In the middle of the room lies a chair with bent legs, he walks around it, then quickly starts shaking hands. No one asks what he's doing here, maybe the older woman told them about him. Well, he says, it looks like something's afoot—the others nod—so I guess I'll take off. He wishes everyone a good day. On his way out, he tries to set the chair back on its feet, but since one of the legs is bent at a right angle, it immediately falls over again. Apologizing for this failed attempt to create order, he turns back to the silent group, one of the staff members is slurping coffee again. Was that Rashid? Richard asks, pointing at the chair, and the others nod. The light in the stairwell has calmed down again, the hurler of thunderbolts is nowhere to be seen or heard.

Downstairs at the exit, one of the security guards is on the phone. Richard asks the other one what's going on and is told that it looks as if the men will have to move tomorrow, to a facility located in the middle of the woods, nearly five miles outside Buckow.

Outside Buckow? Tomorrow?

I have no idea. I'm the security guard, that's all I know.

It takes at least an hour to get to Buckow, even in a car with no traffic. That's ridiculous, he says. The guard shrugs his shoulders.

Today at two o'clock they're holding an assembly, here's the flyer. Someone from the Berlin Senate might come.

Richard had planned to do his shopping today, but now he's too worked up to think about shopping. People wouldn't throw rulings like this around, he thinks, if they understood what it means to do serious research. He's only just started his interviews, and now obstacles are being strewn in his path. Even at the university there were bureaucrats like this who thought it was more important to get all your travel receipts stamped, renew your health insurance forms, and record the number of hours you spent in the office on some ledger, than it was to have time to do the work you'd been hired for, such as investigating whether there were ratios that determined the beauty of a line of verse just as reliably as they did the stability of a snail shell. Or finding out where in the literature of the Augustan Age Jesus appears as the last Greek god. Certainly you could spend time changing the password for your work email for the eighth time, or you might ask instead how what an author doesn't know about himself is nonetheless inscribed in his text. And who is the speaker in passages like these?

For this reason—although Richard's already been to enough time-gobbling assemblies to last a lifetime—he sets out twenty minutes before the hour to attend this accursed gathering.

The classroom where the German lessons are held is already filled to the last seat, many men are sitting with their legs wedged beneath the too-small desks. Staff members and security guards stand at the edges of the room, the discussion is just beginning. Since the gentleman from the Senate standing at the front of the room—slight of build, accurately parted blond hair—understands neither English, nor French, nor Italian, much less Arabic, a similar translation procedure is followed to the one Richard witnessed some weeks ago at the occupied school. But we have to be glad the Berlin Senate sent anyone at all, the man standing next to him whispers—one of the staff members he saw sitting at the silent table in the lounge that noon. The blond-headed German words now proclaim: We are completely sympathetic to your position! You contributed greatly to the peaceful resolution of the untenable situation at Oranienplatz! And other, similar sentences. This official doesn't look so happy to be tasked with addressing this malcontent, demanding riffraff. He's probably one of the lowest-ranking members of the Senate administration, or else he was given the assignment as a test. Richard almost feels sorry for him. So what do they want now, these complainers who are already getting three hundred euros a month from the Senate—which has no legal obligation to give them a penny—to tide them over until their cases are individually settled; on top of that, the city is giving them, at least for the time being, free subway passes and twelve part-time staff members to escort them to the doctor or the agencies where their cases are being processed.

The facility outside Buckow, I promise you, is a good solution for all involved, says the man from the Senate. You're not the only ones here in Berlin and the surrounding area who need housing, and if you want to stay together as a group, there aren't so many options.

We want to remain visible until there's a political solution for the problem as a whole, says Rashid, the thunderbolt-hurler from this morning, and rises to his feet. What are we supposed to do out in the woods? What's the point of having reached an agreement with the Senate? You have yet to fulfill a single item included in this agreement.

The beast has been shot and wounded, the shot costs three hundred euros a month per man, plus subway pass and staffing, but the beast remains dangerous nonetheless, it's impossible to tell whether it doesn't have fight left in it after all, maybe it'll attack again, perhaps more unpredictably next time.

These aren't issues that can be resolved overnight, says the man from the Senate, thinking about where best to seek shelter should the wounded beast decide to pounce.

A second man stands up: I've heard that from this *Lager,* it's three miles to the nearest bus stop.

Gaining time is always a good tactic—it lets the blood go on flowing quietly from the wound, weakening your opponent.

A third man: And just like that, from one day to the next!

A fourth: We need showers with doors, everything else violates our religion.

The wounded beast is still twitching, but it's only reflexes.

A fifth: More than four people in a room is unacceptable!

The man from the Berlin Senate waits until all the statements and questions have been translated for him, then he says: I understand your concerns, I'll make a note of everything.

When you're foreign, you don't have a choice anymore, Tristan says. And he isn't wrong either. Well not wrong exactly, Richard thinks, but wishing assumes that a person still lives in the sort of world in which wishing is permitted. Wishing is a form of home-sickness. No wonder, he thinks, so many half-starved prisoners of war of so many different nationalities in different camps during different wars kept themselves alive by exchanging recipes. In truth, what the refugees want from the Senate isn't a four-person room, a shower with individual stalls, or a bus stop just a short walk from the facility where they're housed. What they want is to be allowed to look for work, to organize their lives like any other person of sound body and mind. But the inhabitants of this territory—which has only been called *Germany* for around 150 years—are defending their borders with articles of law, they assail these newcomers with their secret weapon called time, poking out their eyes with days and weeks, crushing them with months—and if that weren't enough to subdue them, they might go so far as to issue them three cooking pots in assorted sizes, a set of bedding, and a document labeled *Fiktionsbescheinigung*.

Tribal wars, you might say.

At home, a little wooden chest on the bookshelf holds Richard's old ID and insurance card. In 1990 he suddenly found himself a citizen of a different country, from one day to the next, though the view out the window remained the same. The two swans he knew so well swam from left to right the day he became a citizen of the Federal Republic of Germany, exactly as they'd done back when it was still accurate to call him a citizen of the German Democratic Republic. A pair of ducks sat on a corner of the dock exactly as they had the day before—this dock for which he'd procured rail-road ties from the *Deutsche Reichsbahn*, which had been obliged to keep its fascist name even during the years of the Socialist repub-lic, apparently because of formalities surrounding the acquisition of the company. Did it matter what something was called? When Richard first encountered the word *Fiktionsbescheinigung* while reading about asylum issues on the internet, he'd assumed it was a term relating somehow to the English word *fiction*, but then the notion that any author among the refugees might be issued a *certificate of fiction* to make it easier for them to break into the international book market seemed far from plausible. As he soon came to understand, this *certificate of fiction* was merely a confirmation that this person existed who had not yet been granted the right to call himself a *refugee*. But the certificate itself didn't entitle its holder to any rights.

Meanwhile no resolution appears forthcoming in the argument between the two parties (the blond Senate representative and Rashid as speaker for the others), as the discussion has gotten bogged down in the back-and-forth translation; suddenly the director of the home appears, a sort of deus ex machina, and takes the floor. He announces that he's just received word that there are two cases of chickenpox in the home. The news renders today's discussion superfluous, since the law requires that any move to another facility be postponed for the length of the incubation period. The Africans don't know what chickenpox is. Agitation begins to spread. Is the Berlin Senate now trying to get rid of them by infecting them with some infernal virus? The blond-headed Senate representative wonders in turn whether there's any truth to the story or if the director is making common cause with the black men. Meanwhile the director is worrying about the delays the outbreak threatens to his construction plans and wonders how grown men can suddenly come down with a childhood illness out of the blue.

As a schoolboy in the 1950s, Richard had to help collect potato beetles in the fields—the GDR's Ministry of Agriculture claimed the Americans were trying to sabotage the harvest by dropping the beetles on the East German fields. In long rows, the children had walked across the fields with canning jars, checking each individual plant and dropping the beetles in vinegar. Later Richard learned that in the Nazi era, party members and even soldiers were deployed to exterminate this scrabbling American secret weapon with its yellow and black stripes. So had the Americans battled first the Fascists and then the Antifascists using the very same weapon? Or does an army of beetles eventually start making its own decisions as to what tastes good? From a beetle's point of view, a potato field around 1941 no doubt looked just as good as one in 1953. On Richard's first work trip to London after the fall of the Wall, an older English colleague told him one evening over whiskey that as a schoolboy he too had been compelled to walk the furrows of English fields to combat the potato beetles that were supposedly being deployed by Germany during WWII as biological warfare. Germany had even conducted experiments to study the devastating effects of this beetle, the English professor of German literature insisted, and near the end of the war had dropped thousands of these pests over fields in the Palatinate—in their own country!—for test purposes. Anyway, I love the German language, he said by way of summation, taking a good slug of whiskey. It's only because of this cryptic concluding remark that Richard remembers the conversation at all.

Chickenpox, in any case—this much is clear—is a viral infection that during an outbreak among adults can remain infectious for a period of two weeks. The move isn't happening tomorrow, so there'll be time to look for other more suitable quarters for the refugees. On his way out, Richard speaks to Rashid the thunderbolt-hurler, who's now calmed down again, and asks whether he'd like to meet tomorrow for their first conversation. No problem, he says, and it really does seem he has no memory at all of seeing the professor that morning when he ran out of his room convulsed with rage.

18

Eid Mubarak is the name of the holiday marking the end of Ramadan, Rashid says, the month of fasting. In the morning, the men gather for the big *Eid* prayer while the women prepare the food at home. Then all of them eat together, from noon until late at night. The children are given presents or pocket money so they can amuse themselves during the two days of celebration. The children should have fun, Rashid says. Everyone wears new robes. My father always bought fabric for Eid Mubarak for all the women in our family, and another fabric for the men: me, my brothers, and nephews. In the year 2000, it was a blue fabric. This blue robe is what I was wearing *that day*, and a cap.

Richard and Rashid are sitting behind a closed door in a tiny little room right next to the entryway. One of the security guards unlocked this room when Richard asked if there was a quiet place to talk somewhere. Now the two of them sit between the flattened boxes that were ordered for the move and the towering stacks of chairs. Rashid has taken down a chair with a burgundy cushion, Richard has taken a yellow one.

On Eid Mubarak, you make peace with everyone you quarreled with all year, Rashid says. You visit your family. You donate for the poor. Do you know the five pillars of Islam?

Richard shakes his head.

The five pillars of Islam are first, trust in God, second, prayer, third, sharing with the poor, fourth, fasting during Ramadan, and fifth, if you can afford it, a pilgrimage to Mecca at least once in your life.

Aha, Richard says.

A person who kills is not a Muslim.

Richard nods.

84

You're only allowed to kill if you want to eat, but you mustn't kill anyone at all, not even the tiniest insect that crosses your path. Even an animal might have babies waiting at home. You don't know. Never.

No, Richard says.

Not even a fly!

Right, Richard says.

A person who kills is not a Muslim.

All summer long, Richard has used the vacuum to suck up the flies and wasps circling around his food. During his first year at the university he formally left the church.

Jesus is a prophet in the Quran too, Rashid says.

Once in his seminar "Jesus, the Last Greek God," Richard compared the scene of Jesus's birth in the various gospels of the Bible with the corresponding scene in the Quran. So he knows that in the Quran, Mary is all alone when she gives birth to Jesus. She gives birth in a remote place and suffers such torments that she exclaims: *Oh, would that I had died ere this and had become a thing of naught, forgotten!* Did his students understand what it meant for Mary to wish to be not only dead but also forgotten? But such things couldn't be taught. All he did in the end was draw their attention to the fact that immediately following Mary's despair, the newborn beneath her suddenly starts speaking—so it's Mary's crisis that gives rise to the miracle of speech. The child speaks to console his mother, he speaks of a rivulet—and the rivulet is there. Then he speaks to her of a tree—and the tree is there. Mary finds herself transported to a paradisiacal landscape, she sits beside the rivulet with a date palm above her, she eats and drinks, and later when she returns to her people with the child in her arms and is asked where this child has come from, she doesn't have to say anything herself, because the newborn prophet speaks in her stead, he's still only 21 inches long and weighs 7¾ pounds.

Paradise is beneath your mother's feet, Rashid says. Richard tries to imagine this man seated beside him wearing a blue robe with a cap on his head. I would like to see my mother again before she dies, Rashid says. She's seventy now. But if I go back to Nigeria, I won't be able to return to Germany.

Why don't you want to just return to Nigeria?

Rashid doesn't answer the question. My father, he says, was very popular. Everyone wanted him to marry their daughter. In the end, he had five wives and twenty-four children. I was the first son after ten daughters, my mother was my father's third wife. In the evening we would all sit around a big table for meals. I was allowed to eat from my father's plate. Every morning at a quarter past seven— my father would still be half-asleep—we older children would line up in front of his armchair, and he would give each of us our lunch money for school. *The sultan holds audiences on a platform, with three steps. It is carpeted with silk and has cushions placed on it. Over it is raised the umbrella, which is a sort of pavilion made of silk, surmounted by a bird in gold, about the size of a falcon. The drums, trumpets, and bugles are sounded. Two saddled and bridled horses are brought, along with two goats, which they hold to serve as a protection against the evil eye. If anyone addresses the king and receives a reply from him, he uncovers his back and throws dust over his head and back, for all the world like a bather splashing himself with water.*

At seven-thirty, the driver of the delivery truck would arrive, Rashid says, and we climbed up on the truck bed. He picked up a few more children from the neighborhood and drove all of us to school.

What subjects did you study?

English, mathematics, and also Hausa.

When Rashid was grown, he enrolled in a vocational training school and studied metalworking.

Four of his sisters attended secondary school. One went to university and became a teacher.

How strange, Richard thinks, that he has only just now remembered *The Travels of Ibn Battuta*. Battuta journeyed from Morocco through Africa and Central Asia to China in the fourteenth century. Richard's school friend Walther—who during GDR times had only ever been cleared for travel to other Socialist countries—learned Arabic for the sole purpose of translating this book into German for the first time. What's become of Walther's manuscript? It never saw print, because the publisher who intended to bring it out went bankrupt right after the fall of the Wall. Richard had helped Walther proofread the manuscript.

Twenty-four children with five women—that wasn't so different from Walther's situation, except that his four wives had never, thank God, been asked to live under a single roof. At Walther's funeral, Richard shook hands with his oldest son in the receiving line and said he was very, very sorry, but the son just looked him right in the eye and asked: what for? Apparently as soon as Walther died, his ex-wives and children started squabbling over his house, which was still his fourth wife's legal residence. Now, in West German times, the house was worth something. Walther's oldest son wore faded jeans with holes in them to his father's funeral. Richard hoped that what people said was true: that the dead and buried know no pain and feel nothing at all.

For Eid Mubarak, all the women always cook together, Rashid says. It's the most important holiday for us; you have to eat a lot, you're celebrating the end of a month of fasting. And for weeks before, the house is tidied up and scrubbed from top to bottom. In the year 2000, the fabric my father bought for our Eid Mubarak robes was blue. Richard suddenly realizes he needs to know everything in great detail: He wants Rashid to describe for him every dish on the table set for Eid Mubarak. Eggplant? Tomatoes? Peppers in oil? Fish? Rice? Yams? Plantains? Veal, chicken, lamb? Did all the women sit together, or did each sit with her children at a special part of the table? Was the table inside the house, on a veranda, or outdoors? Richard would like to be able to ask and ask without stopping. So in the evening, illumination is provided by lanterns with colored glass? After the meal, when it's getting dark, the children hang these lanterns on long stakes and parade around the neighborhood? And they sing as they march? And the adults visit their relatives? The next day everyone strolls with the entire family?

But that evening and the next day didn't happen that year, Rashid says finally.

At around eleven in the morning, Rashid says, we men had just finished praying. The place where we pray is about as far from our house as the bridge Oberbaumbrücke is from Alexanderplatz. We were just about to drive back home to our families to begin the feast when they attacked us. With clubs, knives, machetes. My father was about to unlock his car when they came running, they drove us apart and started beating us with clubs and stabbing us with knives and machetes, then they pushed my father into his car, three of them got in with him, and they drove off, that's the last I saw of him. Three weeks before, he'd celebrated his seventy-second birthday.

Rashid has very strong black hands, they rest on his knees, narrow only at the fingertips, and the skin under his nails is pink.

At the edge of town they burned him in his car.

Richard and Rashid both sit there for a moment without saying anything.

Do they know who did it? Richard finally asks.

Rashid doesn't answer.

It was very bad, he says after a while. Why do people kill other people?

That's a much better question, Richard thinks.

Rashid has a scar under his eye. He walks with a limp, Richard noticed it yesterday.

We tried to get away. My brothers, my nephews, my uncles, the neighbors. Everyone running and screaming. Everywhere people were lying on the ground, there was blood everywhere. One of my younger brothers hid at first in a mango tree at the edge of the square. When night fell, he ran over to the river and hid in the water, all night long he stood there in the water, terrified, they lynched people on the riverbanks, he told me later, he saw it all. I remember the smell of smoke, Rashid says, while I was running and running. The first houses were already on fire.... From Ober-baumbrücke to Alexanderplatz ... *St. Martin rode through snow and wind, on his horse that bore him strong and swift, his heart was light as off he rode, all wrapped up in his nice warm cloak.* In the year 2000, the traditional lantern parade featuring the children of the Nigerian town Kaduna—of whose existence Richard has been aware for a mere two weeks now—wasn't held as usual on the night of Eid Mubarak. The last time it was St. Martin's Day here in Berlin, the neighborhood children marched singing around Schlossplatz with their lanterns, but the young woman from Duisburg who's lived in an apartment building on Richard's street for three years now and in recent months has started making the most peculiar comments when they cross paths while shopping or taking out the re-cycling—she sometimes stands on the sidewalk arguing with an invisible interlocutor—well, while the children were marching around Schlossplatz, singing, this woman from Duisburg crept into the dark snowberry bushes at the edge of the square and howled like a wolf.

We ran home as fast as we could to warn the women. The women took the children and left at once—going to friends' houses or home to their own parents. My mother, too, sought refuge with her parents in their village. I just grabbed a spare robe from the closet and stuffed it in a plastic bag. I was in such a hurry I forgot the pants that went with it. Barely half an hour later, no one was left in the house, and the feast still stood untouched on the table. We didn't even lock the door. Why lock it? The house was tidy and scrubbed from top to bottom for Eid Mubarak. It was tidy and scrubbed from top to bottom and a couple of hours later it burnt to the ground.

From one day to the next I had no father, no family, no house, no workshop. From one day to the next, our former life came to an end. We couldn't even bury our father. I went to see my mother one last time, to say goodbye, then I went to Niger. That was the last time we saw each other. Thirteen years ago. When my mother asks me on the telephone how I am, I always say: good.

Richard remembers that Rashid said to him at the beginning of their conversation: *Paradise is beneath your mother's feet*.

I can't stand the sight of blood anymore.

And only now does Richard understand that Rashid has spent the past two hours answering the question he asked him at the outset.

Our life was cut off from us that night, as if with a knife. It was cut, Rashid says.

Cut.

The two security guards grin when Richard and Rashid come out of the storage room. That must have been some conversation, one says. Yes, Richard replies.

On the way home, he stops at the flower shop and buys an enormous bouquet of colorful asters. It's the first time he's ever bought flowers for himself. He puts them in a large, clear vase on the kitchen table. Now it looks as if his wife were still here. Or his lover.

Last night—he now remembers—he woke up and instead of going to pee, he walked through every room in the house for no particular reason, not looking for anything. He walked through his house in the dark for no reason at all, as if strolling through a museum, as if he himself no longer belonged to it. As he passed among these pieces of furniture, some of which he's known since childhood, his own life, room after room, suddenly appeared to him utterly foreign, utterly unknown, as if from a far-off galaxy. His tour ended in the kitchen. Ashamed, he remembers how he sat down on a kitchen chair and, without knowing why, began sobbing like a man condemned to exile.

What could have gotten into him? He doesn't remember. Or did he just dream it all?

But eat we must, as his mother always said.

He takes a can from the shelf, pea soup, it doesn't take long. Afterward, he puts the bowl in the dishwasher. This dishwasher still makes him smile. There weren't any dishwashers in the East. *Deutschland is beautiful*.

And then, before it gets dark, he goes out to the garden. Maybe he'll clear the leaves from the gutters while it's still light enough to see, and sweep the twigs from atop the awning. It's a good thing his new ladder is so long.

Then in the evening he sits down at his desk to take notes.

For a while he just sits there quietly, and in the end there are only three short sentences on the piece of paper.

There was childhood. There was day-to-day life. There was adolescence.

And under this, in parentheses: *Rashid = the Olympian = the Thunderbolt-hurler*.

The cone of light cast by his desk lamp creates a stage for the letters, even after Richard has already gone to the bathroom to brush his teeth.

19

There's supposed to be a German lesson the next day, but when Richard arrives, the security guards inform him that it's payout day. They've all gone to get their money, the man in the meaningless uniform says. It's a good thing Richard has his shopping list with him.

dish detergent
1 quark
1 butter
jam (black currant? raspberry?)
ham
iceberg lettuce
2 cucumbers
tomatoes, medium-sized
mineral water
½ rye-wheat bread

While out shopping, he runs into Sylvia, his friend Detlef's wife, well, today he unexpectedly has nothing to do, unexpectedly? Surely you're writing, don't you have lectures to write? Not exactly, he says, but that's a longer story. Will you come for lunch? We have tons of leftovers from the birthday party. Sure, why not, I'll drop my groceries off at home, okay, see you in a minute.

What are you working on these days? Detlef asks while Richard's still wiping the bottoms of his shoes. Until five years ago, Detlef was employed as an interior design consultant at a firm specializing in retail spaces, but now he's in early retirement. After the fall of the Wall, he was fortunate to be fluent in Russian: this made him Our Man in the West for the new entrepreneurs in Moscow. His West German employer was pleased at how well he, the former East German, got along with the firm's Russian clients. Sylvia, who still wore a ponytail and had a girlish look about her when she moved into his house, had been a typographer until the fall of the Wall; afterward she'd lost her job, and a few years later the advent of the Computer Age, bringing many new technologies, effectively relegated the profession she'd trained for to the museum. Now that her husband is also unemployed, the two of them have been traveling on their savings, they've gone to Hamburg, and seen Venice, Morocco, the Pyramids, the Eiffel Tower, Stonehenge, and the Croatian coast. Until a year ago when Sylvia fell ill. At Detlef's birthday party, Richard heard her say for the first time: I'm glad I still got to see so much of the world. At the word "still" he'd involuntarily glanced at Detlef, and his friend had asked: Want a beer?

Really? There are Africans housed in the nursing home? I had no idea.

I've seen some of them out shopping a couple of times and wondered.

Apollo, Tristan, and the Olympian now have a place in a German living room with its L-shaped sofa, TV, fruit bowl, and bookshelf. While Richard speaks of the conflicts between the Tuareg and various al-Qaeda groups in the deserts of Mali and Niger, he watches a squirrel outside running across the lawn. While he relates that Tristan's father didn't raise the blinds on the south side of his house in Tripoli until evening, his eyes come to rest on this week's TV schedule lying on the little table next to the sofa. The numeral displayed on the digital clock (wedged between books on the shelf) leaps from 12:36 to 12:37, and he's just finished telling about the blue robe that Rashid, the thunderbolt-hurler, wore on Eid Mubarak and was still wearing when he fled.

I understand, Detlef says from time to time as he speaks. Now that Richard has finished his story, his friend remains silent for a little while, nodding.

So they're only allowed to work in Italy? Detlef asks at last.

Exactly.

Where there's no work.

Exactly.

And the money they get here?

It's only for a few months, until it's been definitively proven that Germany bears no formal responsibility for them.

And then?

Then they get sent back to Italy.

Where there's no work.

Exactly.

Sounds like we have it pretty good here, Sylvia says.

Richard thinks of his father, who was sent to Norway and Russia as a German soldier to produce mayhem. Detlef thinks of his mother, who with the same care with which she'd once braided her hair as a young German girl had later tapped the mortar from pieces of stone as a *rubble woman* helping to rebuild the country. Sylvia thinks of her grandfather, who sent his wife the bloodstained linens of Russian children for their own children: *The stains will come out easily in cold water.* The great achievement of their forebears was, if you will, destruction, the creation of a blank slate that their children and grandchildren then had to write on. And the great achievement of their own generation? The reason they were doing so much better than, say, these three African men Richard was just talking about? The ones sitting on this sofa are postwar children, and so they know that the progression from before to after is often based on quite different principles than punishment and reward. There's no clear link between cause and effect, there's an indirect relationship, Richard thinks, as he's thought many times before in recent years. The Americans had their plans for one half of Germany, and the Russians their plans for the other. Neither the material prosperity on one side nor the planned economy on the other could be explained by any particular trait of the German citizens in question—they were just the raw material for these political experiments. So what was there to feel proud of? What should they have thought of as better, as opposed to something inferior and other? They'd worked all their lives, that's certainly true, and they hadn't been forbidden to work. Then these Easterners were embraced as blood relatives by their brothers and sisters on the other side of the Wall; this blood they were born with, a circumstance beyond their control. Richard's friend Monica's daughter-in-law, breast-feeding her post-Wall baby, always marveled at the apparent miracle by which a glass of Coca-Cola could be transformed inside her body into milk. No one knew for sure whether it was blood, Coke or milk flowing in her veins, nor could any of them answer the question: who deserves credit for the fact that even the less affluent among their circle now have dishwashers in their kitchens, wine bottles on their shelves, and double-glazed windows? But if this prosperity couldn't be attributed to their own personal merit, then by the same token the refugees weren't to blame for their reduced circumstances. Things might have turned out the other way around. For a moment, this thought opens its jaws wide, displaying its frightening teeth.

Sylvia says: I keep imagining that someday it'll be us having to flee, and no one will help us either.

Detlef says: Well, chances are . . .

Sylvia says: And where in the world would we go?

Richard says: I've thought about leaving my old motorcycle parked on the other side of the lake. Then if anything happens, I can row across, hop on, and scoot off to the East. I can't imagine anyone else would go in that direction, so probably it would still be peacetime there.

Speaking of which, Sylvia says, isn't that drowned man still at the bottom of the lake?

Yep, he's still down there.

On the terrace outside the window, an ashtray has been left out

95

in the cold, already rusted. When she got her diagnosis three-quarters of a year ago, Sylvia stopped smoking.

Detlef gets up and says: I'll go bring us something to eat. There's still some duck breast left. And soup.

20

Never use a microfiber cloth on the faucet, the plumber says, otherwise you'll scratch it up, the surface only looks like chrome. Okay. There was also something wrong with the toilet's flush mechanism. *Friday after one, the week is done.* Now it's Friday and after one, and the man is just packing up his tools, sign here, please.

When Richard arrives at the nursing home, they tell him: You're out of luck, Friday afternoon is when the refugees go to pray.

There's no one here at all?

Just the handful of Christians.

Well, I'll see what I can do, Richard says. In 2017 no one opens the door when he knocks, but in 2019 a bleary-eyed young man opens the door to him. A few soft beard hairs are poking out of his cheeks. Probably he's one of the roommates who lay sleeping in bed during his first visit to Apollo.

Richard explains once more who he is and what he wants, and the young man says: Okay.

So you might be willing to speak with me?

The young man shrugs.

Do you understand English?

Yes, he says, but makes no move to invite Richard into the room. Maybe he's nervous about being alone with him.

Should we go out, to a café?

The young man just shrugs again.

So much insecurity on both sides, Richard thinks—both his

own and surely that of this young refugee. But just as Richard is about to excuse himself and leave, the boy takes a step forward; he nods to Richard, shuts the door behind him, and follows him—just as he is, without combing his hair, without picking up a bag, and wearing a jacket that's much too thin.

Not that Richard minds leaving the building for once to have a conversation. The rooms he's gotten to know so far are all filled to the brim with ghosts. He knows that next door in Room 2020, where a plaid and ironed curtain still hangs in the window, all the other furnishings have been smashed to pieces by marauding troops, the bed is flipped over, the wardrobe toppled. Booted feet trample on clothes, dishes are hurled against the wall—only this blue plaid curtain that someone put up for his 102-year-old grandmother remains intact. It casts its shadow on a sunny autumn day on the outskirts of Berlin. In Room 2017 the ghosts of fish await their food, but all eight hundred passengers are still alive. Down by the exit, the storeroom, whose door Richard and the boy in the thin jacket are just passing, holds tall stacks of yellow- and red-cushioned chairs with wooden and metal frames, as if Rashid's large family is about to gather to celebrate the great feast of Eid Mubarak: five wives, twenty-four daughters and sons, and Rashid's father.

It's no problem to leave the building with the young man, the security guard says, as long as he signs out here.

In a suburb of Berlin like this there aren't many cafés. One bakery expanded right after reunification: there's now a glass addition out front, and the bakery sells their raspberry-topped cakes, éclairs, and meringues from behind a twenty-eight-foot-long counter. The old folks who usually meet here at four p.m. are still at home lying beneath their camelhair blankets, taking after-lunch naps. Only a single guest sits near the counter in front of a cup of coffee, reading the paper. Richard seats himself and his young companion as far as possible from this man, at a table at the very edge of the glassed-in room looking out.

What would you like to drink? Coffee? Tea? Hot chocolate? Juice? Water?

The boy shakes his head.

Would you like a piece of cake?

The boy shakes his head.

Tea?

The boy shrugs.

Do you want herbal tea, green tea? Black tea?

Nothing.

Green? Black?

The boy shrugs: black then.

And cake?

The boy shakes his head.

Richard goes to the counter to order black tea and a cappuccino. He never drank cappuccino during GDR times, but he got into the habit when he went to Italy. It would never have occurred to him during the previous forty years that he could ever acquire a habit in Italy.

What's your name?

Osarobo.

Already the black tea is arriving along with the cappuccino with its cap of frothy milk dusted with cocoa and a little cookie on the saucer.

Where are you from?

Niger. Later I stayed with my father in Libya.

The sugar he adds to his coffee slips through the frothy milk into the depths.

Do you still have family in Niger?

A mother and a sister.

How old is your sister?

Fourteen or so.

He stirs the sugar.

And what's her name?

Sabinah.

Do you call them sometimes?

No.

And your father?

The boy shakes his head.

Do you talk about the war with your friends from Oranienplatz?

Sometimes.

Is there anyone here you know from Libya?

No. I lost all my friends.

Soft background music is playing, a woman is buying some cake, that'll be 11.60 euros.

I saw them die. Many, many people died.

The woman leaves the shop with her packet, the sliding glass doors open automatically before her.

Osarobo's tea is standing there untouched. Richard's cappuccino also stands untouched.

Life is crazy. Life is crazy.

Richard wishes he knew what questions would lead to the land of beautiful answers.

Do you go for a walk sometimes? Richard asks, but Osarobo misunderstands, he thinks he's being asked about work.

Yes, I want to work. I want to work, but it's not allowed.

Richard thinks of Mozart's Tamino and how he is tested. In front of every door he tries to open, a voice makes him stop: *Go back!*

What is your mother tongue?

Hausa, and Tebu-Tebu.

How do you say "hand" in Hausa?

Hanu.

And eye?

Idu.

Tea?

Shayi.

I?

Ni.

You?

Kay.

Then he asks: Where in Italy were you?

In Naples, Milan ... In the metro, he says, people get up and sit somewhere else when a black man sits next to them.

Italy stopped being the land of beautiful answers long ago.

So, the boy says. He plucks at the skin on the back of his hand as if he wanted to pull off this annoying husk. Then he looks out the window at the trees outside, from which a few last yellow leaves are hanging. There's something wrong somehow with his left eye, Richard notices only now, since the boy hasn't looked up until this moment.

What happened to your eye?

He shakes his head. Not a word. He looks down again.

How old are you?

Eighteen.

How long have you been in Europe?

Three years.

Do you think about your future sometimes?

Future? he says.

The boy still hasn't taken a single sip of his tea.

Crazy life, crazy life, he says, and then falls silent.

The frothy milk has revealed itself to be utterly inappropriate.

I want to go back to my friends, he says.

Richard doesn't know if Osarobo means his friends in the nursing home or the ones who are dead. With this boy, Richard has run aground. But his failure isn't what matters here. He's not what matters.

That'll be 4.70 euros, the woman says, gazing mutely at the table on which the two beverages stand untouched.

Until they reach the intersection where Richard has to turn off to go home, the boy walks wordlessly beside him. Only when Richard stops to say goodbye does Osarobo suddenly ask: Do you believe in God? He looks at Richard for the first time.

The traffic light at the intersection turns red, and so the entire street falls silent. Not really, Richard answers. And that *really* is already a compromise.

I don't understand how anybody can not believe in God, the boy says. When you are in trouble, you believe in God. Life is crazy. When I'm sick, the hospital doesn't make me healthy again, it's God. God saved me, he says.... He saved me, but he didn't save the others. So he must have some plan for me, right?

He's still looking at Richard with one healthy eye and an eye that has something wrong with it, but when Richard doesn't answer, he collapses back into himself; his jacket is much too thin for a German October, and his gaze slips back into the invisible brambles that seem to fill the air.

Thirty years ago, for his driving test, Richard took a first-aid course. Doing CPR proved to be far more strenuous than he'd expected.

Is there something—anything at all—that you'd like to do if you had the opportunity? he asks the boy, as if he had a personal stake in drawing him back into life, as if he would lose something if this boy from Niger, whom he hardly knows, were to throw in the towel. Something you'd like to do if you had the chance? he asks again. As if the boy's so much as wishing for something would be enough for him to buy his way back into life. If you can just get a person to want to breathe, all the rest can be figured out later.

Yes, Osarobo says.

What is it? Richard asks.

Play the piano, the boy says.

The light turns green again.

Play the piano? At first Richard doesn't believe his ears, but Osarobo is really saying: Yes. Piano.

Then all that's left is for Richard to explain that he has a piano at home, and that, no, there's no admission fee to pay, Osarobo is welcome to come to his house anytime he likes. What about Monday? Or Tuesday?

Wednesday.

21

On Saturday his friend Peter, the archaeologist, comes to visit and reports that it's fortunately still warm enough to go on with his dig.

On Sunday he has an egg with his breakfast. He's been meaning to study this memorandum, the so-called "agreement" signed by the Berlin Senate and the Africans to reclaim Oranienplatz for the use of all Berliners. He's reserved the entire day for this, but to his amazement, the document proves to be only three-quarters of a page long. Even the contracts his phone company sends him are longer, and on his shelf stand two fat binders filled with paperwork regarding the purchase of his house. For a German document to be so short strikes him as astonishing to put it mildly. *We are united in our belief that the conditions for refugees seeking shelter in Europe and Germany must be improved.* This is the first sentence of the agreement. Two parties, then, are seeking to agree on something after declaring themselves at the outset united in a belief. Often in the past, examining a text, it's seemed to him that all he was doing was hunting for clues. Who, for example, is this "we"?

All camping and protest activity in violation of what is legally permissible will be permanently discontinued. The refugees assume responsibility for dismantling all tents and shelters and will take all necessary action for this state to be permanently maintained.

He is particularly taken with the formulation "*what is legally permissible.*" Could his relationship with his lover have been considered at any point "matrimonially permissible"? And might such a designation have sufficed to provide consolation to his lover, who was reduced to tears at least once a week over the fact that he always returned home to his wife in time for dinner? Or were the tears themselves a violation of matrimonial permissibility?

Additionally, mention of the permanent nature of the withdrawal has crept into this paragraph twice. Language is never a coincidence, as he always tried to make his students understand. He himself had been taught this lesson over and over while studying the newspaper *Neues Deutschland*, published by the so-called *Central Organ of the Party*. The designation "central organ" itself was enough to inspire doubt. So the refugees themselves were to publicly dismantle their own camp until it was reduced to a pile of kindling. And what were they getting in return? Richard remembers well how the letters came pouring in those first few weeks after the monetary union: *You're a winner! A brand-new Mercedes! Five hundred million! A villa!* The little paper plaque with "Villa Richard" inscribed in gold still hangs above his desk in memory of his lost Socialist innocence.

The Senator will provide support within the limits of her political jurisdiction. Individual cases will be processed in accordance with all applicable laws. Deportations will be suspended while these cases undergo processing.

A limit, this much is clear, is nothing more than a border. And a period of time during which cases are processed must eventually end. Eternity is being exchanged here for a finite length of time. An actual and *permanent* subtraction of tents and demonstrations from an actual place in exchange for a vague notion of hope: *aid and assistance in pursuing vocational opportunities.* Foreign as the world of lawyers is to him, he sometimes feels akin to them in his obsession with capturing states of affairs in language with maximal precision.

103

So there's one more thing this text communicates beyond the information contained in its individual sentences: the refugees can't afford a lawyer, and they barely understand German. Hope is what's keeping them alive, and hope is cheap.

22

And then there's German class again on Monday.

Richard is wearing his light-blue shirt.

The teacher places pairs of men one behind the other, one next to the other, one facing the other, practicing the use of prepositions and their objects.

To whom does the sun belong?

The sun belongs to God! someone answers.

The sun belongs to us! someone else says.

To whom does Ali belong?

Ali belongs to himself.

The teacher laughs, welcomes this and that latecomer, writes on the board, looks over the shoulder of this and that writing pupil, like an experienced lion tamer she moves among all these men, and after two hours that seem to pass in no time, the lesson is over.

If you want, you can take over the lessons for the more advanced students. As you see, they're at all different levels.

He used his new aftershave today too.

I'll think about it, he says.

And next thing he knows, she's said a quick *goodbye* and darted out.

On Tuesday, Richard once again walks down the hall, seeing the three pairs of shoes neatly lined up on the windowsill as always, and knocks at room 2017. This time it is the refugee named Zair who opens the door. The others are asleep on their cots, and the TV is off.

Do you know where Rashid is, Richard whispers.

Zair points at one of the cots: the hillock under the blanket is somewhat larger than the others.

So it seems that even mighty Rashid—whom Richard has taken to privately calling the thunderbolt-hurler ever since the scene in the stairwell—this powerful man who, clad in his festive blue robes, bears the five pillars of Islam upon his shoulders, can still relent, becoming nothing more than a sleeper among sleepers.

Richard shakes his head when Zair invites him to enter.

Now another door opens, and a half-naked man, barefoot and wearing only underpants, a towel around his shoulders, comes out of one of the rooms, and ambles past him with a nod, heading for the stairs, that must be where the showers are. Then everything is perfectly still again. But there are sounds coming from further down the hall. Richard walks toward them, turning the corner to the right, and finds himself in front of a kitchen. To his delight and surprise, the young German teacher is standing there all alone on a ladder, trying to hang up a poster above one of the three ranges: Bellevue Castle by night, floodlit and symmetrical. One range further, a poster is already hanging on which a beer bottle, cigarette, and pills are all crossed out beneath the legend "Be Like a Bird."

Can I help you? Richard asks.

You can hand me the thumbtacks.

Why are you putting up posters? he asks, poking around in the box of tacks to find ones that are dark blue and green, just like the night enveloping Bellevue Castle, where Germany's federal president resides. Could the teacher have spent the night with one of the men? That would explain her presence here so early in the morning. Maybe with the man Richard just saw coming out of his room half-naked?

Even fish in an aquarium have something to look at, at least a

105

picture of coral and seaweed, she says. Don't the people here deserve to have as much as a couple of fish?

Richard thinks of the flowers he bought last week, which have already wilted since he forgot to change their water. Sometimes he catches himself eating pea soup straight out of the can, cold. And in his living room, the advent wreath has been standing on the table for five years now, its red candles burnt down to stumps from the last Christmas he celebrated with his wife. It's almost Advent season again.

Could you hand me the third poster over there?

Richard hands the roll up to her, and she flattens out the poster against the wall. Whatever corner she isn't holding down immediately curls back up again. When she smoothes down the left side, he sees the left half of the Bode Museum.

Richard's wife always sent him down to the basement punctually, whatever the current holiday was, first to carry up the boxes with the season's decorations, and then to bring them back down again after they had served their purpose: Easter bunnies, eggs made of glass and wood, artificial grass; for Christmas, folding paper stars, nutcrackers, angels, strings of lights, Christmas tree ornaments; for New Year's, sparklers and firecrackers; and then in Carnival season, colorful streamers and the large tin of confetti that seemed bottomless. After her death, he'd packed up the Christmas decorations on his own for the first time ever and brought them down to the basement, but he'd forgotten the wreath, and ever since, it's been sitting there on the table.

Does that look okay?

Maybe a little to the left.

Like that?

And two centimeters higher.

After his wife's death, Richard was at first relieved that the yearly cycle of holidays could now go on without him, each holiday would pass before he'd realized it was coming. Only recently—now that time in its new formlessness has gone on long enough for him to start to tire of it—has he begun to linger in the basement when he has business there, reading off the names of the various holidays in his wife's handwriting and trying for a moment to imagine all the strange beings and things packed into these boxes solely according to their size and fragility but otherwise randomly.

Do you happen to know when the men are supposed to be moving now?

White and light blue, the sky above the Bode Museum. Green and black: the water at its base.

Not soon, in any case—there are two new cases of chickenpox, the beautiful Ethiopian murmurs. As she presses the first thumbtacks into the wall, she holds the others between her lips.

Certainly it's absurd though, she says once she's done and on her way down the ladder, that the men have only been paid out the first half of the money they were promised. They'll get the second half in their new quarters, one of them told me yesterday. As if you could bribe bacteria.

That really is absurd, he says, remembering the potato beetles and his canning jar half-full of vinegar.

I've got to go, she says, actually I'm not allowed to be here, it's off-limits for me according to the staff, but no one's going to check this early in the morning.

Off-limits? But you teach here twice a week.

I'm allowed to be in the classroom, but not up here where the rooms are. They claim I disturb the peace.

He can imagine what the staff might mean by that but says nonetheless: That's unbelievable.

At the same time he feels glad that she didn't spend the night with the half-naked man.

Maybe you'll think more about what I asked you yesterday—taking over the lessons for the more advanced students?

I'd be happy to, he says, and already she's on her way with her

107

hurried *goodbye;* he hears her resolute steps receding down the hall, she's gone in a flash, as always.

He wonders whether any of the men have ever been to the Bode Museum.

23

When Richard gets home that evening, he can't remember how the conversation even started. He hadn't wanted to knock on any more doors behind which men were sleeping. On his way downstairs, he saw the thin man with the broom, sweeping the uninhabited second floor as if he had all the time in the world. Richard's conversation with him lasted far longer than any of the others, and Richard can't really account for this.

I know why it is, the voice says. The thin man is still wearing the yellow sweatsuit pants with holes in them, still holding his broom. Sometimes he pauses for a moment, propping himself up on it with both hands, then he sweeps some more.

Or is it still not over yet?

I look in front of me and behind me and I see nothing.

This was the first sentence uttered by the man on the deserted second floor, and many, many sentences spiraled out from this one. Now Richard is home again and can still hear the man's voice.

When I was eight or nine years old, my parents left me with my stepmother—my father's first wife—and they moved to another village with my two brothers and my sister. When I was eleven, I got my first cutlass—a knife for working in the fields for thirty cents per hour. By the time I was eighteen, I'd earned enough to open a small kiosk. When I was nineteen, I sold the kiosk to go to Kumasi in Ghana.

Richard turns on the lights in the living room, library, and

108

kitchen, just as he always does when he comes home at night.

I went to see my parents, my brothers, my sister, and said good-bye to them. I could only stay with them for one night, their room was too small.

I went to Kumasi and started working as a helper for two merchants who sold shoes on the street. I met a girl, but her parents wouldn't give their permission for us to marry because I was so poor. Then the merchants I worked for went bankrupt.

I went back to my parents, my two brothers, and my sister, and I could only stay with them for one night, the room was too small.

I didn't feel well in my body in that time.

Richard goes to the kitchen, opens the window facing the garden, looks out into the night, and thinks for a brief moment that everything is very quiet now. Then he hears behind him the sound of the broom sweeping the floor.

Something changed, but I didn't know if it was a change for better or worse. I started to work on a farm. My job was to take care of the animals, the goats and pigs. I brought them their food, cut grass, twigs, and leaves. But the owner kept my pay, he said: It costs me this much to feed you.

Richard closes the window again and turns around. The man props himself with both hands on his broom, smiles, and says:

One night I had a dream. My father lay on the ground, I wanted to hold him, but I couldn't grasp him, beneath my arms he was flat, and then he sank down into the ground.

The next night I had a dream again. Three women were washing the dead body of my father. I was supposed to help them, but I didn't know how to do that.

The third night I saw my mother standing next to the body of my father, as if she were watching over him.

One day later I received a message from my village that my father was dead.

Where'd he get the broom, anyhow?

I knew that I didn't have enough money to go to the big memorial ceremony for my father eight weeks later. But a son must come and mourn his father.

Now he goes back to sweeping with calm, broad strokes. Well, it can't hurt, Richard thinks.

For the first week I worked.

The second.

The third.

The fourth.

At the end of the fourth week, the owner said to me that it was only the probationary month and again he didn't give me money.

I found work on another farm. I dug up the fields for planting yams. The first week I worked. From four in the morning until six-thirty in the evening.

The second week.

The third week.

The fourth.

But if a girl hadn't given me food for free, even the money I earned there wouldn't have been enough for me to travel for the ceremony and buy the goat I wanted to sacrifice.

Maybe a cold beer would be a good thing on such an evening, Richard thinks, and goes down to the basement.

I went with the goat in a share taxi to Nkawkaw.

Then I went with the goat in a bus to Kumasi.

I went with the goat in a share taxi from Kumasi to Tepa, then I went with the goat to Mim.

Richard remembers laughing when the man told him how hard it was to squeeze the live goat into a vehicle with all the other passengers.

I arrived on the exact day the ceremony for my father took place. We sacrificed the goat in the customary way. I could only stay with my family for one night, the room was too small. From then on, I alone had to provide for my mother and my three siblings.

In a nearby village I found work on a cocoa plantation.

After one year I decided to go to Accra with the money I earned.

I went to my mother, my brothers, my sister, and said goodbye to them. I could only stay with them for one night, the room was too small.

While Richard is sitting on the sofa with his beer, the man in the yellow pants with holes in them sweeps the living-room rug.

I went to Accra and bought the first four pairs of shoes for my own business. By afternoon, I sold two pairs. I bought two new pairs, and that evening sold another pair. With the profit from the three pairs of shoes I sold, I could buy food, a sleeping mat, and a tarp for sleeping on the street. During the night someone stole the tarp.

Richard's gaze comes to rest on the advent wreath that's been standing on his living room table for five years now.

The rainy season had just started, so I went around in the city. Now I had eleven pairs of shoes total, I always showed one shoe, and another was in my backpack. At night I sometimes got wet if it rained through my new tarp. During the day I was sometimes so tired that I sat down and fell asleep. Finally I had wood cut for a counter. I found someone who would lock up my bag of shoes overnight for me. But I still slept on the street with the money in my pocket, and I was always afraid of being robbed. I gave five pairs of shoes on commission to a man who said he would help me sell them. But he took the shoes and didn't come back.

Now the man in the yellow pants with holes turns the broom upside down and plucks the lint from the bristles, dropping it right back on the floor next to him. What does he think he's doing? Richard wonders, but then thinks: Let him do what he wants.

I went to see my mother and siblings. I could only stay with them for one night, the room was too small.

I asked myself: What is wrong with me?

I asked myself, and I also asked God.

It's all right to have bad times. But if you *never* know where you'll sleep and what you'll eat? Was there really no place in the entire world where I could lie down to sleep?

I looked in front of me and behind me and saw nothing, but I told my mother things were good with me.

And my mother said to me that things were good with her.

But I knew: she didn't own any land. If I didn't give her money and if no one else ever gave her anything, she couldn't cook anything for herself and my siblings.

My silence and her silence met when we looked at each other.

Then I worked helping with the harvest on a plantation.

The first week.

The second week.

The third week.

He turns the broom around again, but remains standing there.

I thought: if I wasn't there anymore, no one could ask me for anything else, and then I sat down at the edge of the field and cried.

It's like that, many people in Ghana are very desperate.

Some of them hang themselves.

Others take DDT. They drink water afterward, then they go into the house, close the door behind them—and die.

I sent a kid to the store where they have DDT. But the seller asked the kid who sent him. He looked for me, and then he talked to me for a long time and said I should think about it carefully. For three days after this conversation I sat in the mosque and thought about it.

Then I didn't have the strength to do it anymore.

And after that I got sick.

Richard gets up and walks across the hall to the library. He sometimes sits in the armchair there to talk on the phone. Maybe he needs a book to clear his head before he goes to sleep.

If the DDT seller hadn't talked to me then, I'd have died a long time ago.

Of course there's plenty of dust in the library too. Richard watches the thin man for a while as he turns over the chairs surrounding the round table and lifts them to the tabletop. He's leaned his broom against the bookshelf, the section devoted to German Classicism.

Then I went back to Accra. I hired a helper. At some point I had two and a half sacks of shoes, almost three hundred pairs. Now I almost had enough money for a room.

But then selling on the street was declared illegal.

I looked in front of me and behind me and saw nothing.

I carried five pairs of shoes around and sold them in secret. All day long I walked back and forth across the city. I let my helper have the last twenty or thirty pairs for cheap. With the profit I bought a sack of *athfiadai;* someone told me they make medicine out of it here in Europe. *Paracetamol.*

When Richard has a headache, he takes A.S.S., the aspirin product still favored by East Germans, but he doesn't know if it contains the active ingredient paracetamol.

Then I went home to my mother and siblings. I stayed with them for just one night and told them what they should do to help me. All four of them went into the bush to collect this fruit that looks like a small apple, you dry it, then it splits open, you collect the seeds, the seeds are dried in the sun for two or three days, and then you grind them in a mortar. In the end it's a black powder. The fruit is rare, and it's a lot of work to get the powder; but finally a second sack was full, and my mother sent it to me in Accra.

Richard would like to turn out the light and go to bed. But he remains sitting until the thin man has finished sweeping under the sofa and the secretary, he waits until he's taken the chairs back down from the table and put everything neatly in its place.

I went to the market with the two sacks.

On the first day, no one came to buy the powder.

Not on the second day either.

Not on the third day.

After that, I heard that the year before, some sellers put a powder that looked similar in sacks to cheat the buyers.

Now Richard turns off the light. The voice is waiting for him in the hallway.

I left the sacks with a friend and went to my mother and siblings to say goodbye. I could only stay one night, no longer, because the room was too small.

I gave my mother half of the last money I had, and with the other half I paid a smuggler to take me to Libya.

That was in the year 2010.

It's nice, actually, Richard thinks, that sweeping doesn't make any noise, and he wonders why, on the rare occasions he cleans, he always grabs the vacuum cleaner.

My money was only enough to get to Dakoro in Niger. The smuggler loaned me the rest. The others and I lay under the false bottom of a pickup truck squeezed in so tightly that we couldn't even turn around. The smuggler kept us alive with pieces of watermelon that he shoved into our hiding place.

For the first eight months in Tripoli, I worked on a construction site just for the smuggler. When my debts were finally paid, the war broke out. We couldn't leave the construction site. All around us we heard shooting. Eventually the man who always brought us our food and drink stopped coming. We held out for three days, and on the fourth day we had to go outside. The streets were completely empty. There were no foreigners left anywhere, but no Libyans either. No people at all. Finally we managed to get on a boat at night. A friend lent me the two hundred euros for the crossing to Europe.

When I called Accra from the camp in Sicily, the man I'd left the two sacks of powder with said that the stuff had gotten old.

Yes, I said, just dump it out, I said.

And now the thin man begins to sweep the stairs from bottom to top, the opposite of how Richard always saw his mother do it,

114

moving upwards as he sweeps one step at a time, with the dust from each step falling on the one just below, the one he's just cleaned.

For as long as I was in the camp in Italy, I received seventy-five euros a month, and I sent twenty or thirty of that to my mother.

But after a year the camp was closed. They gave us five hundred euros. With that, I stood on the street. I went to the train station to sleep there until a policeman woke me and sent me away because I didn't have a train ticket.

Outside was a man from Cameroon. He said he had a brother in Finland. We called the brother. Yes, I could go to Finland and stay with him. I went to Finland, but the brother of the man from Cameroon didn't answer the phone.

For two weeks I slept on the street in Finland. It was very, very cold. Then I went back to Italy. I walked around with my bag on my back. One day I threw away a pair of shoes and some pants, because the bag was so heavy.

I spent a total of one year and eight months in Italy.

Then I went to Germany.

All my money was gone, the five hundred euros.

I looked in front of me and behind me and saw nothing.

The thin man has now reached the top of the stairs with his broom and seems to be heading in the direction of the guest bedroom, but when Richard follows him, carrying a volume by Edgar Lee Masters, and looks around on the upper floor, there's no one there.

24

On Friday, Richard told Osarobo he'd pick him up at eleven a.m. on Wednesday for some piano. But when Richard knocks on the door of Room 2019, a long time passes before the door finally opens. Osarobo stands there disheveled and sleep-dazed and says: How are you? When Richard asks if he doesn't want to come play the piano, Osarobo says: Oh, sorry, I forgot.

Richard says: I'll wait downstairs.

He feels irritated, but why is he so annoyed? Because this African isn't as happy and grateful as he expected? Because he was so easily able to forget him, the only German from outside the home who voluntarily sets foot here? Or maybe because this African isn't desperate enough to understand that Richard is offering him an opportunity? Or is it more that Osarobo's carelessness has casually made clear to Richard that his offer to let Osarobo play his piano isn't really an opportunity at all but at best a way to pass the time, only marginally more attractive than sleeping? Back when he and his lover had their penultimate arguments before she left him, she'd said several times that it wasn't so much the disappointment of his expectations that was the problem, but the expectations themselves.

One flight down, no one's sweeping today.

The sorts of things he'd asked of his lover were, for example: calling him on such and such a day at five p.m., or wearing that blue miniskirt he liked so much to their next assignation, or—when she was coming back from some trip—letting him know in advance what car of the train she'd be getting out of. He would start looking forward to each date the moment they made it, and so his anticipatory pleasure lasted far longer than the date itself. This anticipation almost replaced its object, but even so it remained inextricably linked to the bit of reality it referred to, and if it ended in disappointment, that nullified the entire segment of the past leading up to it retroactively. At first his lover had jokingly referred to all these things he looked forward to as his *vanishing points*, an expression she later replaced with a different one: *happy-ending terrorism*, and during the final phase of their relationship, she'd terrorized him in turn by allowing herself deviations from their agreed-upon plans.

116

Richard nods to the pool players he's already passed by a moment before on his way upstairs. One of them gives a two-fingered victory salute.

She'd call him eight and a half minutes late, or not at all; she gave the blue skirt to her sister; she didn't arrive at their favorite café by crossing the square diagonally from the subway station as usual, allowing him to recognize her at a distance by her upright gait, but instead she came swooping around the corner from the opposite side, locked her bicycle to a lamppost, and sat down at his table sweating with dirty hands.

The security guard says: No one home?

I found who I was looking for, Richard says, but I'll wait outside.

A second guard holds the door open for him.

Only on the surface had it been perhaps a question of whether the causes for his lover's negligence were rooted in some completely different mode of being, a system different from his own point of reference—such as a new love affair she must be keeping secret from him, or maybe it was just that her dress size had changed, or because new bike lanes had been installed in the city center. Fundamentally though—even if it was never openly articulated—she was seeing what remained of their relationship, what was really there in the first place once the rituals he kept trying to bind her to were suspended. In any case it was certainly true that no human being could be one hundred percent known to another, and it was unfortunately also true that he, Richard, found this fact impossible to accept, particularly as it pertained to his lover.

You know where you can put your vanishing points! she'd shouted at him during their last argument, and then: What if I urgently need to reach you at 11:27 p.m. some night when you're lying in your goddamn master bedroom with your wife and I haven't requested a phone date in advance? Enraged like this, she'd appeared to him particularly attractive, and he'd smiled looking at the frantic patches of red that appeared on her neck. The smile had been a mistake. His final mistake—after that, she hadn't given him any more chances to make mistakes.

But wasn't finding shared points of reference—standard units of measure—crucial in any relationship?

He's also annoyed now that he's having to wait and doesn't have a book with him. Not even a newspaper.

Yesterday, in an article about German aid to developing nations, he read that as a matter of policy the first thing one aid organization did on beginning work in a new country was to establish standard measures and norms corresponding to the German system. For trade, the article explained, an authoritative scale of this sort was indispensable, but of course Richard knew that a scale like this was also, and above all, an instrument of domination. Well, after all, even domination was a sort of relationship. To be sure, the Treblinka Death Camp Revolt could be planned only after the SS had installed a new camp leadership that strictly adhered to its own rules and therefore was predictable. Anything predictable and rigid can be undermined and broken. Only chaos disrupts and remains. And then it occurs to him that just now he was thinking like his lover.

Whatever.

White and as full as a moon, in any case, is what her rear end had looked like in happier times under that blue skirt he so loved to see her wear.

Finally the door opens and Osarobo appears, again wearing his too-thin jacket.

I'm sorry, he says.

It's perfectly all right.

And they set off.

Hey, did you know you can play soccer here, Richard asks, indicating the gravel-covered playing field on the left.

Everybody you mean?

Of course—everybody.

Without paying?

Exactly, without paying. Do you have a ball?

No.

Is anyone watching him walk down the street with this dark-skinned young man? He wonders what such a person might be thinking. Every time they turn a corner, Richard stops and draws the boy's attention to the name of the street, so he'll be able to find his own way the next time.

Did you know that this used to be the East?

Osarobo shakes his head. East?

Probably this isn't the right way to ask this question when speaking to a person from Niger.

Did you know that there used to be a wall in Berlin that separated one half of the city from the other? he asks.

I don't know.

It was built a few years after the war. Did you know there was a war here?

No.

A world war?

No.

Did you ever hear the name Hitler?

Who?

Hitler. He started the war and killed all the Jewish people.

He killed people?

Yes, he killed people—but only a few, Richard says quickly, because he's already feeling bad about getting carried away almost to the point of telling this boy, who's just fled the slaughter in Libya, about slaughter that happened here. No, Richard will never tell him that less than a lifetime ago, Germany systematically murdered so many human beings. All at once he feels deeply ashamed, as if this thing that everyone here in Europe knows is his own personal secret that it would be unreasonable to burden someone else with.

And an instant later, just as forcefully, Richard is seized by the hope that this young man's innocence might transport him once more to the Germany of *before*, to the land already lost forever by the time he was born. *Deutschland is beautiful.* How beautiful it would be if it were true. Beautiful is hardly the word for it.

Then they have arrived. The entryway, the hall, the kitchen, the living room with its view through to the library, the stairs leading up.

You live here with your family?

My wife is no longer alive.

Oh, I'm sorry. You have children?

No.

You live here all alone?

Yes, Richard says. Come, I'll show you the piano.

The piano is in the tiny room next to the entryway that Richard and his wife always called the music room. Christel, who'd been a violist until her orchestra was disbanded, used to practice here. Sometimes Richard accompanied her on the piano, but that was all an eternity ago. Nowadays he comes here only to assemble the year's bills and invoices when it's time for his accountant to do his taxes. The shelves lining the room are covered with binders and folders, along with photo albums, old reel-to-reel tapes, cassettes, records, and a handful of scores.

Richard folds back the dusty cover from the keyboard, clears the stack of paper from the piano stool, and asks: Do you need music?

He doesn't know if the boy can really play the piano. Maybe he worked as a waiter somewhere in Libya and the bar pianist gave him lessons. Or maybe Osarobo had just started improvising on some piano that was standing around somewhere.

Bach? Mozart? Jazz? Blues?

Osarobo shakes his head.

Okay, then I'll leave you to it. Come, sit down.

Osarobo sits down on the stool and turns around to look at

Richard. Richard nods at him, leaves the room, and shuts the door behind him.

Richard has just reached the living room when he hears the first notes. Osarobo plays one, two, sometimes three notes at a time— dissonances, high notes, low notes, over and over. This isn't Johann Sebastian Bach, nor is it Mozart, jazz, or blues. Osarobo has never touched a piano in his life, this much is clear. Richard lies down on the sofa with a newspaper, reads an article, reads another, then gets tired and falls asleep under the camelhair blanket, and the notes keep falling into his late-morning dream, one, two, sometimes three at a time, they rub up against each other, then fall silent, then try once more here, there, and the silence between the notes remains alive, as if each dissonance were relating something to the one that follows, and then the next one had a question, and the third waited for them to finish. When Richard eventually wakes up again, he goes back to flipping through the newspaper. It took him approximately seven years of practicing the piano as a child before he was able to listen to himself and understand that what he was doing was making music. Probably it's only this listening to oneself that turns the notes into music. What Osarobo is playing isn't Bach, nor is it Mozart, jazz, or blues, but Richard can hear Osarobo's own listening, and this listening turns these crooked, lopsided, harsh, stumbling, impure notes into something that, for all its arbitrariness, still is beautiful. He lays down the newspaper, goes into the kitchen, and puts on water for coffee. Only now does it occur to him how long his daily life has been lacking sounds other than the ones he himself makes. He was always the most content, back in his old life, when his wife practiced the viola while he was sitting at his desk one room away, working on a lecture or article. *The joy of the parallel universe* is how he'd described it to her. She, on the other hand, had always insisted—above all in her final years—that the full happiness of marriage required each of the partners to look at one another, but really they had to touch. Unfortunately these discussions had increased neither his nor her happiness.

During his childhood, his mother had sometimes done her ironing while he sat at the piano practicing, that's why to this day when he hears Bach's *Inventions* on the radio, it always seems to him he can smell freshly washed clothes.

When the water boils, he goes to the front room, knocks, opens the door a crack, and asks Osarobo if he would also like to have some coffee, or tea, or water. Osarobo shakes his head.

Are you enjoying playing the piano?

Yes.

I'll bring you a glass of water.

He sets down the glass to the left of the low A, and shows Osarobo how to place the five fingers of one hand one at a time on the keys. There's a key beneath every finger. Osarobo's fingers are weak and keep collapsing, and he soon forgets the pinky finger altogether. But that doesn't matter. Once more. And again. Here in the middle is the keyhole for the keyboard lid, here is middle C. And make your hand heavy. Osarobo's hand is not heavy. Just let it fall. The hand doesn't get any heavier, and why? Because Osarobo won't let go. Let it fall. He can't. The black man and the white man look at this black arm and this black hand as if at something that is causing problems for both of them. Your hand has weight, Osarobo shakes his head, yes it does, of course it does, just let it fall. Richard holds Osarobo's elbow from below and sees the scars on this arm that the arm's owner is trying to control, the hand is prepared to jerk back at any moment, the hand is afraid, the hand is a stranger here and doesn't know its way around. Let it fall. Richard thinks of how, in the café last Friday, Osarobo plucked at the back of his hand, plucked at the black skin that will cover him all his life. Exert himself as he will, Osarobo is unable to put an end to his own exertions. Where does Mozart begin?

And because nearly three hours have passed, Richard asks him if he would like to eat pizza. No problem, Osarobo says. Richard goes out. As he puts the frozen pizza in the oven and sets the table for two—something he hasn't done in a long time—he hears the five notes being played in the correct order, one note per finger, and then a pause, and then the five notes again, and again. The left hand too, he shouts, and since Osarobo doesn't understand, he goes back to the room again and shows him that the left hand must do the same exercises as the right, just the other way around.

Osarobo eats only a small piece of pizza, that's all he wants, thanks. And water, yes, water from the tap, not fizzy water from a bottle.

Do you know how to get back to the home from here?

I don't know.

Richard takes out a map of Berlin, and on the special pull-out section for this part of town, he shows Osarobo the name of the suburb, then his street, and then he traces his finger along the lines: Here you turn to the left, walk down So-and-so Street and here along the edge of the square, then turn right and cross the street to the home. He sees Osarobo trying to understand the map, and then he knows that Osarobo, who traveled from Niger by way of Libya to Italy, and then from Italy to Berlin, has never before seen a map of any city or country on earth.

Then he gets up along with Osarobo, puts on his brown shoes—the most comfortable ones—and walks him back to the home.

25

Today the Ethiopian teacher is wearing her hair up, but a few loose strands curl around her face. While she gets started with the reading exercises for the pupils who are illiterate, Richard is off in one corner of the room setting up a conversation course with the two advanced students she's assigned to him. *Guten Tag*, he says: Hello! How are you, what's your name? What country are you from? How old are you? How long have you been in Berlin? Yussuf is from Mali, and Ali is from Chad. Richard is glad to be holding class in the same room as the teacher so he can see how she explains things, how she dictates words to her students, helps them with their writing, wiping away a word here and there on the board with the ball of her hand to write something in its place, then asks a question of the group as a whole. Sometimes she even glances over at the advanced group. Meanwhile, he's begun a discussion about professions with Ali and Yussuf: In Libya I worked on a construction site and in Italy as a nurse, Ali says. As a nurse, really? Yes, for a while. And Yussuf? In Italy I worked in the kitchen. Aha, Yussuf, so you're a cook? Richard stirs an imaginary pot. No. What did you do in the kitchen? I washed plates. Oh, so you were a dishwasher. How do you say that? Dish-wash-er. His advanced student hands him a pad for him to write down the word. Then Yussuf reads it. Dishwasher. Richard makes him practice the *a* sound, and then his pronunciation is as good as perfect: Dishwasher! Dishwasher! I am Yussuf from Mali and worked in Italy as a dishwasher! Richard observes this laughing Yussuf from Mali, a short, extremely dark man who, before coming to Germany, worked in Italy as a dishwasher. His pronunciation is perfect. The sentence is perfect. As a statement—of this he is quite certain—it spells Yussuf's doom. Richard has now learned enough about German and European immigration law to understand this. Without meaning to, he thinks of a line from Brecht: *He who laughs has not yet received the terrible news.* Did you have any sort of professional training, in Libya maybe, before you went to Italy? No, Yussuf says. And in Mali? No, Yussuf says, I wanted to go to school, but my parents didn't have any money. And again he laughs: Now I'm here and can write and read, I speak Arabic, French, Italian, English, and soon also German— now I know much more than pupils in Mali!

124

Richard finds this claim perfectly plausible.

And you? he asks Ali.

I only went to Arabic school. My father said I had to finish Arabic school before I could start French school. In Arabic school, we learned to recite the Quran from memory. You can recite the Quran? Not the whole thing, only around three-quarters of it. You can recite three-quarters of the entire Quran from memory in Arabic? Yes. But then we fled to Libya. I learned English in Italy, from my friends. And I learned Italian from the old woman I took care of, in only three months, but German is more difficult.

The Ethiopian teacher is just reviewing the material from two weeks ago with her pupils: for the German past tense form known as *Perfekt*, you always need two verbs, the main verb and the auxiliary verb *sein* or *haben*. That's how Richard first made her acquaintance, she was swimming past the blackboard (*ich bin geschwommen*), flying past it (*ich bin geflogen*), walking past (*ich bin gegangen*). The joy of the parallel universe. Ali, what sort of profession would you like to train for? I'd like to become a real nurse. And you? he asks Yussuf. I'd like to be an engineer. In the pause that now ensues, Richard considers what to say as a resident of a country that has seventy thousand vacant apprentice positions with no one to fill them, a country that suffers from a shortage of trained workers but is nonetheless unwilling to accept these dark-skinned refugees; these people can't just fly over Italy, Greece, or Turkey like birds in springtime without setting foot on the wrong soil—they can't be accepted as applicants for asylum, much less taken in, educated, and given work. In this brief pause, Richard, absorbed in these thoughts, glances over at the teacher: to practice the *Perfekt*, she's placed pairs of men at the front of the classroom, one of them representing the auxiliary verb, the other the verb being declined. Khalil and Mohamed, she says, are friends, right? Yes, all the men say. And Moussa and Yaya too, right? Yes, all the men say. Moussa is the one with the blue tattoo on his face whom Richard noticed back at Oranienplatz. And now, since the teacher wants to clarify the grammatical opposition between the past and present tenses, she asks who among them is always completely alone, who has no friend and doesn't speak with anyone. The silence that follows resembles the silence that emanated from Richard after Yussuf said the word *engineer*. A murmuring follows, and out of this, a name gradually emerges, and the name is Rufu. Rufu comes to the front, as an example of someone who is always alone, he advances obediently to have his singularity observed. An engineer, Richard thinks, good Lord, and he sees that the teacher too has fallen silent. Rufu stands in front at the blackboard as an example of the present tense, which requires no auxiliary verb. *Ich gehe*, the teacher says now, noticeably more quickly, I go. *Ich schwimme*, I swim. And: *ich fliege*, I fly. So the verb in the present tense is always alone. Now you can all sit down again. And the two pairs of friends, Khalil and Mohamed and Moussa with his blue facial tattoos and his friend Yaya, sit down in pairs in their seats, and Rufu goes alone. In turn, Richard says to his two advanced students: No matter what profession you want to practice someday, it's definitely a good idea to learn German.

Rufu's face.

In the Wismar Cathedral, Richard once saw a Madonna standing with both feet upon the head of a moor lying on the ground. As he later read, it wasn't the head of a moor at all, it was supposed to be the moon, which, back when the altarpiece was carved, around 1500, had been painted silver, but the silver paint had darkened over the years. It took five centuries, but eventually it looked as if the Madonna were stepping on a black moon; five centuries after it was carved, this moon had a face resembling that of Rufu, who is all alone in the world, who has no friend and speaks with no one.

At least the teacher and Richard are spared the question of how the lesson should continue, for all at once Apollo comes racing in the open door, his vivacious hair leaping up and down on his head, he speaks to the others loudly and fast in Hausa, then in Italian, then in French, and then in Hausa again. All of them now start arguing in various languages, they pack up their notebooks, get up, and leave the room. The lesson seems to have ended on its own. On his way out the door, Tristan (Awad) says to Richard:

How are you?

Fine, but what's going on?

The move to Spandau that was supposed to happen tomorrow has been postponed again because of the sickness.

Because of the chickenpox?

Yes.

And what's this move to Spandau?

It's another house. We all packed our things already.

You too?

Yes.

Aha.

Take care, Tristan says. He waits until Richard actually looks at him and nods, and then he's out the door and gone. Take care—it's been a long time since anyone's said that to him. Meanwhile, the teacher has wiped the board clean, now she's packing up her letters. Richard asks her: Did you know about the move?

No, she says.

Goodbye, she says, and picks up her bag.

Goodbye, Richard says. He is surprised she hasn't left yet.

That thing with Rufu—I'm really sorry, she says.

Listen, he says, I've done things like that too—perfectly normal sentences come out sounding completely different here.

Even so.

Then she does leave the room.

It pleases him that she's dissatisfied with herself and that she's gone so far as to confess this to him. It pleases him perhaps even

127

more than her hair, breasts, nose, and eyes. People concerned about their failings are always the wrong ones, he thinks, the ones with the least to reproach themselves for, but they torture themselves all the same. Like his gray-bearded colleague in Archaeology who lost no time in posting a self-critical statement on the bulletin board the morning after the fall of the Wall, announcing that he'd thought he was working to advance what he believed to be the will of the people, and that now he knew better. His junior colleague in Byzantine Literature, on the other hand, who, as a Stasi informant, had submitted a conspiratorial report on Richard's extramarital affair, had not posted words of self-criticism in the immediate aftermath of the Wall coming down or at any later point. Richard had discovered the report in his Stasi file in 1995: *Subject's areas of weakness include habitual arrogance and documented marital infidelity (active liaison with Assistant Professor XXX, employed by Prof. XXX). In general, subject displays pronounced fondness for members of the opposite sex and is easy to approach. Unpredictably vacillating political-ideological positions. In time of political crisis, subject tends to show poor political judgment, sometimes going so far as to make statements of an antagonistic-negative character. Subject unsuitable for conspiratorial collaboration according to Directive 1/79.* This Byzantine colleague now holds a professorship in Basel. The gray-bearded Archeology professor died five years after what everyone's now calling the *Wende*: the change. GDR history might now, if one so wished, serve as a subject for study by archaeologists, Richard thinks, and for a moment imagines Honecker, chairman of the GDR State Council, giving his speeches in Latin—he grins vacantly for a moment before he realizes what he's doing. Could this grinning, which he's been noticing himself doing more and more often in recent weeks, be a sign of senility? Or perhaps of serenity? Then he turns out the light and leaves.

26

In the *Kaufhalle* that's now a supermarket, Richard picks the short-est check-out line. Only as he's unpacking his items at the cash reg-ister does he see that Rufu, the black moon of Wismar, has gotten in line right behind him. He recognizes him by the pained expres-sion of his mouth that he'd noticed in the classroom, the bitter-ness so clearly imprinted in this face that it serves as an identifying feature like a wound or a scar. Richard nods to him and says good morning, and Rufu recognizes him and says, *Come stai?* He's buying a bag of onions. Richard's purchase includes lettuce, tomatoes, bell peppers, cheese, and noodles, that'll be 16.50, but when he reaches for his wallet, it isn't there. No, the checkout clerk can't put it on a tab for him, all she can do is set his purchases aside until he returns with the money. There's really no other way to handle this? She knows him, after all. Alas, no. Rufu says: *Hai dimenticato la moneta?* *Sì.* Richard is still hunting around, in his left coat pocket, his right coat pocket, his inside pocket. Just as he's wondering whether Rufu might have ... but no, he doesn't want to think that ... although he's standing right here behind him and could easily have slipped his hand into his pocket—just at this moment, Rufu hands the ca-shier a twenty-euro bill. No, that's out of the question, Richard says. You'll give it to me later, Rufu says. I can't accept that. *Non c'è un problema*. Are you going to make up your minds before tomor-row? the cashier says, and Richard does at last thank Rufu and lets him pay for his groceries. When they're outside, though, he insists on giving him back the money right away and won't take no for an answer. He says he's about to make lunch anyway, and Rufu is most definitely invited. Just as obediently as Rufu went up to the blackboard yesterday when called upon to serve as an example of someone without a single friend—just this obediently he now walks beside Richard. The wallet is lying on the floor in the hall, right where Richard bent down to tie his shoes. Richard tries to give the moon of Wismar two ten-euro bills, but the moon shakes its head and accepts only one of them. Please take both of them! Rufu shakes his head. Then take at least the 16.50. Or at least 15! Rufu refuses the second bill, he won't accept another 6.50 or even 5, no, absolutely not. Richard places the spurned banknote on the console in the hall, and there it remains.

Would you like to read something while I'm getting lunch ready? Rufu says: *Si, volontieri*. The only book in Italian that Richard owns is Dante's *Divine Comedy*. For years he'd been planning to read it in the original, but at some point the plan slipped his mind. For years, the Italian dictionary has stood beside it on his shelf. *Nel mezzo del cammin di nostra vita / mi ritrovai per una selva oscura / ché la diritta via era smarrita*. He can still recite the opening lines in Italian from memory. *Midway upon the journey of our life, I found myself in a dark wood, the right road lost*. Maybe not such a bad choice after all, he thinks, and hands the refugee—who's gone half a world astray—the burgundy-linen-bound first volume; and now while Richard is cooking, Rufu sits reading at the table, looking up just once when Richard steps on the pedal of the garbage can, making the lid pop up. Rufu gets up for a moment, steps on the pedal himself, the lid pops up, and Rufu—the man suffused with bitterness whose face is usually contorted in pain—smiles. Then he sits down again and goes on reading. When Richard tells him that lunch is ready, he puts the book aside and thanks him.

So where are you from, actually?

Burkina Faso.

Richard has forgotten where this country is situated. On the coast? Or in the interior of the continent?

In any case, Rufu's skin is extremely dark.

Say, do you know the guy who's always cleaning up, the one with ... Richard briefly gets up from the table and mimes the movement of sweeping, because he doesn't know how to say *broom* in Italian.

Con una ramazza?

Yes. The thin guy, from Ghana.

What's his name?

I don't know.

No. I don't know him, Rufu says.

After lunch, Rufu clears his plate and wants to do the dishes.

Oh, just leave them.

Then Rufu puts his shoes back on, and Richard also puts on his shoes, the brown ones, his most comfortable pair. The ten-euro bill is still lying on the console—no, Rufu still isn't willing to take it.

If you'd like to read more, just call me, I'll give you my number.

Richard types his name and number in Rufu's cell phone, then the two of them set off together, turning first to the left, then down So-and-so Street, then along the edge of the square and so on until they see the home.

In the evening, Richard pulls out his map of the city to see how far it is to Spandau. It's far. Even by car it would take at least three-quarters of an hour.

27

His head is practically splitting in two from the pain, Awad doesn't want to think, but he has to, the thinking has been locked up in his head and is pounding at his skull from the inside. It's been like this since three thirty a.m., he's dizzy with exhaustion, and still he can't stop surrendering to this out-of-control thinking, he doesn't want to think but has to, doesn't want to remember but has to, since three thirty a.m. he's been nauseous from all the thinking and remembering, since three thirty he's been awake. At first he sat on the edge of

131

the bed, hoping it would stop so he could go back to sleep. Around seven thirty he started walking up and down, over and over, up and down, up and down. His walking woke his roommates, who eventually went downstairs to the pool table, now it's ten thirty, and there's still no prospect of peace inside his skull, then there's a knock.

Since the door doesn't immediately fly open, Awad knows it's the polite older gentleman even before he sees him. Hasn't he told him everything about himself already?

Awad opens the door, greets him. How are you, fine, and offers him a cup of tea, the thought of the shattered window he escaped through is lodged in his head, and so is the thought of blood, and the older gentleman sits down and says he has a few more questions, if it's possible, and the thought of his father is lodged in his head, he can't manage to extract all these thoughts from his head all on his own, all the shards are lodged in there while he puts the water on to boil, the thinking is lodged in his head like a shattered animal; if only his head were a different one, but in wartime there's nothing but beatings and bullets, beatings and bullets, in wartime everything is in shards, you see the war and nothing else, and what the older gentleman would like to know is what he, Awad, had been planning to take with him when he moved to Spandau—the move is no longer taking place today. What he'd packed and prepared for this move, as he mentioned doing yesterday, what his baggage was. The move is no longer taking place today. Here, this bag, Awad says. That's your bag? the older gentleman asks and pulls out his notebook. And besides that? Nothing else, Awad says. Can you tell me what's in the bag? Awad dictates, and the older gentleman, who is very polite but perhaps also crazy, writes everything down carefully in his notebook.

4 pairs of pants, 2 from the home in Italy, 2 from Caritas Germany
1 blazer, a gift from a friend in Italy

3 t-shirts
*3 pairs of shoes (2 from the Caritas collection, 1 pair bought for him by
  a German)*
1 pair of sandals
1 sponge
1 cocoa butter lotion

Butter? the visitor asks. Awad pulls the bottle of lotion out of the
bag to show him.

Aha.

Then Awad finishes his list:

1 towel
1 toothbrush
1 Bible in English (the Jehovah's Witnesses gave it to him)

Do you have a sweater?

No, Awad says.

A winter jacket?

No, Awad says.

The move is no longer taking place today.

The older gentleman was alive on the day when Awad's father
was beaten to death or shot, and he is still alive today.

Now there's a knock at the door, which flies open at the same
moment, it's a staff member:

Pardon me, he says to the older gentleman. Hello, he says to
Awad, how are you? We're just taking blood samples to see who's
been infected with chickenpox in the past, would you like to come?
And again to Awad's visitor: We're checking to see which of them
might already have antibodies in their blood, would you mind explaining that to him?

Awad says: I don't understand.

A blood sample, the staff member says, it's voluntary, so only if you want to, Awad. We'll be waiting upstairs in Room 4015. Then he's gone.

The elderly gentleman says, a test like that is a good idea. Because of the sickness.

Awad says, I don't want to.

What would his father have counseled? One day he, Awad, will have a wife and a son, he'll give his son his father's name. And when he talks to his son, he'll call him: Daddy. Then his father will be with him every day, transformed into a child.

What's this lotion for? the older gentleman is asking now, picking up the bottle again to read the small print on the back.

Daddy. What will the kitchen look like where he'll cook for his son? What will the bathroom look like where he'll show him how to dry his back with a towel, where he'll later show him how to shave? What city will this be in, what country? Italy? Germany? France? Sweden? Holland? Switzerland? Or Libya, where he was at home? Where there's still war? In wartime, it's only the war you see. Now he has to watch out that he doesn't start walking up and down again. He knows his roommates spend the entire day beside the pool table because they can't stand it when he's walking up and down. He has to be calm, he has a visitor. If you want to arrive somewhere, you can't hide anything. What did the older gentleman just ask him? He's still holding the lotion he showed him.

The light here in Germany makes our skin patchy, Awad said. The light here isn't good for us.

The older gentleman looks over at the blue plaid curtain, behind which the gray sky is hung like a piece of felt.

You get ugly white patches, Awad says, and only the cocoa butter helps.

Involuntarily, the older gentleman looks at his hands, which are full of brown spots. He says: The German light gives me spots of a different sort. He puts down the bottle and shows Awad his hand.

Awad holds his dark hand next to it, and there really are spots that look as if someone tried to rub the color off.

Awad will never forget what his father's hands looked like. Where are these hands now? Under the earth, or were they eaten by dogs or birds?

And may I ask you something else? The visitor rubs one of his hands over the back of the other, as if he could wipe the age spots away.

Of course.

At the assembly last week, someone said that the showers have to have individual stalls. Is that really a matter of religious belief?

So Germans really didn't know that the aura of a man extends from his navel to his knees, and that no one except your wife is ever allowed to see an adult Muslim naked?

No, I didn't know that, the visitor says, but it's very interesting. He writes it all down carefully in his notebook.

When Awad arrived in Italy, at the camp, at first he couldn't believe that the men were expected to stand side by side to urinate, shamelessly, like animals.

Okay, the visitor says and shuts his notebook. You probably should go for that blood test now.

Why?

Do you know what chickenpox is?

No, Awad says.

Didn't you see the ones who got sick?

No.

You get bumps all over, it itches a lot and is very unpleasant.

Do you die from it?

No. But still.

For a moment Awad is very happy that his father is telling him what to do. His father is strict but just. He wants only the best for his son.

135

When they arrive in the staff room, there's already a dark-skinned man sitting on a chair in the middle of the room and the old lady working there is just disinfecting the spot on his arm where she's about to stick the needle.

Awad asks: Why isn't there a doctor here?

I used to be a doctor, she says.

Awad doesn't know what this is supposed to mean. Until now this lady was a staff member who helped him fill out forms. Will she be a judge or maybe a policeman tomorrow if no one else is available to play the role? Might the older gentleman suddenly become a salesman or truck driver? What's this strange play the Germans are putting on for them here? And why?

Have a seat, the older gentleman says, pointing to the chair that now stands empty, waiting for him. What are the Germans doing to us here? Awad thinks and notes the panic rising up in him. Maybe he'll get lucky and succeed in escaping before they catch him. He says: I'll be right back, nods to his visitor, turns around as inconspicuously as possible, walks out of the room and then down the stairs very slowly, very very slowly to his room, which can't be locked from the inside, but at least he shuts the door behind him and stands as silently as he can with his back to the wall. He takes shallow breaths. If someone were to come in now, he'd be hidden behind the door, and that's better than nothing. Only after a little while does he calm down again, realizing that no one's come after him. Then he sits down again where he was sitting before, on the edge of the bed.

28

Aren't their applications supposed to be getting processed one of these days? asks Richard after Tristan has left the room.

Yes, one of the staff members says.

Have they started yet?

No.

And why not?

We don't know, the staff member says.

And you'll go on taking care of these men until their applications for asylum are accepted?

The first thing that'll be decided on is whether or not they're allowed to apply for asylum.

Thrush, blackbird, finch, and starling made the mistake of stopping over in Italy. Richard had almost forgotten.

But aren't they a group—all of them driven out of Libya under exactly the same circumstances?

True, but they all originally came to Libya from different countries.

Aha.

Would you like a coffee? (The coffeemaker's gurgling again.)

In terms of the physics of the thing, it surely makes sense to divide a group into individual cases, Richard thinks, and says: Yes please.

Have the men received the second half of their money yet?

No, because the decision hasn't been made yet.

And all of you are elder-care professionals, if you don't mind my asking?

Richard takes a sugar cube from the box and pours milk into his coffee.

No, we're all social workers, or retirees from related fields, like the doctor here. We're only under contract for six months. It's part of the Oranienplatz agreement. We're supposed to accompany the refugees on all their trips to the various agencies.

Which agencies?

The doctor sets down her needle and comes over to the coffee table. To the Foreigners Office, she says, the District Office, the Social Welfare Office, sometimes to a doctor, sometimes a lawyer.

For the ones who've committed some infraction?

No, for the ones who can afford a lawyer.

How much does it cost?

For asylum applications, 450 euros. Often the lawyers will let them pay in installments, but even then it's 50 or 100 a month.

Richard calculates: 357 euros, minus 57 for the transit pass makes 300, minus 100 to send to a mother in Ghana, say, so that's 200, minus the cheaper lawyer makes 150. Maybe also a prepaid card for a cell phone. That leaves less than 5 euros per day to live on.

How many staff members are there for this group?

Twelve half-time positions.

He hears Apollo's voice saying: They give us money, but what I really want is work. He hears Tristan's voice saying: *Poco lavoro*. He hears the voice of Osarobo, the piano player, saying: Yes, I want to work, but it is not allowed. The refugees' protest has created half-time jobs for at least twelve Germans thus far, Richard thinks.

If I might ask something completely different...., he says.

Of course, the former doctor replies, pulling off her rubber gloves and sitting down.

Why are the men paying full price for their transit passes?

Because they don't receive the benefits covered by the Asylum Seekers' Law.

Because they still aren't allowed to apply for asylum?

Exactly.

That's why they receive 357 euros, not just 300, says the staff member in charge of the coffeemaker.

Richard stirs his coffee and for a while says nothing. But then he starts up again:

Were they already receiving these payments at Oranienplatz?

No.

What did they live on?

Donations.

Richard remembers the cardboard box with the word "donations" that he saw at Oranienplatz, and the two men waiting behind it.

And once the individual applications have been processed?

Then it'll be clear who is entitled to benefits and who isn't.

I understand, Richard says. He takes a sip of the coffee. It tastes exactly the same here as it would in the waiting room of a tax accountant, or a car dealership, or a notary.

Do you think he'll be back? he asks, nodding in the direction of the door.

I doubt it, the staff member says.

Have many of them come to have their blood tested?

Not really.

They're funny about blood sometimes, says the third staff member, who's been sitting half in shadow beneath the slope of the roof and hasn't said anything until now.

On his way downstairs, Richard glances quickly down the empty corridor of the first floor. There's no one to be seen. Down beside the exit, Apollo, who wants to go out, is just showing his ID to the guard on duty. *Vse v poriadke.* Outside Richard catches up with him and asks whether he might have time over the weekend to help him in his garden. Paid work, of course. *Kein Problem*, Apollo says in German: no problem.

On Wednesday, the piano player will visit him again, that's set now, and surely Rufu, the moon of Wismar, will come by soon to read more Dante. How long has it been since the director of the senior-living facility told Richard that it might be better to speak with the refugees in the home and not, say, at Richard's house? Just a suggestion, the director added. What exactly had he meant? A suggestion. After six weeks, Richard is now chafing at the man's words as he walks home. And the dead man is still lying at the bottom of the lake. Assuming he hasn't since dissolved.

In the evening, when Richard starts undressing for bed, he ponders whether he, too, has an aura such as Tristan described. The terrain from his belly button down to his knobby knees has seen better

139

days, he thinks, looking down. Even the hair growing there is now completely gray. Could he ever lie in bed with the young Ethiopian, or take a shower with her—or simply just stand somewhere embracing? Or with any other woman, ever again? Learning to stop wanting things is probably one of the most difficult lessons of getting old. But if you don't learn to do that, it seems to him, your desires will be like a bellyful of stones dragging you down into your grave.

29

In the beginning was an undifferentiated whole that contained everything: feminine and masculine, space and time, sameness and multiplicity. This totality sank down through the emptiness and revealed itself in multifarious forms. The feminine is dense and corporeal, it is made of primordial matter and was there at the beginning, then the masculine arrived, lighter in substance and mobile. In just this way, space and time came into being. But all these manifestations are mutually dependent, none stands above the other, rather each complements the other, and in all their multifariousness they remain a whole, a single body. In just this way, individual human beings in society are parts of a living totality—like the different organs in a body, they perform different functions but are inextricably connected. And finally there is also a political body made up of its various constituents. The Tuareg say that in the 1960s the French, by dividing up the region they had traditionally inhabited into five different countries, cut their political body into pieces.

Richard is reading.

Richard's reading began with Herodotus, who described the Garamantes, the ancestors of the Tuareg, back in the fifth century B.C.

The Greeks learned the art of steering a chariot from the men of this Berber people, and from the women, they learned poetry. To this day, the older women sit out in the open before sunrise, when it's still night, and sing:

Even when a person is prosperous and rich,
Death is still near.
Death is greater than time, death envelops time.
Even now he sends out his arrows, and they fall
in the middle of the herd.

The ancestors of the Tuareg are said to have come from today's Syria more than three thousand years ago, perhaps even from the Caucasus, crossing Egypt to reach North Africa, which in antiquity was known as a whole as Libya (in other words the region encompassing today's Tunisia and Algeria). In the course of time they traveled even farther to the West and South: all the way to Timbuktu, Agadez, Ouagadougou.

Richard reads, and as he reads, he experiences a shifting in his conception of the Greek pantheon—his area of specialization, after all—and suddenly he has a new understanding of what it means that for the Greeks the end of the world was located in what is now Morocco, at the edge of the Atlas Mountains where Atlas pressed the sky and earth apart so Uranus wouldn't slam against Gaia and do her harm. The regions now known as Libya, Tunisia, Algeria were, in antiquity, understood to be the territory just before the end of the world. It was on Libyan sand that Gaia's son stood, the giant Antaeus who drew his strength from his connection with his mother, and who was vanquished only after Heracles raised him up and held him in the air. Owl-eyed Athena, described by some scholars as a *black goddess,* grew up in the home of her foster father, Triton, on the banks of Lake Tritonis in modern-day Tunisia. The Amazons, originally Berber warrior women known as Amazigh,

141

the first to worship Athena, would dance on the shores of the lake before heading into battle—they spoke Tamasheq, the same language that the young man in room 2019, whom Richard recently started calling Apollo, speaks; at the time Richard still utterly mistook the lay of the mythological land.

Richard reads.

Medusa, too—the Gorgon with hair made of snakes coiling atop her head, who turned to stone all who met her gaze—was, it's said, once a beautiful Libyan Berber girl and a successful warrior. Only after Poseidon, the sea god, had slept with this beauty (in a temple to Athena on the Libyan shore) did the indignant Athena give the Amazon her frightening aspect, and later she gave Perseus the mirrored shield that would allow him to avoid the Gorgon's fatal gaze so he could finally cut off her head without being turned to stone. The drops of blood that fell on the Libyan sand after her beheading turned into snakes, Richard reads. No, it's surely no coincidence that today the Tuareg's herds and tents belong to women, and that the women can choose their own husbands and divorce them as they please, that they go around without veils while their menfolk are covered, that property is inherited from woman to woman, and that even today Tuareg women are celebrated for their poetry and song, that it is they who teach their children to write, using the same script that Herodotus saw with his own eyes.

Much of what Richard reads on this November day several weeks after his retirement are things he's known most of his life, but today, thanks to this bit of additional knowledge he's acquired, it all seems to come together in new, different ways. How many times, he wonders, must a person relearn everything he knows, rediscovering it over and over, and how many coverings must be torn away before he's finally able to truly grasp things, to understand them to the bone? Is a human lifetime long enough? His lifetime, or anyone else's?

When he considers the path the Berbers may have taken: from

the Caucasus by way of Anatolia and the Levant all the way to Egypt and ancient Libya, then later into modern-day Niger (and then back from Niger to modern-day Libya and across the sea to Rome and Berlin), it's nearly a perfect three-quarter circle. This movement of people across the continents has already been going on for thousands of years, and never once has this movement halted. There were commerce, and wars, and expulsions; people often followed the animals they owned in search of water and food, they fled from droughts and plagues, went in search of gold, salt, or iron, or else their faith in their own god could be pursued only in the diaspora. There was ruin and then transformation and reconstruction. There were better roads and worse ones, but never did movement cease. To explain to a student that he is speaking not about a moral law but a law of Nature, Richard would only have to point out the window, where so many of the leaves whose appearance in spring cheered him now lie on the grass, while the branches are already studded with next year's buds. But there's no student here asking him about any of this.

Richard continues to read.

He reads about the lost cities of the Garamantes—their sand-swept fortresses and clever underground irrigation systems in the once thickly settled oases at the beginning of the trade routes leading through the desert to the south. Well, now that Gaddafi has been deposed, satellite images have finally proven that the original inhabitants of Libya weren't bandits on the margins of civilization but rather people who were technologically on the cutting edge of their time. He reads this on the two-year-old website of the transitional government. Now it's hoped, he reads in this two-year-old present tense, that archaeology in Libya will enjoy a renaissance after having been criminally neglected by Gaddafi all these years. Soon, he reads, the people of Libya will, for the first time, have the opportunity to acquaint themselves with their own history, so long

143

suppressed. At the moment, the website goes on, the professor in charge of this research has evacuated because of the riots, but as soon as security has been restored, he will go on with his investigations, for which he's received grant support from European agencies. Richard, who lives in this now two-year-old future, knows that since the overthrow of Gaddafi by various militias, whose aims are increasingly unclear, the entire country has been turned into a battlefield. The people of Libya have by no means been devoting themselves to delving into their pre-Islamic roots—they've had their hands full just trying to survive. It's true enough that Gaddafi allotted the Libyan archaeologists only meager resources for their research, but now even the Europeans have frozen their aid, the archaeologists themselves have no doubt been in exile these past two years, and the only aficionados of antiques left studying the fortresses, cities, and villages of the Garamantes are men in uniform systematically stripping them of all their treasures that can be converted into cash. The descendents of the Garamantes are now regarded as foreigners in today's Libya, for which reason they were forced into boats two years ago with all the other foreigners and sent to Europe. What span of time should you consider if you want to know what qualifies as progress?

Richard reads and reads.

For which reason he hasn't even eaten lunch yet when the phone rings, and his friends propose he join them for a walk. It'll be getting dark soon, Sylvia says. And Detlef shouts in the background: Thomas is coming too.

Doesn't Thomas have to stay home all weekend to look after his wife? asks Richard.

No, her cousin has come to visit.

Chubby Thomas—a former economics professor, now a computer specialist—lights a cigarette as they walk.

Only six left, he says, shaking the pack before he puts it back in his coat pocket. It must be the last of the three packs his wife allows him every week.

That's all I get till Monday, he says.

His friends nod.

Richard, Thomas, Sylvia, and Detlef all live less than ten minutes apart by foot, but they would probably never get together if Sylvia didn't occasionally just call them up as she's done today.

How are the Africans doing? Detlef asks.

They're moving soon.

What Africans? asks Thomas, and now he hears the short version of the story that Richard recently shared with the other two. Richard also tells them about the goddess Athena, and Medusa, and Antaeus, and finally his appointment with Apollo.

But Apollo was from Delos, says Thomas, who, even though he studied economic history, has always been at least as well informed about everything else as Richard.

Sure, Richard says, but I'm talking about a refugee. Tomorrow he's coming over and helping me, I want to get the garden ready for winter and I can't drag the rowboat out of the water by myself anymore. *Haul up your ship upon the land and pack it closely with stones all round to keep off the power of the winds which blow damply, and draw out the bilge-plug so that the rain of heaven may not rot it.*

Works and Days, says Thomas.

Works and Days, says Richard. Thomas is the only one among his friends who, like him, can recite Hesiod from memory.

If my back would cooperate, I'd help you, says Detlef.

I know, says Richard.

This Apollo is a Tuareg? asks Thomas.

Yes.

From Niger?

Yes.

Well, give him a once-over with a Geiger counter before you say hello.

145

I know, Richard says.

How come? asks Sylvia.

There's more uranium in Niger than nearly anywhere else in the world, Richard says.

As they walk past the pine trees and oaks, and while the dog that always pulls away from the old couple he belongs to comes running up to them—his name is Cognac, Richard tells Detlef and Sylvia, who probably don't even know exactly where Niger is, about the French-government-owned corporation Areva that holds a monopoly on the mines and dumps its waste in an area where the Tuareg used to pasture their camels. And where they live, he says.

In the sky, a few birds try to arrange themselves in a triangle as they fly, for the trip to Africa. A mailbox in front of a completely overgrown property has been painted pink ever since the owner began renting it out to students from Berlin.

In Niger, Richard says, the drinking water has been contaminated, the camels are done for, people keep getting cancer without knowing why—but in France and here in Germany we have plenty of energy.

Here in Germany, Detlef repeats. Richard isn't sure whether Detlef is astonished at what Richard's just told him or by his use of this formulation. After all, the country known as Germany existed until a very short time ago only on the other side of the wall. Well . . . , says Richard, as if to excuse himself for verbally unifying these two German-speaking countries.

Besides which, Thomas says, Areva's yearly profits are ten times the size of the total revenues of the State of Niger.

How in the world do you know that? asks Richard.

You know, I read it somewhere, says Thomas, flicking his ash into the Brandenburg sand.

It's really awful, Richard says. There was a Tuareg uprising back in 1990, and they got massacred, so things were quiet after that. A few years ago, the same thing happened.

146

Someone has leveled out the dips in the sandy road with chunks of brick and tile, no doubt to spare the bumpers of his car.

And the only government that tried to kick out the French was quickly deposed in a coup, Thomas says. By God knows who.

Shall we turn around? asks Sylvia, as she asks on all their walks when they reach the end of the row of houses. Then they return by the path that curves through the woods, where it still smells of mushrooms, even though all the mushrooms have probably rotted by now.

Al-Qaeda knows about the uranium too, Richard says. It just remains to be seen if they'll ally themselves with the Tuareg against the government of Niger. Then again, maybe they won't.

Probably one doesn't exclude the other, Detlef says.

Yes, Richard says, the desert is certainly big enough to contain several fronts.

Actually what Areva is doing is exactly the same thing Richard was talking about before, Sylvia says. Heracles lifts Antaeus from the earth, and that's what makes him lose his strength.

Detlef says, doesn't the Nuremburg soccer team have Areva on their jerseys?

Could be, Richard says, thinking. He thinks as they pass the property of that local functionary who's constantly threatening her neighbors with a two thousand-euro fine for every minor infraction—they are passing it in the other direction now that they're on their way home—and then the property where the head of the Anglers' Club has hoisted the German flag, and then the swimming hole that's been deserted all summer. Richard thinks as he watches Sylvia link arms with her husband Detlef, watches Thomas scowl into his cigarette pack and then put it back in his coat pocket without extracting a cigarette, he thinks at precisely this moment that these four people here, including him, are like the parts of a single body: hand, knee, nose, mouth, feet, eyes, brain, ribs, heart, and teeth, each of them some part or other.

What will happen when Sylvia—who sometimes picks up the phone out of the blue and calls him or Thomas or a few other of their Berlin friends—is no longer here?

30

All summer long, the boat lay moored beside the dock, but because of the dead man in the lake, Richard didn't use it even once. A couple of times over the last few nights heavy rain fell, so now the boat is full of water, and it wouldn't take much to make it sink. The two men lug the skiff toward the shore like a drunken whale until it touches bottom and they can climb onto the seats to bail it out.

Say, when were you born exactly? Richard asks.

In '91, Apollo says.

Richard thought as much.

What month?

January 1.

In other words: eight months after the massacre to put down the Tuareg rebellion that he told his friends about yesterday. You're lucky, he says, that's perfect timing for New Year's fireworks.

The Italians say it's January 1 if you don't have a document.

I understand, Richard says.

Then they go on bailing.

Say, Richard says after a while, I saw on the internet that in Niger they dig very deep wells. And then a donkey pulls up the bucket of water. Is that really true?

Yes, says Apollo, the donkey has to walk for the same distance as the length of the rope with the canister. And then it turns around and walks back. Every day, back and forth like that for three or four hours.

That sounds labor-intensive.

The animals need water.

Why don't you just roll up the rope with a crank?

It won't hold in the sand.

Then it must be dangerous to dig these wells.

Yes, many people were buried.

Now they place round logs under the boat, pieces of a sawed-up tree, and use them to roll the boat across the grass to the edge of the lawn. Yesterday Richard read that because of the enormous quantities of water needed to flush the uranium out of the stone, groundwater levels have dropped noticeably all around the mines.

Do you know Arlit?

Of course. My region, Apollo says.

Soon the world will once more have occasion to speak of the Tuareg, since the French minister intends to vigorously pursue the completion of this undertaking. When one day, perhaps quite soon, the Sahara Railway is a reality and the steam-snorting iron horse takes its place upon the desert sands as a rival to the nimble camel, these sons of the desert will no doubt experience distress. The Tuareg will do their best to arrest the course of Culture, but their attacks will be countered with well-aimed peloton fire and brandy until, like the Indians in America, they cede their land to the Civilized. This was written in 1881 in the journal *Gartenlaube* shortly after the invention of journalism. The planned Sahara Railway came to naught, but a mere one hundred years later, the French just as undauntedly began to pursue uranium mining in their former colony.

Culture, Richard thinks. Progress, he thinks.

Okay, he says, listen, start tipping the boat from that end, and I'll push it from the other side.

He holds the boat while Apollo takes some logs to place underneath it. Then they turn the boat slowly until it comes to rest upside down.

But you didn't work in the mines in Arlit, did you?

No, we had camels.

You traveled with a caravan?

149

Yes.

What did you trade in?

We sold the camels in Libya.

How old were you?

Around ten. Starting at ten you go with the men.

How long does a caravan travel?

A few months, sometimes a year.

Across the desert?

Yes.

How do you find your way?

We know the way.

But how?

The young Tuareg shrugs. We just know it.

Richard would like to understand. He's still standing beside the inverted rowboat with this young man, who traveled more than two thousand miles to help him with his yardwork.

Can you tell by the stars?

Yes.

And during the day, when there are no stars?

The men know what happened along the way.

When?

Always.

Everything that ever happened?

Yes.

They tell what happened?

Yes.

While they're walking?

We don't walk, we ride.

Right.

They tell the stories in the evening.

They find their way by these stories?

Yes.

They find it by remembering?

150

Yes.

Richard falls silent. Of course he's always known that the *Odyssey* and the *Iliad* are stories that were passed on orally long before Homer—or whoever it was—wrote them down. But never before has the connection between space, time, and words revealed itself to him so clearly as at this moment. The backdrop of the desert shows it off in sharp relief, but really it's always been just the same all over the world: without memory, man is nothing more than a bit of flesh on the planet's surface.

Then they rake the grass and carry the garden furniture from the terrace to beneath the roof of the shed, they deflate the rubber dinghy that Richard hasn't tried out a single time this summer, carry broken branches from the woods to the fire pit, and disassemble the grill. Then Richard pays the refugee, who looks exactly the way he always imagined Apollo would look, fifty euros.

31

On Monday Richard puts on the black shoes that aren't his most comfortable pair but go better with his gray slacks. What stories will he tell about the path he takes to the nursing home? Will he say that someone drowned once in the lake? That many years ago someone bred peacocks on that property over there and you could hear their crazy shrieking for miles around? That yellow apartment building was always the turning-around point when he went for walks with his mother, back when she was still alive and capable of walking, and he would pick her up every Sunday for lunch, a walk, and coffee. That restaurant on the square is where he celebrated his silver anniversary with his wife not long after they moved here. The storefront on the corner that now houses a snack bar was once a tool shop—until one morning the owner was found hanging from a rope. No one knew why he hadn't wanted to go on living. The low building that in GDR times had held the local *Konsum* stood empty for a long time, now it's a branch of the bank Sparkasse. And then that building that was just torn down, the pale sand of a lot is all that's left. And the digital sign that always lights up red when someone drives too fast. Some day in the future, walking or driving past this building made of brick, he'll think: this is where the Africans were housed.

Will he too occupy some place in their stories? Maybe. Does it matter?

But then he's already at the home, and one of the security guards holds the door open for him, not out of politeness but because the door, as always, is locked from the inside.

And now he learns that the language lessons are being permanently discontinued—the teacher's left already, and the men are just getting ready because today at eleven the official language course will begin at a community college in Kreuzberg.

I see, he says.

He doesn't even have her phone number.

I'm so sorry, you must be disappointed, one of the guards says and offers him a chair.

Thank you, he says but doesn't sit, instead he goes on standing there and notices that the air suddenly has weight to it. What should he do?

He's still standing in the vestibule when the first of the men begin to gather in preparation for their departure. The man with golden shoes appears—Richard hasn't seen him here in the nursing home before, but remembers him from his first visit to Oranienplatz: Hermes. He wears glasses with very thick lenses and gleaming braids that lie close to his head. The two good friends, Khalil and Mohamed, appear, one wearing a fake gold chain around his neck, the other with his pants pushed so far down that his buttocks in their underpants are visible not just at the top but almost in their entirety. Apollo appears, his eyes encircled with a line of black kohl and a scarf wrapped around his head to make his hair stand up, *come stai, tutto bene*. Rashid appears wearing a t-shirt on which a leopard is printed, *everything good*? Tall Ithemba appears, also from Room 2017, and despite the gray November weather outdoors and the fluorescent light in the hall, he's got on mirrored sunglasses, *a real school, is more better*. Tristan appears, wearing on his feet his good pair of shoes that, as Richard now knows, a friendly German once bought for him, *how are you*? Tristan, too, has sunglasses, but he's put them on backwards, with the lenses behind his head. Osarobo appears, Richard sees him clean-shaven for the first time, he's wearing many strings of beads in different lengths around his neck and pants with enormous pockets below his usual too-thin jacket, but this time he's pulled it only halfway on so the collar sits at his elbows like a diva's boa, *crazy, eh*? he says and grins when he discovers Richard in the middle of the crowd. Zair appears, the one who was once in the same boat as Rashid, today he's looking dapper in a white shirt, suit trousers, and a blazer, and Yaya appears as well, Richard remembers Yaya from the last German lesson, he's got the Statue of Liberty on his t-shirt, and also Yaya's friend Moussa. Around his hips is a scarf the same gray-blue shade as the tattoos on his cheeks, and Abdusalam, the singer, appears, today with his head held high despite his squint, and Yussuf, the dishwasher from Mali, in the company of Ali, the future nurse from Chad (both of them Richard's advanced students), and now the three pool players enter, who are always motionless and mute, but today for the first time Richard sees them talking and laughing. Indeed, all the men are talking and laughing, exchanging greetings, there's a smell of cocoa butter and shower gel. The crowd includes many whom Richard knows only by sight, but at the very back he finally spots the thin man from the empty second-floor hallway, the one he's been looking for. The man stands perfectly still at the edge of the crowd, smiling over at Richard across all the braid-covered heads and the heads of the security guards and the staff members who are suddenly standing here as well.

And then it's time to go: the first outing to a proper German school, an outing right into the future. One staff member asks if everyone has their transit passes, and only now does it occur to Richard that there's someone missing: Rufu, the moon of Wismar. Okay, but it's too late now, the staff member says, it's time. Richard notes down the name of the school, and then the ceremonial procession begins: Chieftains and princes with heads held high depart the gleaming palace with ropes of cowry shells around their necks, peacock feathers bobbing atop their heads, they are wrapped in shimmering vestments. Joyful trilling fills the air; the gate opens as if by magic, tame antelopes and a unicorn join the delegation, and the rear of the train is brought up by three white elephants upon whose mighty backs the three staff members sway in jewel-encrusted seats. Until this glorious pageant has vanished beyond the horizon, the servants who opened the gates to all this splendor can be seen still bowing with their foreheads in the dust.

Richard doesn't have to think for long before he goes up to the third floor and knocks on the door to Room 2018: the door that's never before been opened. The nameplate beside the door says Heinz Kröppcke. What if Rufu disappeared without anyone noticing because he's always alone? What if he isn't even alive? Richard carefully presses down on the door handle, but Heinz Kröppcke's door is locked. Rufu, he shouts down the hallway, on the off-chance of being heard. Rufu. He goes down the hall. Rufu! And then a door opens at the very end of the hallway, right next to the kitchen where recently he helped the German teacher hang the Bode Museum on the wall. Rufu, the moon of Wismar, sticks his head out. Dante? he asks.

No, Richard says, today's the start of German lessons at a real school. Come with me.

Rufu looks solemn, as always, but he nods and says, *un attimo*, before he shuts the door again and, five minutes later, he appears in his jacket and cap.

Richard doesn't know if they'll really get there that much faster traveling by car, but he hopes so. Only after his wife's death did he buy his first GPS—until then, his wife, Christel, had always sat in the passenger seat with the road atlas open on her knees, telling him when to turn right or left. Christel. Her name is still alive, unlike the person to whom the name belongs. Now, when he drives, the voice of a woman to whom he isn't married says to him: Turn right, turn left. This voice served him well on a trip to Rügen, and then a trip to Weimar.

Do you know how to drive? Richard asks Rufu sitting silently beside him.

No, he says.

It takes Richard three red lights to type in the address, then the woman in the tiny machine suddenly says to him: If possible, make a U-turn. She must think he's still on his way back from Weimar.

Startled, Rufu asks: What is that?

She tells me where to drive.

Aha, Rufu says, frowning.

In two hundred feet, continue straight ahead.

Why do you need it? Rufu asks, pointing again at the GPS.

I don't know my way around so well in the West, Richard says, then he remembers his conversation with Osarobo.

Continue straight ahead.

Did *you* know that there was a wall between the Western and Eastern parts of Berlin for almost thirty years?

No, Rufu says.

Richard is already acquainted with these conversational shoals, so he says only: There was a border, and crossing over from the East into West Berlin wasn't permitted. Some people were even shot trying to cross the border.

Ah, *capisco*, they didn't want them in the West.

No, they didn't want to let them leave the East.

Okay.

In five hundred feet, keep right, says the female voice of his GPS, which even has a name in the instruction manual, though he can't remember it now. Annemarie maybe, or Regina.

But if they got across, did they get a passport in the West?

Yes, without a problem. As if they had always been citizens of the West.

Why?

Keep right.

Because they were Germans. Brothers and sisters, Richard says, and he thinks again of the crowd of weeping West and East Berliners he'd had to force his way through after the opening of the border crossing.

All of them were brothers and sisters?

No, of course not. Well, some were, but not all.

Okay, Rufu says, but Richard sees that Rufu doesn't really understand.

Do you think the wall was as high as the fence in Melilla?

Something like that, Richard says.

The Spaniards sent a friend of mine back to Morocco right away, Rufu says. Even though he got over the fence. His brother lived in Spain. But they still sent him back.

Was his brother a Spaniard?

No.

Well, that's it, don't you see?

What don't I see?

Yes, what is Rufu supposed to see? Annemarie or Regina isn't prepared to answer Rufu's question either, all she says is: In twenty-five feet, turn left.

Richard considers whether he should explain to Rufu about the Soviet War Memorial tucked away behind the trees they're just passing but decides not to. Should he start explaining in Italian something that is difficult enough to understand in German, namely that the monument depicts a Soviet soldier carrying a German child to symbolize the rebirth of Berlin after this final battle of the World War in which eighty thousand Soviet soldiers fell fighting to liberate a city that didn't want to be liberated in the first place? And that the Soviet soldiers were heroes. In part anyhow. Richard doesn't know how to say "rape" in Italian.

A quarter of a mile later they cross the invisible line on the asphalt that used to be the border and shortly afterward drive past a watchtower that still stands in the middle of a park, a relic of the time when this border still existed, crossing an area that used to be filled with barbed wire and landmines buried in the sand.

Richard says nothing about this either.

It's almost as if Rufu were sick or hard of hearing, and he, Richard—his visitor—didn't want to go to all the trouble to utter the sentences that might lead to a conversation. Too much would require explanation. Too much is missing.

A moment later, Annemarie or Regina chimes in again: Turn left.

A church, a taxi stand, a restored firehouse, and buildings from the century before last come into view.

Rufu says: Beautiful.

Why weren't you ever here? Oranienplatz isn't far away.

The subway runs underground, you don't see where you are.

I understand.

Sotto terra, Rufu says. *Sotto terra*.

They arrive at the school just in time, the staff members from the home are standing in the corridor with the director of the school working out the schedule. One of the staff members points at a door when he sees Richard with Rufu. And indeed, behind this

157

door is a large room where the Africans are already seated at tables. There's a card with questions to fill out so the teacher assigning the men to their course groups can tell which of them can read and write the Latin alphabet. Admitting that you don't know how to write strikes Richard as no less intimate than taking off one's clothes at the doctor's. He's about to leave, but then Tristan asks him if he has to fill in this blank here. And Osarobo doesn't have anything to write with. The teacher, who's getting on in years, is having difficulty understanding the Africans' English. Would you do me a favor and help me collect the forms after, to get the names right? Sure, of course. And so he sits down on a chair at the edge of the room while the men silently labor, each of them at pains to fill out the form as well as possible, and the oldish teacher sits at her desk, quietly sorting her papers.

Finally all are finished. Rashid says: I can help you. After all, he knows all the men and together with Richard, he goes from table to table while Richard makes a list, trying to clarify in each case which is the first name and which the last: this is Awad Issa from Ghana, this is Salla Alhacen from Niger, this is Ithemba Awad from Nigeria, this is Yussuf Idrissu from Mali, this is Moussa Adam from Burkina Faso, this is Mohamed Ibrahim, and so forth. The last names are patronyms, so it can happen that one of the refugees has the first name Idrissu, while Idrissu is also the last name of another. To make the confusion complete, some of the men put their last names first when introducing themselves, as is also customary in the Southern German countryside and also among the Austrians. Richard still remembers Möstl Toni quite well, the owner of a tavern specializing in young wine that Richard and his wife wandered into one day, after which they regularly ordered crates of his Riesling for years. Christel. Finally the list is finished, and Richard now knows (though in truth it's none of his business) that five of the approximately forty men can neither read nor write the Latin alphabet, including Hermes, the myopic fellow with the golden shoes, and also Khalil, Mohamed's best friend, whose gleaming chain is assuredly not real gold, and Abdusalam, the singer.

For the drive back, Rashid unhesitatingly claims a seat in Richard's car—well, who's ever heard of a thunderbolt-hurler taking public transportation? And Abdusalam's joining them too, so Richard moves a few empty bottles from the back seat to the trunk, and since there's room for three in the back, Rashid quickly summons tall Ithemba, who has to tuck his head in, car is more better than S-Bahn! While the three Nigerians squeeze into the back, laughing and shoving, Rufu, the moon of Wismar, sits solemn and silent up in front beside Richard. On the drive home, Richard learns that Rashid knows how to operate not just cars but also bulldozers, but his driver's license isn't recognized here, since he has neither a residence permit nor proof of identification. Abdusalam begins to sing, and Richard tells his passengers that there's even a German song about rides like this one, and he begins in turn to sing: *I've packed my wagon nice and full, packed it full of Africans!* Of course he knows that the original ditty speaks not of Africans but of women young and old—but the word "Africans" fits handily into the old folksong. Stopped at a red light, still singing at the top of his lungs while the men in the back seat clap the rhythm and hoot—with even Rufu nodding his head to the beat—Richard happens to glance into the car next to his, which holds a young family: father, mother, two children, all with their heads turned facing Richard's car, speechless and aghast at the sight of all these exuberant blackamoors and a white man apparently out of his mind. As he starts driving when the light turns green, singing, *Gee up, coachman!*, Richard hears the chorus of honking horns behind the car of the family still frozen in shock.

32

The next day, Richard does a little tidying up, then he takes out the garbage, by which time it's already almost eleven thirty, he changes the sheets, and goes out to the shed to look for a tape measure. It's surely bad timing to go visit the men during lunch, so he vacuums as well, and while he's at it, he cleans the kitchen and bathroom, then the whole house will be tidy and clean when the piano player comes to visit tomorrow. Before he knows it, it's evening, soccer, a talk show with everyone monopolizing the floor, a car chase, a burning eighteen-wheeler, two people kissing, the late news, the weather report. Not until bedtime does he google the keywords "Ethiopian" and "language teacher," but of course he knows, even as he's typing, how ridiculous this is.

The next morning Richard's phone rings at ten after eleven, it's Osarobo, who's standing at an intersection somewhere nearby and can't remember how to get to Richard's house. Richard says: Read me what it says on the street sign where you are, then he says, I'll come get you. And wonders what the others would do in such a situation: Hermes, Khalil, Abdusalam, who can't read a street sign or the name of a subway station.

Osarobo stands at the intersection, and even at a distance Richard can see that he doesn't have the slightest idea what direction Richard is coming from to pick him up. The way he's standing there, he looks like a blind man, Richard thinks. I'm not smart, Osarobo says after their hellos, knocking on his head with his knuckles. The gesture reminds Richard of Osarobo plucking at the black skin on the back of his hand in the café. It has nothing to do with being smart, Richard says. Life is crazy. Meanwhile, Richard has an idea of what Osarobo has in his head instead of these few suburban street names.

The scale, C major. How to execute the crossing over and passing under with the fingers, and then attempting a simple bass line. Explaining what sheet music is and that every key corresponds to a note on the page, and every so often going out again to do nothing in particular, taking advantage of the presence of another person who's alive and makes sounds (in this case notes) that turn the simple passing of time inside the house into something that resembles normal everyday life. Today there's pumpkin soup with bread for lunch, again Osarobo eats very little and drinks only tap water, and after lunch Richard carries a second chair into the living room and places it beside the desk, have a seat, he says, sitting down as well, and now he shows the young man a video so he can see how this one excellent pianist, for example, plays the piano: Osarobo shakes his head, marveling. Is he marveling at Chopin? Or at the beautiful young woman who, even before she finishes playing the frenzied piece of music, smiles herself at what she's doing. Richard asks Osarobo if he'd like to hear another pianist—yes, please—one who doesn't even take off his watch to play and nonetheless understands so much about Schubert, isn't that wonderful?—yes—and then to conclude, there's one more they really have to watch—no problem—a man who, sitting on the low piano stool, stares at his own fingers the entire time he's playing. For a long time the old man and this young man sit there side by side at the desk, watching and listening as these three musicians use the black and white keys to tell stories that have nothing at all to do with keys' colors.

It's been a long time since Richard last listened to his music together with another person, a long time since anyone has shown any interest in these recordings he so loves. Another two or three hours pass, and Osarobo says, maybe I'll go now, and—okay—

Richard hands him his thin jacket from the hanger on the rack beside the front door.

Can you find your way back to the home by yourself?

No problem.

Richard gazes after him to make sure he's going in the right direction, then he goes back inside. What would it be like for this young man from Niger to hear Bach's timpani and trumpets for the first time in his life? He sits back down at his computer and orders two tickets for the *Christmas Oratorio* in the Cathedral.

33

When Richard shows up at the home the next day, the security guards tell him that the chickenpox epidemic is finally over: The men have one day to pack, and then tomorrow they'll be moving to Spandau.

A couple of Africans are just coming down the hall, they say "how are you" in passing to Richard and then enter the little storage room where he sat some time ago with Rashid among the stacks of chairs to retrieve the folded moving boxes to start packing.

Go, went, gone.

Today Richard takes a walk all the way around the lake, it takes two and a half hours. After his brief visit in the red-brick building he didn't go back home, but instead turned to the right when he got to his street. Maybe a circular walk could hold something together. The lake? The drowned man? After all, he's also walking around this man who lies at the bottom of the lake or has dissolved in it. And also around the schools of fish that inhabit the lake, and the depths whose existence he knows about but will never see because they are concealed by all the water that fills them, he circles the

162

coots and swans whose nests are gradually becoming visible amid the pallid reeds. And with his walking he also draws a circle around the houses built directly beside the water and the properties on whose banks the docks stick out into the water like tongues. He walks between the fields and forest on his right, the houses to his left. He walks and walks, and perhaps one of the neighbor women sees him walking when she lifts her eyes for a moment to glance through the kitchen window, or else one of the men, raking leaves or standing on a ladder to affix tar paper to the roof of his shed. But Richard, by walking past, is drawing a circle even around some who don't see him: the dogs asleep in the houses, the children sitting in front of TV sets inside, or even some lost drinker sorting out the empty bottles in his basement.

Spandau.

But maybe they'll have it better there, Sylvia says on the telephone that evening. Maybe the move is a sign that they're going to be accepted. After all, according to what you've said the place in Spandau is a proper asylum-seekers' facility.

I don't know, Richard says.

I'm sure the Senate wants everything settled by the holidays.

That's certainly possible, Richard says.

Let me put Detlef on.

Okay.

Why don't we get together again for a few rounds of Skat? What do you think? asks Detlef.

Good idea.

How about Friday?

Friday's good, Richard says.

By the way, it's much quicker to get to Spandau now that they've finished that new stretch of highway.

I know.

You'll see, it's not that far once you know the way.

You know, one of them was at my house just yesterday, and he hadn't heard about the move yet.

Maybe he's happy about it.

I suppose it's possible, Richard says.

34

Rashid has a single room, that's why he's sitting in the room shared by Ithemba, Zair, and another man who lies on the bed at the back of the room, asleep. Three beds, three chairs, one table, one cupboard, one sink, one TV, one fridge.

It's normal here, Rashid says, we're happy.

Normal? What does that mean? asks Richard.

There are children here, Rashid says. We're happy. It's been so long since we've had children around us, families.

Zair asks Richard: How many children do you have? How many grandchildren?

None.

Really, you don't have children?

Richard shrugs his shoulders.

I'm very sorry for you, says Zair, in a tone of voice that suggests someone has died. Obviously he's operating on the assumption that only a terrible misfortune could lead to a man Richard's age not having offspring.

That's what we decided, my wife and I.

Really? asks Zair. Then he falls silent, but Richard can tell by looking that he doesn't understand how someone could voluntarily decide to die all alone.

Tall Ithemba, who went out for a moment and has now returned, puts a large plate of steaming food in front of Richard: meat and spinach with a sort of dumpling in the middle. He takes a container of fruit juice out of the cupboard.

Richard still clearly remembers his calculation of five euros per day. He is moved, but hates how he gets when he feels that way. Africans in Germany are delighted by the ticket machines in the subway, and Germans on safari are delighted by the Africans' hospitality.

Isn't that much too much for me alone? he asks—without really expecting that this hospitality that's turned him into a sentimental idiot will suddenly cease.

Not too much, eat! More is more better, real African food: *fufu*.

This morning Richard left his house feeling as if he were on his way to visit someone in prison, and here he is enjoying a nice lunch in the asylum-seekers' residence. The food tastes good, down in the courtyard you can hear the children running around and playing—Romanian, Syrian, Serbian, Afghan, and also a few African children. When it's time for Richard to leave, Rashid accompanies him to the exit like a man who's received a visitor in his home.

It's normal here, he says.

In the course of the next two weeks, Rashid finds jobs for his people as volunteers. Without pay, they rake leaves in Berlin's parks, they mop the floors in preschools and schools, they wash dishes in a community center. We're glad when we have something to do, Rashid says.

And still Richard can't help thinking every time he pays a visit in this two-story building: a desperate man can't throw himself to his death from a second-story window. The wing for the terminally-ill cancer patients at the Charité, where his mother died, had the best views from the hospital's top floor, but all the windows were sealed shut.

In the Foreigners Office, the first applications are being processed, the first interviews held.

Dear Mr. XXX: you have been registered as Oranienplatz Agreement Participant No. X.

Richard thinks about the three-quarters of a page.

To determine your residency status, you are requested to appear, bringing this document, on the Xth at X o'clock at the address below, waiting room C06.

What is *Totensonntag*? Khalil asks Richard on *Totensonntag*, the last Sunday before Advent on which the dead are honored.

Why do you ask? Richard responds. That morning he'd paid a visit to the cemetery in Berlin-Pankow where his parents are buried.

The club we always go to was closed last night.

What kind of club?

We go dancing there, they let us in without paying. Yesterday there was a sign on the door that said *Totensonntag*.

On *Totensonntag*, says Richard, you're not allowed to dance, and movie theaters are closed too.

Why?

It's to remember the dead.

Oh.

Already the face of the young man who wanted to go dancing last night has been transformed into the face of a young man who's fled across the sea and doesn't know if his parents are still alive. Khalil was separated from them the day they were driven onto the boats, Rashid told Richard not long ago, adding that now he doesn't know if his parents are still there, if they were shot, or if they too were forced to get on a boat, and if that was the case, he doesn't know what country they landed in, assuming they landed at all.

Richard keeps hearing reports of capsized boats in the Mediterranean. The corpses of African refugees wash ashore almost daily on Italian beaches. Where are they buried? Who knows their names? Who informs their families that they didn't make it to Europe and are never coming home? Someone on the internet calling himself *DontCare* writes: *The only ones I really feel sorry for are the coast guard workers! Why should they have to keep going out there to drag bodies out of the water?* Another one, who goes by the name *GodOfSlaughter*, writes: *The planet's already incredibly overpopulated anyhow. Nature used to take care of that directly (influenza, plagues, etc.).* And in the part of Germany where, until twenty-five years ago, the words "proletarian internationalism" served as a slogan for countless banners, the campaign posters for an increasingly popular party now proclaim: *Let's save our cash for Granny—not the Roma and Sinti.* Whenever Richard sees opinions of this sort being openly expressed, he always remembers the poem by Bertolt Brecht in which a group of postwar Berliners tear the flesh from the bones of a horse that's collapsed in the street. *And me still alive! Hadn't yet done with dying.* Even as the horse is being torn to pieces, it's overwhelmed with concern for its murderers: *This coldness, why? Now what / In all the world can have come over them! / Who's bugging this lot / to make them act / As if they're cold right through? / Help them. Be quick too.* But what war have people now just been through?

I saw them drown, Osarobo said not long ago. He sat at the piano, his hands still on his knees, shaking his head as if he refused to believe it, as if he were incapable of believing it. Was he talking about the friends of his who'd died during his own crossing? No, he'd only seen a news report on a recent shipwreck. He saw people drowning, and in these drowning figures he recognized himself, his friends, and those who'd sat beside him.

Approximately a hundred years ago, the young revolutionary Eugen Leviné, speaking for the last time before the court of law that condemned him to death by firing squad, described himself and his Communist comrades as "dead men on holiday." These days, the difference between the refugees who drown somewhere between Africa and Europe and those who don't is just a matter of happenstance. In this sense, every one of the African refugees here, Richard thinks, is simultaneously alive and dead.

That morning, before driving to Spandau, Richard covered his parents' grave with fir branches, as he does every year the Sunday before Advent. Even during his childhood, cemetery visits were part of everyday life for his mother and him, though his father never joined them. As a child, he helped his mother rake the sandy path in front of his grandparents' grave (*make it pretty*), and later, when he was stronger, he would fill the watering can for her at the cemetery fountain or carry bags of potting soil from the cemetery flower shop to Plot A XIV/0058. In the spring, his mother would plant pansies, in summer, begonias, in autumn she would deadhead the plants, and on *Totensonntag* she'd cover the grave with winter foliage. At some point her husband too—Richard's father—lay there in the earth, and a few years after that, so did she. Now Richard prunes the box hedge surrounding the mound all by himself, using the same shears his mother always employed for this purpose, he rakes the same sand in front of the gravesite using the same little iron rake he'd held as a child, and just before winter he pulls the withered flowers, roots and all, from the earth, and on *Totensonntag* he covers his parents' grave with fir branches. He knows that his mother liked to call this day Eternity Sunday instead of Sunday of the Dead, and sometimes she just called it Judgment Day. Because of this, he'd always been afraid of this day as a child, believing that some November sooner or later it would be his turn to be judged—judged for all eternity. He would sit with his mother in church, listening to the tolling of the bells as the minister read out the names of congregation members who had died, his name too might be among them at any moment; he sat there in silence with all the others until the sound of the tolling bells faded away: *Let us listen as the sound of the bells dies away, a reminder for all of us that our flesh too will one day turn to dust.*

Fir branches the last Sunday before Advent, and lighting a candle on the grave to be extinguished sooner or later by the wind, and then the stillness of winter, a few weeks from now only the green of the box hedge will be left peeking out from beneath the snow— and all of this just as it was almost sixty years ago. Owning a cemetery plot where three generations can lie at rest is, if you will, a sort of luxury, but this thought has occurred to him only in the last few weeks.... For much of his life, he's hoped in a tiny back corner of his soul that people from Africa mourn their dead less. Death there has been a mass phenomenon for so long now. Now, this back corner of his soul is occupied instead by shame: shame that for most of his lifetime he's taken the easy way out.

35

In preparation for the holiday season, shops across the city have retrieved their Christmas trees from storage and set them up in the same spots as last year, pre-adorned with ornaments and ribbons. Everywhere you look are wreaths, strings of lights, and Christmas pyramids revolving. When Richard goes down to the basement to get a beer, he reads the words "Christmas season" in his wife's handwriting on two or three of the boxes on the bottom shelf.

Richard lends Rufu, the moon of Wismar, volume one of Dante. Ithemba's fish soup tastes very good too. I'm a little bit fine.

And so the first Advent Sunday arrives.

Rashid accompanies Richard to the exit after every visit, as befits a gracious host, and once they run into a woman with short hair whom Rashid greets with a handshake, introducing her to Richard as a Senate delegate, and Richard to her as a supporter. Speaking German, the delegate tells Richard in a half-whisper that the Foreigners Office has received instructions from very high up to be as strict as possible when processing the men's applications. She says she's worried. Richard wonders if she'll tell Rashid this as well. But maybe it's just a rumor.

Richard tells Apollo: Listen. Apart from being in Libya, as a Tuareg back in your own country, Niger, you belonged to a persecuted minority—say that when you have your interview. When I have my interview, I will tell my story. Yes, Richard says, but also mention the rebellion. I will tell my story just as it was. If I have to go, I can go, Apollo says. I don't have a family to support. I'm free. In Italy I lived on the street for six months once.

Richard thinks that he's heard the word *freedom* used in Germany to mean quite different things.

The second Advent Sunday arrives.

It's drizzling.

I would never have expected goat meat to taste so good, Richard says to the cook, Ithemba. Once more he is sitting before a full plate.

Some of the refugees now greet Richard in German: *Guten Tag, wie geht es?* And Richard says: *Gut*.

Tristan (Awad) asks Richard to call his lawyer and ask how things stand with his case. Richard calls the lawyer, who says: He came here via Italy.

Yes, Richard says.

Well, that's a problem, the lawyer says.

I know, Richard says.

And he was born in Ghana.

Yes, Richard says.

Ghana is considered a safe country, that doesn't help.

But he grew up in Libya, Richard says.

Unfortunately, that won't be taken into consideration, the lawyer says. Procedural errors by the agency processing his application will get him a bit of an extension, but after that there probably isn't much I can do.

Khalil doesn't know where his parents are, he can't write very well, so he's sketched out the stations of his flight in a notebook. Richard sees a boat that looks like a very thin sickle moon, with a lot of water underneath.

Zani is the older refugee with the damaged eye, he was sitting on the back of the German park bench the first time Richard came to Oranienplatz. He shows Richard copies of newspaper articles: *Massacre*, Richard reads, flipping through them: *massacre, massacre*. That was in my hometown, Zani says, that's why I fled to Libya, it wasn't easy to get these articles, but I need to have proof for the interview.

Throughout Advent, Richard knows that the agreement Dublin II regulates only the responsibility of each signatory country, but he says nothing.

36

Despite the cold, the men often sit on benches in the courtyard and watch the children, and sometimes they play soccer with them.

The day they hear on the news that holding refugees in custody pending deportation has been abolished, they are beside themselves. Ithemba, the cook, is waving his arms around. Zair and Tristan are arguing, but Rashid (the thunderbolt-hurler) is eerily silent as he sits at the table, a mute colossus. When Richard asks what's wrong, Rashid replies: So they won't lock people up before deporting them, but they've confirmed that the deportations themselves will continue. They really don't want us here, he says. They really don't want us. He shakes his head.

Later he gets up to accompany Richard to the exit.

When the temperature sinks below freezing for the first time, Tristan says: I'm really happy that I can have a place to sleep inside.

Last winter a few of our tents collapsed under the snow.

Another day, everyone's sitting around a laptop watching a film in which a farmer folds his lambs' soft ears down over their eyes before they're slaughtered, to calm them. The lambs don't resist when they're seized by the feet and laid on their sides, they tranquilly await their end. When the little Afghan girl from across the hall comes by, Ithemba gives her a piece of candy.

Two or three times Richard picks up Osarobo to practice the piano, and once he brings Tristan with him to rake the leaves—two hours of work, twenty euros.

Richard's friend Anne, the photographer, calls to say that her mother's home health-care aide is going home to Poland over Christmas to spend time with her family, and no one's responded to the notice she put up at the nursing school. I'm not strong enough to lift my mother without help, Anne says. Richard gives her the phone number of Ali, his advanced student who wants to be a nurse one day—assuming some European country will let him.

Now that the letters from the Foreigners Office have started to arrive, now that each of the men is waiting for his interview or has already finished it, time feels different. At one point, Richard tries to begin one of his conversations, asking: How do you bury the dead in the desert? But as if this question were a cue in a theatrical production whose director remains hidden, a siren inside blares at precisely this moment, and it doesn't stop blaring. Might this siren—itself torture—be warning of torture? Or an air raid? Are the buildings between Oberbaumbrücke and Alexanderplatz on fire? Richard's mother had sat with him in a Berlin bomb cellar when he was just an infant. Can Richard remember the fear he felt as an infant, or his mother's fear? It's nothing, Rashid, the thunderbolt-hurler says, they do that sometimes. It's just a drill, says Zair, who's still lying in bed, having been woken by the alarm. Richard puts his hands over his ears, but it doesn't help. The siren is murderously loud. Could there be a fire after all?

Richard goes out into the hall, where a plump woman is just shuffling in the direction of the kitchen. Is something burning? But since Richard is holding his ears shut, he can't understand the plump woman's reply, she shrugs her shoulders, keeps walking, and disappears into the kitchen, where ten stoves stand side by side. Nothing is burning in the kitchen; the plump woman turns on the water and busies herself with her pots. The siren blares and blares. Richard now runs in a gentle gallop in the direction of the entrance, and lo: at that very moment, the alarm suddenly stops. Was there really a fire somewhere? No, the man at the entrance says, that was just a drill, but someone's always leaving a stove on in the kitchen, that has to stop, they've got to learn. Now another staff member comes running across the courtyard, shouting to his colleague: He cut through the wire! A moment later, the refugee Yaya comes bolting out of the building, all worked up, followed by his friend Moussa, the one with the blue facial tattoos. Yaya gesticulates, shouts. Quickly a group forms around him.

The staff member shouts at the group: We're kicking him out! He'll never set foot in this building again. He intentionally destroyed the alarm system—who's going to pay for it?

How do you bury the dead in the desert?

Richard, though he can't say so, is glad Yaya shut off the murderously loud alarm by simply cutting the wire. *Murderous* is the right word. Can an infant remember a war? Tristan said once: We were sitting in the barracks when the European bombs fell over Tripoli and we were afraid one of them would hit us.

In the courtyard, a shouting match now ensues between the staff member and Yaya, who cut the alarm system's wire.

When Richard gets back to the room where he'd just tried to start a conversation, tall Ithemba is putting on water for tea, and Zair is still lying in bed. The day is still young on a morning like this, and if you don't sleep through half the morning, it can be very long indeed.

37

By the week preceding the third Sunday of Advent, Richard has become quite familiar with the route from the suburbs to the Spandau residence.

Fried plantains are also a delicacy. Is more better? African shops all carry them, Ithemba explains, and there's one quite close by.

Visit after visit, Rashid accompanies Richard to the exit.

Meanwhile, Anne has met with Ali, Richard's advanced German student, and introduced him to her mother. At first, she recounts on the telephone, my mother was scared of him because he's black, but it'll be okay. Richard says: He speaks German amazingly well, don't you think? Yes, she says, and you mustn't forget that she belongs to a completely different generation. Richard only nods, but of course Anne can't see that over the phone. Otherwise I really don't know what I would have done with my mother over Christmas, she says, so thank you.

When Richard returns to the residence at the end of the week with the ticket for the *Christmas Oratorio* on Sunday in a red envelope, Osarobo isn't there.

Where is he?

In Italy, to renew his papers.

Richard suddenly remembers what Rashid said a few days ago, talking about the deportations: They really don't want us here. They really don't want us. What if the piano player is gone forever? What if something happens to him? When he dials Osarobo's number, no one answers. Richard has already bought him a Christmas present: a keyboard that can be rolled up. It can even fit in a small backpack, Richard thought, and if Osarobo ever needed to, maybe he could earn a little money playing it on the street. What an unworthy thought, he thinks now, standing there with the red envelope in his hand. *Exult and rejoice!* Would he have considered a roll-up piano a possible plan for the future of his own son if he had one?

A future for 65.90 euros? When did he turn from a man filled with great hopes for mankind into an almsgiver? Surely not when the Wall came down—but maybe not so long afterward. At some point along the way he must have buckled, and now he's just trying to "do his part" on a small scale, with the occasional gesture, wherever the opportunity presents itself. Has he now truly relinquished all hope?

38

I *miss my places.*

I only have myself to rely on.

Only God can judge me.

Richard knows that the men who have smart phones use a free app to send each other texts, photos, and voice messages. They upload profile pictures and write so-called status updates about how they're feeling. Some of them update their status daily, while others let it stand for weeks or months at a time.

I miss my best friend Bassa.

Dont worry what other people think about you.

Im at school.

A little while ago, Richard started copying down these messages. Sometimes, when one of the men falls in love with a young Berliner and she doesn't want to marry him, he'll write:

I just want to be with you.

But sometimes there are messages like this:

Remain true to yourself.

Or:

The mistake is in the selection.

May I ask you something? he says to Apollo the week before the fourth Sunday of Advent.

Of course.

How can you afford such an expensive phone and internet service?

I don't have a family. I don't have anyone I have to send money to.

Richard sees the plate covered with aluminum foil still on top of the refrigerator. Two days ago it was there, and when Richard asked about it, Apollo lifted the foil to show Richard what he had cooked. On the plate was something like couscous, a shallow portion of which only one quarter had been eaten. Richard couldn't help thinking of the heaping portions Ithemba always placed before him when he came to visit.

It's enough for a couple of days, Apollo said.

This one plate?

Yes. If you eat more, you become like an infant.

Like an infant?

Too spoiled.

I see.

You can never know what is coming. It's possible that you'll have to go hungry again or that you'll have nothing to drink, and you have to be able to endure that.

On TV Richard once saw a report about a Jewish girl in the Nazi era who knew she was going to be deported soon to the East and for that reason she went to school wearing low-cut shoes instead of boots: *I want to harden myself for Poland,* she wrote in a letter to her parents. Richard remembered this two days ago when Apollo showed him his plate with that shallow portion of which only one quarter had been eaten, and he thinks of this again when he sees that the plate is still there—the plate like the face of a clock from which Apollo eats one quarter of an hour each day.

I don't have a family. I don't have anyone I have to send money to.

Nor has Richard ever seen Apollo drink anything but water. Water from the tap, without bubbles. None of the men here ever drinks alcohol. No one smokes. None of them has his own apartment or even his own bed; all their clothing comes from donations. There's no car, no stereo, no gym membership, no outings, no travel, no wife, no children, or even the prospect of having a wife or children. Indeed the only thing that each one of the refugees owns is a phone, some have a phone with a broken display, some a recent model, some with internet access, some without. *Broke the memory*, Tristan said, when he told Richard how soldiers rendered the captives' cell phones inoperable back in Libya.

I see, Richard says.

It's possible, Tristan tells him, that his father's friend is still alive and fled to Burkina Faso. Someone Tristan knows sent him a message. It really was the same name, and now he's hoping his friend can get him the man's telephone number. Burkina Faso. If my father's friend is really still alive . . . Tristan stops in the middle of the sentence.

Rashid says: I haven't seen my mother in thirteen years, just sometimes when I contact her on Facebook. Does she have a computer? No, but one of her neighbors does. Rashid always sits in such a way that his mother can't see the scar over his eye. How are you, son? Good, he says. Sometimes I don't go to the phone when she calls, Rashid says—nothing has changed here for two years now, what am I supposed to say to her?

For Khalil, Rashid says, I've been trying for two years to find his parents on Facebook. Recently, Rashid says, he sat in my room again crying. Richard remembers Khalil's drawing: A boat flat as a sickle moon, with a huge amount of water underneath. On every one of his visits, Richard notes that the men feel more at home in these wireless networks than in any of the countries in which they await their future. This system of numbers and passwords extending clear across continents is all the compensation they have for everything they've lost forever. What belongs to them is invisible and made of air.

Rashid recognized me by my phone, the thin man with the broom says. His cell phone is pink, made of cheap plastic, held together with tape, a discarded girl's phone. I've had it since Lampedusa, almost three years, he says, holding it aloft. But now there's a loose connection sometimes. In his contacts he has Italian, Finnish, Swedish, French, and Belgian numbers—of African friends who, like him, are drifting through Europe, friends who also come from Ghana originally, or who worked in Libya on the same construction site, or were with him on the same boat for the crossing, friends he met in Lampedusa, in the camp, in some train station or Caritas housing. All of them friends who, because they have no work, also have no apartment and no address, who aren't registered anywhere. Their first and last names are notated in Latin letters on their temporary IDs without much accuracy.

How could I ever find them again without their phone numbers?

The thin man doesn't have his broom with him today; he leans against the door to the terrace, the black rectangle behind him concealing what in daylight is quite simply referred to as the garden.

When my best friend and I arrived in Europe, he says, we decided to go our separate ways, in the hope that one of us might get lucky and then that person could help the other one. Richard thinks of Grimm's fairy tales, which he so loved reading as a child, he thinks of the brothers sent out into the world by their father to make their fortune, to find a beautiful princess, solve riddles, and earn their inheritance. There are brothers who follow arrows shot in four different directions, or princes who part ways at a crossroads. Others are set on horseback by their father—a black steed for the oldest, a bay for the middle son, a white horse for the youngest—so they can gallop off to prove their mettle, then one day they return home with chopped-off dragon heads and gold in their luggage, they've become men, and their brides sit before them in their saddles.... Or else one is left behind, transfixed by a spell, waiting for one of his brothers to release him from an enchantment, he is trapped in some distant forest, transformed into an animal or turned to stone, or tongueless, or chopped into pieces in the cooking pot of a witch.

In these tales, the world is always something that begins at a cross-roads, a forking of paths: from there, the story takes you to the north, south, east, or west. In these tales, salvation always comes. When the blade of the sword turns rusty, you'll know I need your help. A prince needs no passport. Not so long ago, Richard thinks, this story of going abroad to find one's fortune was a German one.

39

Just as initially, when the men were still living in the suburbs, he'd considered their cell phones a luxury (though admittedly a luxury of the most modest sort), he also couldn't understand why each of the refugees required his own transit pass. Why did a person with no job and no money for museums need to travel around the city? Couldn't they just go for walks around the lake? And if one of them did want to travel to the city center, why didn't he just dodge the fare and ride without paying? As long as they were being denied legal status here, shouldn't they at least enjoy some of the benefits of that condition? Maybe there should be an "illegal transit pass" for illegal aliens, he thought at one point, suppressing a grin, as he's periodically caught himself doing since his retirement. Meanwhile he's learned that for these few months of deliberation during which the Berlin Senate is providing the refugees with language instruction and there are appointments with various agencies at which they are required to appear, the State is legally obligated to furnish them with transit passes. Just for this period of time, of course, not longer.

We're not giving away anything for free, the law says, unrelenting and hard as iron.

And what if one of them—the thin man with the broom, for example—takes the fifty-seven euros and instead of buying a transit pass, sends it to his mother in Ghana?

When a refugee is caught dodging the fare on a bus, S-Bahn, or subway, just as he dodged German visa requirements when entering the country, he must pay a fine of forty euros for the first infraction like any other first-time fare-dodger. The second time he's caught, the law proclaims, a penal order will be issued, giving that refugee the choice of prison or paying a fine calculated according to his income and the number of days he'd be sentenced to for the offense in question. For even the poorest of the poor in Germany, a fine is calculated in multiples of ten euros. A sixty days' fine at ten euros apiece following a third apprehension would be a slap on the wrist for a German who'd rather pay than do time. Anything less than ninety days would not result in a criminal record. But for a foreigner, a fifty-day infraction constitutes grounds for expulsion; in other words, a refugee who commits such an offense forfeits all right to asylum. And so the relatively modest fine he's being charged in no way lessens the severity of his punishment, since his application for asylum can only be rejected—and rejected for all time.

The iron law knows all of this.

Now that Richard has spent weeks observing how the men spend their days, he knows that in a life like this, a transit pass is no luxury.

We call our friends, the men have said, we arrange to meet.

Richard remembers that when the group was evicted from Oranienplatz, they were divided among three different shelters. The suburban nursing home was only one of the three. Other men were sent to Friedrichshain and Wedding: friends who'd lived together for a year and a half in tents on Oranienplatz with rats nesting under them, with or without snow, with or without one warm meal a day, and—after a German attack on the sanitation trailer—only four instead of eight toilets for 476 people. There were waiting lists to use the showers in a building run by the Social Services of the Lutheran Church.

And what do you do when you meet?

We cook together. We talk. Or we go to Alexanderplatz, the market's there now.

The Christmas market?

Yes.

Do you ride the roller coaster or the carousel?

No, the men say, it's too expensive. But the market is beautiful.

The profile photo of one of the men shows him and a couple of his friends standing around a fire barrel beside a sausage stand, warming their hands.

During the summer, we went to the soccer field sometimes when people were playing. But mostly we go to Oranienplatz, that tent is still there.

The men mean the information tent that has remained on the square as part of the agreement with the Berlin Senate, it's been set on fire three times by xenophobic Berliners and has been put up again three times.

What do you do there?

We stand around and talk.

I will always revere the memory of Oranienplatz, Tristan said back at the very beginning of Richard's conversations.

When Richard opens the newspaper two days before Christmas, he remembers that one of the provisions of the so-called agreement was that the cases of those refugees who'd already submitted applications for asylum elsewhere in Germany in ignorance of European law could still have their cases decided in Berlin. To make it possible for the group to remain together there.

Whenever possible, the agreement had said.

And only, of course, where permissible by law.

The iron law.

But then it turns out that unfortunately the law doesn't permit this after all. Two days before Christmas, the law rises up with a loud creaking of joints. Richard reads in the paper that when the new year begins, the first of the men who belong in Magdeburg, or in a dormitory made of recycled shipping containers on the outskirts of Hamburg, or some Bavarian mountain village, will be sent back to these places.

Even Richard—who's been familiar with this law for a few weeks—knows what this means. It means that this, that, and the other man will be sent back to Magdeburg, Hamburg, and the Bavarian village, where they'll be informed soon after that because they arrived in Germany through Italy, Italy is the only European country where they're allowed to live and work. It'll be two or three months at the most, Richard estimates, before the fingerprints of thrush, blackbird, finch, and starling are located and analyzed. For another two or three months, these people will be allowed to go on living in Magdeburg or the Bavarian village or the shipping containers on the outskirts of Hamburg as individual applicants for asylum, receiving a salary of three hundred euros per month, but then they'll be sent forever and irrevocably back to Italy.

Round up the boys and girls and send them back to where they came from, the voice of the people declares in the internet forums.

Does it really make such a difference, during these two or three months, while a refugee's case (which really isn't a case at all but a life) is being investigated, if that refugee is far from all his friends in a random facility or remains here in Berlin with the others?

Apparently it makes a difference.

But these cretins, these flipped-out n***s say they won't even take the money as a reward for moving to another town, they'd rather say no thank you to two or three hundred euro payouts. They'll just write it off, they've got plenty anyhow, they're all drug dealers or African mafia.

Apparently it really does make a difference whether the group remains united here in Berlin, or whether—after the initial division into three large groups—it continues to be divided into smaller and smaller units.

Why else would the iron law have been awoken from its slumber by the authorities?

Apparently it makes a difference.

A friend, a good friend, is the best thing in the world. Indeed, the men say that they would rather stay in Berlin without any money, even illegally if need be, as a group.

Criminals, delinquents, the nation writes in the internet forums.

The all-male sextet that sang "A Friend, A Good Friend" in 1930 during the Great Depression proved somewhat later to be of half-Jewish descent. Three of the singers were able to escape with their lives by fleeing to America, while the other three were accepted into the *Reichskulturkammer*. From then on, there was no more talk of friendship.

Malcontents who've banded together to make trouble, say the politicians in Berlin. The politicians also say: *There'll be no exceptions.* They say: *Whatever happens, no new precedents—otherwise three days later we'll have another two hundred of them sitting on Oranienplatz.*

Every four years there's an election for mayor in Berlin.

But we don't want a decision for us alone, Rashid says, we want a decision that will count for all the refugees in Europe. That's why our camp at Oranienplatz was called a protest camp. The law can't stay the way it is.

But now the law opens its mouth up terrifyingly wide and laughs without making a sound.

After it's laughed its sinister laugh long enough—in other words after due consideration of all the contingencies—the iron law, the German law, speaks:

A case may be transferred to another state within the Federal Republic, Berlin for example, only if the purpose of the transfer is to unite family members.

Unfortunately not a single one of these men has family here, O you dear, lovely law. Just a few friends.

Friends don't constitute a family, the law replies and begins to grind its teeth.

Dear Law, what are your intentions? What will happen now? What do you think?

Today for dinner the law will devour hand, knee, nose, mouth, feet, eyes, brain, ribs, heart, or teeth. Some part or other.

40

Detlef and Sylvia plan to spend Christmas with Detlef's son at the home of Marion, his son's mother, and her husband in Potsdam. You want to all sit around the Christmas tree together? Richard asks. The first wife and the second wife, the son from Detlef's first marriage, and both husbands? Oh, you know, Sylvia says, that was all a long time ago, and if Markus is coming all the way from China for Christmas ...

Peter, the archaeologist, has promised his twenty-year-old girlfriend that he'll visit her parents in Bamberg for the first time. Her parents are five years younger than me, he says. Well, in that case, says Richard. But Bamberg is supposed to be really pretty. No doubt, Peter says.

The daughter-in-law of Monika (the professor of German literature) and her mustache-wearing husband refused to invite them for Christmas, so they've booked a flight to Florence. Just imagine, she wouldn't even accept my homemade cookies, but later I secretly gave the tin to my granddaughter. In earlier days, the two of them often went on vacation together with Richard and Christel, but now that Richard lives alone, they've stopped asking him, maybe because traveling with two men is too much for Monika.

Richard's advanced student, Ali, has been staying with the photographer Anne for several days since her mother's home health-care aide left to visit her family in Poland before the fourth Sunday in Advent.

And? How's it going? asks Richard.

Just imagine, Anne says, this is the first time in his life he's had his own room.

I can't imagine, Richard says. How is he? Helpful?

The two of us can lift my mother together very well. He's learning a lot from me.

I understand, Richard says.

He's nice, she says, really. But my mother is still afraid of him.

That goddamn Nazi education, Richard says. Things like that show up again in old age.

Could be. But he's really making an effort. Just imagine, he kissed her on the forehead because he saw me doing it.

And did she scream?

Well . . . I explained to him that here in Germany only her daughter would be allowed to do that.

Richard still remembers how it felt when he took his first work trip to America. When people asked how he was doing, he started to explain that he was doing very well and tried to ask the same of them, but before he could finish, the salesman or doorman or waiter would have already moved on. At the cash register in the supermarket, his groceries would be placed in innumerable plastic bags and the cashier would give him a strange look when he tried to help pack. The tap water tasted awful. The windows could only be pushed up a few inches, not really opened. At the beginning of April, lawns were unrolled in front of the biggest mansions, and from one hour to the next everything would be green. After two or three days, Richard was beside himself with the foreignness. Would *he* have any idea how to look after an African grandmother? *Nana*?

Richard got through Christmas perfectly well last year in the company of Andreas, the Hölderlin reader. Without a Christmas tree or Christmas goose, the two of them had sat together drinking whiskey and enjoying *Some Like It Hot*, a movie that should be watched as often as possible—the two of them always agreed on this. This year, Andreas left for a spa in early December and wasn't expected back until the end of January. Richard knew about this all along, but only now, looking at the empty shelves in the supermarket's freezer aisle on December 23, does he suddenly realize he'll be the only one in his circle of friends spending Christmas Eve alone.

He's only just gotten off the phone with Rashid—who said *no prob-lem,* and Richard replied *fine*—and already he's standing in the front hall tying his shoelaces and glancing at his watch—here's hoping the Christmas tree stand is still open, here's hoping he can still find some organic goose that is too expensive for anyone else to buy. The Christmas tree doesn't have to be large, but there has to be one, a real fir tree in a living room, that's probably something no Nigerian has ever seen. The Christmas tree turns out to be not so small after all, and then he can't find a goose anywhere, so he contents himself with a few goose legs, precooked and packed along with their gravy, and then some instant bread dumplings and a jar of red cabbage—*a dash of vinegar and two cloves, and it tastes like home-made*—that had been his wife's Christmas line year after year. The tree had to be put up by the evening of the twenty-third: *give the branches time to unfold*—that had been Richard's Christmas line. He curses when the tree doesn't slide easily into the heavy cast-iron stand, even though he's whittled down the end of the trunk with his axe, then he crawls under the tree to rotate the trunk so the big-gest branches point to the side, allowing one to still squeeze past to get to the terrace door. The fetching up of boxes from the basement that still bear Christel's handwriting on their sides: *Christmas season.* And distributing the angels around the house, the nutcrackers, the stars. He still knows all these gestures well—gestures that he might easily have never performed again now return to him with startling ease. What other things might be lurking in the dark reaches of his memory that will never again be dragged out of storage, before closing time arrives and the lights go out for good?

Although the fourth Sunday of Advent has already come and gone, he places four red candles in the glass wreath that's been standing on the living room table for five years now, so tomorrow he'll be able to explain to his foreign guest what *Advent* means. The morning of the twenty-fourth he decorates the tree and, as a final step— with the goose legs already braising in the oven—he puts together the big Christmas pyramid from the Ore Mountain region, topped with a propeller that stands a couple of inches taller than him when it's set up on the table. He arranges the small wooden angels on the highest tier, and the middle platform soon houses Mary, Joseph, the cattle, donkeys, lambs, shepherds, the Kings of Orient, and of course the manger with the tiny Jesus inside. The "underground" level of the pyramid holds the miners' chapel: the largest, bottommost platform. If you don't carefully even out the weight, a single out-of-kilter angel can throw everything off balance, even the miners, or maybe one miner's drum is a tenth of an ounce heavier than his colleague's flute on the opposite side, and this surplus weight is enough to bring not only the miner's own comrades but even Mary and Joseph and eventually the entire heavenly host toppling over—and indeed, if one is clumsy, this falling can easily spread from one flimsy level to the next, a motion communicated via the Holy Family above to down below, or just as easily from below to above, sending lambs tumbling atop the Christ child and Mary crashing down into the mines, her virginal light-blue robes coming to rest atop the tangled heap off to one side where a drum major, a little drummer boy, and an Ore Mountain trumpeter have already landed, their instruments caught in the halos of a few small, chubby-cheeked cherubs that have plummeted down from Heaven, and all because Richard let his mind wander for just an instant, or

187

because his hands are much bigger than those of his late wife, who always used to be the one to set up the figurines, and so he keeps bumping things as he works, or maybe it's just that he's miscalculated the figures' weight.

41

The world seems emptied-out in the afternoon these last few hours before Christmas Eve. On the way from the asylum-seekers' home, Rashid, looking out the car window, asks: The fields here— do they belong to the government? No, I don't think so, Richard says. *Junker land into peasant hand.* He'd have no trouble explaining the agrarian reform that took place just after the war, but the fate that befell the GDR's agricultural cooperatives after 1989 is something he himself isn't too sure about. Is it difficult to convert a Socialist collective into a capitalist business venture? Does a planned economy bear any resemblance at all to an international corporation? He'll have to ask his friend Thomas some time, the professor of economics.... When the metal gate to Richard's property slides open automatically, Rashid says: I used to build gates like this— that was my job. When Rashid sees the lake, he asks: How long has it been here? Richard doesn't understand the question. I'm saying, when did they make it? Who *makes* a lake? he says. Well, the government. No, Richard says, this lake has been here for a few million years, since the last time there was an Ice Age. A few million years—really? Rashid shakes his head incredulously.

And now Richard, an atheist with a Protestant mother, stands with his Muslim guest before the illuminated, heathen Christmas tree on which, as was always the rule with Richard and his wife, only candles of real wax are burning. The St. Thomas Choir is singing, the goose legs are in the oven keeping warm, the dumplings will float to the top of their pot any minute now, and the red cabbage is simmering with its vinegar and cloves. And now the guest—since Richard has no other gift for him—must select a winter jacket from the closet and try it on, and they do find one that was always too big for Richard and fits the thunderbolt-hurler perfectly and pleases him. Thank you, I really appreciate that. When it's time to eat, they sit where it's most practical, in the kitchen, even if it's not so festive—no, what do you think, I like it, it's nice here, very nice! But what about the burning candles on the tree? says Rashid. Don't worry, the candles will go out by themselves, Richard replies, as if long acquainted with this particular innovation of the West. Rashid seems to be enjoying the meal. Say, does red cabbage grow in Nigeria? After dinner, Richard leads his guest from angel to angel, as if in a Christmas museum, then explains to him the meaning of the star, what an Advent wreath is, and ends by lighting the candles of the Christmas pyramid standing beside the TV. Rashid apparently has difficulty believing that the heat of the candles is enough to set this marvelous contraption in motion, he looks behind the table it's standing on for a plug and electrical cord. Richard explains to him that the warm air rising moves the blades of the big propeller, which are mounted on the diagonal, making the pyramid revolve. Rashid watches for quite some time as the miners, the livestock, the shepherds, the Holy Three Kings, the Virgin Mary, the child in the manger, Joseph, and all the angels on top go spinning past over and over.

You know, Jesus also is a prophet in the Quran.

I know, I know, Richard says, remembering the five pillars of Islam.

And one of them is black, Rashid says, pointing to one of the three Holy Kings.

Yes, that's Caspar, Richard says.

Did you build this pyramid? asks Rashid.

No, Richard says. He explains while blowing out the candles what's so special about the fretwork produced in the Ore Mountains.

Then they go out to the terrace for a moment to get some air.

Richard remembers how, several years ago, his wife once set the roast goose to cool on the table outside, right in front of the window, because the roasting pan wouldn't fit in the refrigerator. When she was ready to warm it up again, the pan with its goose had vanished. Which meant, he thought at the time, that right here in the middle of Germany several years after unification, there were people poor enough to steal a holiday dinner. The roast his neighbors had placed outside two doors down had been stolen as well. The footprints of the robbers were clearly visible in the snow, but of course neither he nor his neighbor had filed a police report.

This year there's no snow at Christmas, the temperature is several degrees above freezing. It drizzled yesterday, but tonight the sky is clear, and you can already see the first stars.

My son was almost three, and my daughter was already five years old when I left, Rashid says.

Are they still there? Richard asks.

I'm a metalworker. At the beginning, says Rashid, when we'd arrived in Agadez after flying from Kaduna and then continued on to Libya, I didn't even know how to say metalworker in Arabic, or in English, says Rashid.

Should we go back in? asks Richard.

In Tripoli we had a living room like this, and also a parlor like that there, and we had three bedrooms, a hallway, a bathroom, and a kitchen, Rashid says. They are sitting on the sofa inside, and the pyramid has come to a halt. Since Rashid doesn't want to drink beer, Richard has made a pot of peppermint tea and lit the four red candles, even though Advent is over.

For breakfast there was always yam, plantain, or eggs. At eight o'clock we left the house, I brought the children to school. Ahmed was already almost three, and Amina was five years old. From our house to school it was about as far as from Oranienplatz to Wedding. My wife worked in a different district.

My shop was close to the school. In two buildings, unfinished on the outside, but very nice inside. And a courtyard. It was almost as big as the shop I had in Kaduna. The rent was five hundred dinar, which is approximately three hundred euros.

At twelve thirty or one when school was over, Ahmed and Amina would come to my shop. They'd take off their school uniforms and put on their regular clothes to play until it was time to go home. I always made sure they didn't come into the workshop so they wouldn't get metal dust in their eyes.

Sometimes my wife picked us up in the afternoon, sometimes we didn't meet until we got home. I always cooked for us in the evenings. My son was allowed to eat from my plate. After dinner the children went to bed, and then around ten thirty we did too. Sometimes my son would come to us in the middle of the night. He always had a lot of dreams. Ahmed. Then I would let him sleep beside me, and my wife would go spend the rest of the night in the children's room with our daughter. Amina.

His peppermint tea is probably already cold. Richard sits perfectly still and completely forgets about reaching for his teacup. He knows that this story Rashid is telling him is something like a gift.

There had already been unrest once, and we stayed inside our house for five days. On that day, at first everything was normal. I had finished a large metal gate for a driveway. It takes me two days to make a gate like that. In the early afternoon it was picked up and I was paid the third installment, five hundred dinar. The children were playing in the courtyard.

Then my wife called me from work, she said something was happening and she was afraid to go home alone. I said: I'll pick you up.

I didn't realize that many blocks in my shop's district had already been cordoned off. The children and I couldn't get through. The soldiers brought me, my children, and also three of my black employees to a camp. Ahmed was almost three, and Amina was five.

Some of these scraps of sentences Richard is hearing now sound familiar, Richard's heard them uttered by Tristan: *Dead people everywhere in the streets. Blood everywhere. Barracks. Not just men: women, children, small infants, old people. They broke the memory.* The soldiers, Rashid says, took the money I'd received for the gate and all the change I had in my pocket. I was still wearing my work clothes. I actually had an account at a Libyan bank. Maybe it still exists. The number is 2074.

Richard looks at the quietly burning red candles and nods his head, although nodding at this point makes no sense at all.

For five days we were in the barracks, there were air raids by the Europeans, and we were afraid the bombers would think that our camp was an arsenal. The children especially were terrified, and I didn't know how to explain to them why their mother wasn't there.

After five days we were forced onto the boat. Altogether around eight hundred people. Zair was there too. The Europeans bomb us—so we'll bomb them with blacks, Gaddafi said.

Rashid looks very tired. So tired that Richard asks him if he wants to lie down.

No thank you, Rashid says. I often can't sleep at night, but it's okay.

One man jumped out of our boat and tried to swim back to shore, but they shot him in the water.

For the first seven days the food and water we had on board was enough. There wasn't much in any case, but finally, we adults stopped eating and drinking and gave everything to the children.

Then the compass broke.

For three days we just went around not knowing our direction.

The captain missed a few buoys at night and the boat scraped against rocks. The motor was kaput. Everyone was in a panic.

For two days the boat rocked crazily back and forth. We couldn't steer it any longer. We didn't know where to steer to.

Five days total without anything to eat or drink. All of us were in very bad shape. Some people died. And the ones who were still alive had no strength left at all. I was so weak. So weak. Everything looked blurry.

But then suddenly the rescue boat arrived.

There was a commotion. The people from the rescue boat wanted to help us, they threw us food and bottles of water, and everyone tried to catch something, but this made the boat start rocking.

And then it tipped over.

Just like that.

From one moment to the next.

It happened so fast.

Within five minutes, not more, in only five minutes, hundreds and hundreds of people died. The people I'd just been sitting next to, people I'd just been talking with.

Cut, Richard thinks, cut.

I can't swim, but somehow I caught a cable. Sometimes I was above the water, sometimes below. Under the water I saw all the corpses.

For a while, Rashid says nothing, and Richard doesn't feel compelled to ask any questions. The Advent candles burn. The pyramid is dark and still.

Approximately 550 of the 800 people drowned. Most of them couldn't swim, and the people who were below deck couldn't get out before everything flooded. Fishermen came with their boats to help us, but so many were already dead. The bigger rescue boats couldn't get close enough to us because of the cliffs. The fishermen pulled us into their boats. Everyone was crying and screaming. Us and the fishermen too. One boy was saved, but his parents and brother drowned. Many were looking for their husbands, their wives. Everyone was crying and screaming.

For a week after we were on land, I would wake at night thinking I was under water. The day I didn't come to pick up my wife at work in Tripoli, she had managed to escape to a UN office. I had to tell her on the telephone what happened. I stood there in a telephone booth in Agrigento. One year ago, she divorced me. She lives in Kaduna now and has a new husband. She's pregnant again.

Even today sometimes I think I see one of our children suddenly walking in the door.

After a rather long pause during which both men stare at the black TV screen as if there were something to see, Richard says:

Could you draw me a sketch of that gate you'd just finished working on that day?

Of course, Rashid says, you know, this was my work.

And while he begins to draw the first lines on the small square-ruled pad Richard has fetched from his desk, he says:

You know—the measurement is always the first thing to do.

Then he draws, corrects, goes on drawing, until Richard can clearly recognize what the gate looked like that Rashid had built for his final commission in his life as a metalworker, a gate that surely still guards the entrance of some property in Libya.

And in the end I put the design in the middle. If you could see me doing my work, says Rashid, whom Richard has always called—with perfect justification, he sees now—the thunderbolt-hurler, if you could see me doing my work, you would see a completely other Rashid. You know, he says, for me working is as natural as breathing.

42

The Polish health-care aide returns to Berlin and her job taking care of Anne's mother before New Year's arrives. She would have liked to spend a few more days with her family in Poland, Anne says, but you understand....

What a shame, Richard says.

Actually Christmas was really nice, Anne says. I'll send you a photo.

That evening, Richard looks at the picture on his computer: to the left of the Christmas tree, Anne's ninety-year-old mother sits in a wheelchair with a blanket covering her knees, her head inclined in such a way that you might almost think she was gazing encouragingly through the thick lenses of her glasses at Ali, who sits to the right of the tree. Ali is smiling. It looks peaceful, this Christmas composition, just as peaceful as all those photographs of all-white German Christmas Eves, in which it's equally impossible to tell what topics are being avoided or argued over before and after the release of the shutter.

Anne writes in her email that when she asked Ali once how his German was so good, he replied: The German language is my bridge into this country. He actually said *bridge into this country*, she writes Richard. He's incredibly talented. Under different circumstances, he'd no doubt already be enrolled in medical school.

Monika and Jörg return from Italy during the week between Christmas and New Year's. They invite Richard, Detlef, and Sylvia over for coffee to show them their pictures of Florence. They report on Giotto's tower, Michelangelo's handsome David, and the Christmas crèches in all the churches: entire landscapes like for a model railroad! They report on the food: a restaurant with forty different kinds of mozzarella! The Christmas dinner was served beautifully in the hotel restaurant—so much less work than doing it yourself at home! There were garlands of lights in the streets stretching for blocks, you get dizzy just looking at them! And enormous Christmas trees, so imaginatively decorated! On the other hand, they add, there were Africans everywhere. Everywhere. We rented a car to go to Arezzo, since Jörg had his heart set on seeing the Piero della Francesca frescoes, and we were expecting a lovely drive through the Tuscan countryside, so we took a side road instead of the highway, there was even snow on the ground. But then—this is incredible—out in the middle of nowhere we see all these black women—Africans!—standing at the side of the road soliciting. Right in the middle of the countryside, with hardly any traffic! Wearing boots and these short little jackets. Just standing there in the cold, in the snow—lots of them! There was something creepy about it.

Richard's met a few refugees here who are struggling to get by, Sylvia says, handing the tablet with the picture to her husband.

Oh really? asks mustached Jörg.

And Monika adds: You really have to be careful, a lot of times they're carrying illnesses—hepatitis, typhus, AIDS. Or so I hear.

These refugees Richard knows are men, Sylvia says.

Oh, I see, Monika says.

Richard says nothing, he's looking at the screen Detlef just handed him. The picture shows female figures standing isolated from one another like chess figures scattered across the snowy landscape, waiting beside the road or on the crests of the gently rolling hills.

No customers anywhere in sight, Monika says.

And the next picture is already of the frescoes in Arezzo: a woman standing behind another, who is kneeling, with a long white cape attached to her dress; the question she's asking the woman kneeling before her can be read only in the position of her hands.

I'd never have thought I'd be able to just get in a car and visit that church someday, just like that, Jörg says.

What does "freedom of movement" mean if not the right to travel? asks Monika, his wife.

During the week between Christmas and New Year's, Peter the archaeologist also returns from visiting the family of his twenty-year-old girlfriend. He sits on Richard's sofa, a glass of whiskey in hand, and says: Want to come with me to a New Year's Eve party Marie's friend is throwing? Otherwise I'll be the only old guy there.

How was her family?

Complicated, he says, I think they think I'm some sort of pervert.

Well, she's their daughter.

The father's jealous in any case, and I think the mother wouldn't mind having a go at me herself.

Good thing they're far away.

It sure is.

Peter takes another sip.

The main thing is that the two of you get along.

Yes, so will you come to the party? And Richard agrees.

During the week between Christmas and New Year's, Osarobo too finally comes back from Italy. Richard invites him over, plays him the Christmas song "*Leise rieselt der Schnee*" ("Softly drifts the snow") on the piano, singing along as best he can. "*Still schweigt Kummer und Harm*," he sings, then he translates: "Silent are worry and grief." Christmas, he says, is supposed to be a festival of joyousness.

Okay, Osarobo says.

How were things in Italy?

Well . . .

What city were you in?

Milano.

Nice, Richard says.

Well . . . , says Osarobo. In the subway the Italians get up and sit somewhere else if I sit next to them.

Richard remembers that Osarobo told him this the first time they met.

They think I'm a criminal. Every black man.

Surely not.

It's true. It doesn't matter if we're criminals or not.

But of course it matters, Richard says. Did you at least get your papers?

Yes, I can pick them up in eight weeks.

Eight weeks? So you have to go back there?

Yes.

How much does that cost?

The bus ticket is one hundred euros.

So two hundred euros for the round trip?

Yes. Osarobo plays a few high notes. And eighty euros for the *marca da bollo*, he says.

For the document?

Yes, Osarobo says. *Pling, pling, pling*. And besides that you need an Italian address.

What does that mean?

There are people who give you an address. That costs another two hundred euros.

Private people who take money from you?

Some African guy who has a room. But I can live there, too. Until the appointment. Sometimes they check.

Richard would really like to know whether the law of supply and demand is in fact a law of nature.

In other words, he says aloud to Osarobo, you need a total of 680 euros for the two bus tickets, the address, and the fees?

Yes.

And what about eating while you're there?

Osarobo shrugs.

That surely costs more than you get here to live on for two months.

The *permesso* expired last spring already, Osarobo says. But I didn't have any money then.

What *permesso*?

The document, the *permesso di soggiorno*, the Italian residence permit.

Is that really necessary?

Without that we have no papers at all. Without a *permesso* there's no health insurance.

You have insurance from Italy?

Yes.

I see. So you lived with the African guy?

Until my appointment.

And after that?

Well ..., Osarobo says, hitting a couple of low notes on the piano, life is crazy.

Did you sleep on the street?

Osarobo doesn't answer. *Pling, pling, pling*. Consecutive fifths have been forbidden in the Western musical tradition for six hundred years now. Only now does it occur to Richard that he still has a Christmas present for the future street musician: the roll-up piano, he almost forgot about it.

I appreciate that very much.

They unroll it on the kitchen table, plug in the cord, and try out the different instruments: percussion and English horn, saxophone, harp.

It also works with batteries, Richard says.

Oh, very good.

And with the buttons over here, Richard says, you can set an underlying rhythm, like cha-cha-cha or tango.

Only in the pause between waltz and march does he hear the doorbell: Sylvia and Detlef spontaneously decided to visit him.

What's going on, a tea dance?

This is Sylvia and Detlef, my oldest friends, he says to Osarobo as he leads them into the kitchen, and this is Osarobo.

Osarobo stands up and shakes hands with both of them, but his eyes are flickering back and forth, and it looks as if he'd rather he were someplace without people he doesn't know suddenly walking in the door.

Go on and play some more, Richard says, and we'll sit in the living room and talk for a little while, then I'll drive you home.

No, no, Osarobo says, it's okay, I'll go home on the S-Bahn.

Do you have a transit pass?

Osarobo shakes his head.

While Osarobo is putting on his shoes in the hall, Richard takes sixty euros out of his wallet—the cheapest transit pass costs fifty-seven euros, for people who don't have to use the buses and trains before ten a.m. Welfare recipients and asylum-seekers receive a discount, but not these refugees, who aren't even permitted to apply for asylum. Richard hands Osarobo the two banknotes and gives him the bag containing the rolled-up keyboard.

Do you know how to go?

Yes, don't worry. Osarobo looks at the ground and says: God bless you.

It's my pleasure.

So how was the *Christmas Oratorio*, Richard asks his friends when he goes back to the living room. After his disappointment at Osarobo's sudden departure, he'd given them the two tickets.

Oh, it was so beautiful, Sylvia says.

They did a great job with that aria with the echo, Detlef says, they put the other singer on a little balcony next to the choir loft.

Nice idea, Richard says.

43

The day before New Year's Eve, it snows. Richard has bought birthday presents for Rashid, Apollo, and Ithemba, all of whom he knows now celebrate their birthday on January 1: winter sweaters in various colors. He's just about to tramp across the courtyard to their building when he spots a figure sitting on the bench in the cold and recognizes the thin man. How are you? Good, he says. Isn't it too cold to be sitting here outside on a bench? I was waiting for you.

How could the thin man—whom he hasn't seen for weeks—know that today of all days he would be walking across the courtyard? No matter, Richard decides.

Can I show you something? the thin man asks.

Of course.

From the inside pocket of his jacket, he pulls a police summons: *For the failure to provide valid ID.*

What happened? asks Richard.

The day before yesterday they stopped me on Alexanderplatz and said that wasn't me in the photograph.

The man in the photo really does look quite different, but maybe the thin man wasn't always as thin as he is now. Richard reads the name: Karon Anubo.

Your name is really Karon?

Yes, the thin man says. He hands Richard the summons.

Police Station Berlin-Mitte, Rm. 104, H. Lübcke, Mon.–Fri. 9:00 a.m. – 4:00 p.m., no appts.

I'll take you in the car, Richard says.

There's a traffic jam in the city, like always in Berlin after the year's first snowfall, streetcars are stuck between stations, drivers scream at each other from the windows of their cars. Here and there you hear a high-pitched whistle followed shortly after by a rocket exploding—apparently some people can't wait for New Year's. Richard spends an hour and a half crisscrossing Berlin with Karon, from Spandau all the way to the police station in Mitte, *Turn right now . . . turn left . . . enter the traffic circle and take the second exit.*

Thank you for bringing me, Karon says, otherwise I'd have to buy a ticket.

You don't have a transit pass?

Normally I send 150 euros to my family, but this month I also sent an extra fifty euros because my brother cut himself with a cutlass while he was working in the field, and he had to go to the hospital.

I'm so sorry. There wasn't anyone else there who could help him?

It's the culture, the thin man says.

The culture?

That means this is what is proper: the oldest son must provide for the family.

Because of his wife, Richard once went to a meeting of Alcoholics Anonymous, where the men and women also told stories like this, stories that always began with something perfectly simple and always ended in calamity. A hamster escaped from its cage and wouldn't come out from behind the wall unit, so the entire thing had to be dismantled. And what was in the bottom cabinet that hadn't been looked at in years, hidden behind the dish towels? Countless empty bottles left over from the days of addiction. And at once the thirst returns.

The effects are indirect, not direct, Richard thinks, as he has thought many times now in recent days.

How old is your brother?

Thirteen, the thin man says.

The police station in Berlin-Mitte. When they arrive, it's 3:25 on a Tuesday, but Ms. Lübcke isn't here today, the woman at the registration desk tells him. Why not? She's stationed somewhere else today. But here it says: *Mon.-Fri. 9-4, no appts*. Richard's so worked up that he pronounces the abbreviation "appts," practically spitting the plosives through the holes of the intercom. I just told you that Ms. Lübcke isn't here. And now? You'll have to come back, sorry. And what if Mr. Anubo had made the trip here all by himself, all the way from Spandau? The whole round-trip journey, two different transit zones to pay for? I'm very sorry. The police official isn't sorry, let alone *very* sorry, Richard sees this quite clearly, but in any case Ms. Lübcke is unavailable.

When they get back to Spandau, it's already dark, and Richard's really not in the mood for a birthday party with three honorees; already on the drive back he's decided to postpone the presentation of the sweaters until the new year. Before he lets the thin man out in front of the home, they sit for a few minutes in the car, talking.

If I can't stay in Germany after the interview, Karon says, where can I go? Where can I find a job in Italy? How can I feed my mother and siblings? Where in the world is the place where I can lie down to sleep in peace? The problem is very big, Karon says. I have no wife and no children, he says—I am small. But the problem is very big, it has a wife and many, many children.

The Africans have to solve their problems in Africa, Richard's heard people saying many times in recent weeks. He's heard them say: It's incredibly generous of Germany to be taking in so many war refugees, in the same breath they say: But we can't feed all of Africa from here. Then they add: Economic refugees and asylum fraud are using up resources that ought to be going to the actual refugees.

It would be better to solve the problems in Africa there.

For a moment, Richard imagines what a to-do list would look

like for the men he's gotten to know over the past few months.

His own to-do list would look something like this:

Schedule repairman for dishwasher
Urologist appointment
Meter reading

The to-do list for Karon, on the other hand, would be more like this:

Eradicate corruption, cronyism, and child labor in Ghana

Or for Apollo:

File lawsuit against the Areva Group (France)
*Install a new government in Niger that can't be bribed or blackmailed by
    foreign investors*
Establish the independent Tuareg state Azawad (discuss with Yussuf)

And for Rashid the list would read:

Broker a reconciliation between Christians and Muslims in Nigeria
Persuade Boko Haram to lay down their arms

Finally Hermes, the illiterate with golden shoes, and Ali, the future nurse, would have to join forces to complete these two tasks:

Prohibit the sale of weapons to Chad (from the U.S. and China)
Prohibit U.S. and China drilling for oil in Chad and exporting it

Say, Richard asks Karon, how large would a property in Ghana have to be for your family to feed themselves?

Karon thinks for a moment and says: About one-third the size of Oranienplatz.

And how much would that cost?

Karon thinks some more and says: I think between two and three thousand euros.

The summer before last, Richard almost bought himself a surfboard for 1495 euros, but before he finished making up his mind, autumn arrived, and then last summer the drowned man who never resurfaced from the bottom of the lake rendered all such considerations moot. A robotic vacuum cleaner though (799 euros) would be a much better investment, and he would certainly get good use out of a video projector (1167 euros) for watching movies with his friend Andreas. If Christel were still alive, the two of them might have decided to buy themselves a new video camera for Christmas (1545 euros), or a tablet with sufficient memory (709 euros) that would be easier to take along with them on trips than a computer—but these were all things he could easily do without. On the other hand, he's already firmed up plans to finally buy one of those so-called riding mowers in the spring (999 to 2999 euros).

Or at least the plan was firm five minutes ago.

How big is your family, did you say?

My mother, my sister, and two younger brothers.

So, four people?

Yes.

If they had land, what would they plant?

Plantains, cassava.

And that would make them independent?

My mother would sell part of the harvest or trade it for other things she needs, and the family would eat the rest.

What would you say if I were to buy a piece of land for your family?

Richard is now expecting to see the African at first incredulous, perhaps, then speechless with excitement, and finally overjoyed, jumping into the air with relief and pleasure, throwing his arms

205

around Richard or at least bursting into tears.

Nothing of the sort happens.

Karon is calm and very solemn and looks as if he is thinking very hard.

At least you wouldn't have to worry about your family anymore.

Karon still doesn't say anything.

What's the problem?

It will be one year before the first harvest, Karon says, thinking.

Karon is right.

But there's one more thing Richard understands at this moment: Karon's worries have ground him down to such an extent that he's even afraid to hope.

44

And then the new year arrives. The young friends of Peter's twenty-year-old girlfriend have been dancing and drinking, chatting about hairstyles, the new movie showing at Kino International, the mustache worn by a female pop singer, bands Richard's never heard of, but also Richard Wagner, Harry Potter, Kierkegaard, Virginia Woolf, handsome men, and the new shopping center at Alexanderplatz. Several of the guests have French-kissed and then gotten into arguments as the evening advanced, with one girl bursting into tears just before midnight, having to be comforted and held by her best friend; one of the young men drank too much and stumbled over the threshold on his way out to the balcony, falling, bleeding, requiring the application of a band-aid across his nose in the final seconds of the old year. How long has it been since Richard was so young? His friend Peter is in fine form; he and his girlfriend (who answers to the lovely name Marie) are dancing to Queen's "We Are the Champions." Richard wonders if Marie is just being nice when she puts on music that reminds her boyfriend—over thirty years her senior—of his youth, or does she just like the song?

At exactly midnight when the corks start popping, guests hug and kiss, rockets are fired off and sparklers waved around. Richard just stands there, wondering what the beginning of a new year really means. He's never quite understood what's supposed to be departing in that final decisive second, while at the same time something new—something you can't know yet—suddenly presents itself. Sometimes in past years he's tried to concentrate on this future that was apparently arriving at just this moment. But how do you concentrate on something you don't know yet? Who's going to die? Who'll be born? The older he gets, the more grateful he is to have just as little idea as anyone else what is in store.

The first day in this new year was a Wednesday, so most of the officials in the Berlin Foreigners Office have profited from this by taking nearly the entire week off using only two vacation days. Not until Monday, January 6, do they set foot in their offices once again and turn the little wheel for the year on their date stamps one click forward. They flip through various binders and papers, typing up this and that, and on Tuesday they send out a few letters. On Wednesday, January 8, lists arrive in Spandau as well as Friedrichshain and Wedding with the names of the first 108 men, who, on the morning of Friday, January 10, are to move from the asylum-seekers' residences to Magdeburg, for example, or to a dormitory made of shipping containers on the outskirts of Hamburg, or to a Bavarian mountain village, where approximately two years ago, knowing nothing of European and German regulations, these refugees more or less randomly filed applications for asylum. Places from which they set out for Berlin two years ago and protested the law forbidding them to pursue a livelihood independently or even move around within Germany while their applications were being processed. The law is still the law and now, starting at eight on Friday

morning, its grand moment will arrive. Even though forcibly trans-
porting the refugees to remote locations that have jurisdiction over
their cases is not legally permitted, the police have been charged
with evicting them from the rooms in the facilities they've been
inhabiting in Berlin.

Rashid took a picture of the list and messaged it to Richard on
Thursday. Twelve of the Spandau residents are on the list, including the singer Abdusalam, who has a squint and is just learning to
write, along with Zair, who was on the same boat as Rashid and
only survived after it capsized because he clambered over the railing
while the boat was tipping until he was clinging to the bottom. And
there's one more name on the list that Richard really doesn't want
to see there: Osarobo. Only now does Richard understand why
the Berlin Senate insisted on making identification of the refugees
by name part of the Oranienplatz agreement. Only when a name is
known can there be a list like this. Thursday night, Richard sleeps
poorly and wakes before five a.m. Where will Osarobo go now?

When Richard arrives in Spandau shortly before eight, there are
already twenty squad cars parked either right in front of the residence or in nearby lots. The entryway has been fenced off with
metal barricades. A few residents are standing on the sidewalk in
front, including a few women and children. No, you're not allowed
to go in, the guards tell him, who do you want to see? Rashid, he
says, pointing at the thunderbolt-hurler who is in the courtyard
talking and gesticulating among a group of other refugees. No,
it isn't possible to visit today, the guards say, but just then Rashid
spots him and begins shouting when he sees that his guest is being
barred from entering. I'm not in prison, he shouts, I'm not a criminal! You can't keep my friend from coming to see me! Now police
officers in riot gear get out of the first of the squad cars, wearing helmets with visors lowered, carrying truncheons and pistols.

And the place of assemblage was in turmoil, and the earth groaned beneath them, and a din arose. The officers take up position, four men across the gate. Richard asks himself whether forty heavily armed men are really necessary to remove twelve African refugees from a residential facility, not to mention the other 150 or so police officers waiting in the squad cars for their signal. Tomorrow—this is already clear to him—the newspaper will report on the high cost of this deployment, and this country of bookkeepers will be aghast and blame the objects of the transport for the expense, as used to happen in other periods of German history, with regard to other transports.

So a border, Richard thinks, can suddenly become visible, it can suddenly appear where a border never used to be: battles fought in recent years on the borders of Libya, or of Morocco or Niger, are now taking place in the middle of Berlin-Spandau. Where before there was only a building, a sidewalk, and everyday Berlin life, a border has suddenly sprouted, growing up quickly and going to seed, unforeseen as illness.

At the New Year's Eve party, standing with his friend Peter on his girlfriend Marie's friend's balcony gazing out into the darkness of the old year about to become the darkness of the new, Peter told him that for the Incas the center of the universe wasn't a point but a line where the two halves of the universe meet. Is this the scene unfolding before Richard's eyes at the entrance to the asylum seekers' residence? And are the two groups of people facing off here something like the two halves of a universe that actually belong together, but whose separation is nonetheless irrevocable? Is the rift dividing them in fact a bottomless chasm; is that why such powerful turbulences have been released? And is it a rift between Black and White? Or Poor and Rich? Stranger and Friend? Or between those whose fathers have died and those whose fathers are still alive? Or those with curly hair and those with straight? Those who call their dinner *fufu*

209

and those who call it stew? Or those who like to wear yellow, red, and green t-shirts and those who prefer neckties? Or those who like to drink water and those who prefer beer? Or between speakers of one language and another? How many borders exist within a single universe? Or, to ask it differently, what is the one true, crucial border? Perhaps the border between what is dead and alive? Or between the stars and the lump of earth we walk on every day? Between one day and the next? Or between frogs and birds? Water and earth? Air filled with music and air with no music? The blackness of a shadow and the blackness of coal? Three-leaf and four-leaf clover? Fur and scales? Or millions of times over between inside and outside, when you consider a single human being or a single animal or plant as a universe unto itself? Richard gets along well with his organs, he's made his peace with the raw flesh of his interior that keeps him alive, not just him but also his thoughts—thoughts about the beauty of Helen, or the best way to slice an onion.

When taking all these possible borders into consideration, it seems to Richard that the difference between one person and another is in fact ridiculously small, and perhaps there isn't any chasm opening up here at the entrance to the asylum seekers' residence in Berlin. Perhaps on this level of the universe, there is no such thing as difference, there are no two halves—it's just a matter of a few pigments in the material that's known as skin in all the languages of the world, meaning that the violence on display here is not at all the harbinger of a storm in the center of a universe but is in fact due merely to an absurd misunderstanding that has been dividing humankind and preventing it from realizing how enormously long the lifespan of a planet is compared to the life and breath of any one human being. Whether you clothe your body in hand-me-down pants and jackets from a donation bin, brand-name sweaters, expensive or cheap dresses, or uniforms with a helmet and visor— underneath this clothing, every one of us is naked and must surely, let's hope, have taken pleasure in sunshine and wind, in water and snow, have eaten or drunk this and that tasty thing, perhaps even have loved someone and been loved in return before dying one day. Enough grows and flows in this world to provide for all, and none-theless—as Richard can clearly see, gazing at these twenty squad cars—a struggle for survival is apparently taking place here. Should he assume these police officers have been deployed to defend the interests of those Germans who are so poor that all they can serve up for the holidays is a stolen goose? Probably not, he thinks, oth-erwise he'd no doubt have seen these twenty squad cars parked in front of various bank branches and officers dressed in riot gear cart-ing away the managers who've embezzled so many billions. Yes, he thinks, this spectacle unfolding before him looks like theater, and theater is all it is: an artificial front concealing the real front behind it. The audience bellows on cue, thirsting for sacrifice, and on cue the gladiators carry their own real lives into the arena. Have people forgotten in Berlin of all places that a border isn't just measured by an opponent's stature but in fact creates him?

Rashid is shouting that he's had enough, he's going to set every-thing on fire, tear down the building, blow it all up, smash the fur-niture, tear off the roof, kick down the doors—and while Rashid is shouting things of this sort in the courtyard, Richard stands out-side listening to the director of the residence and his assistant qui-etly confer about whether it's time to kick the hothead out. Then the column of forty police officers in their military costumes be-gins to move. Marching in lock-step, they advance, but not toward Rashid, instead they turn off and rapidly disappear into the front building where, as Richard knows, no refugees are housed—these are the administrative offices. A few minutes later, the men in uni-form emerge again, still marching in lock-step, and resume their earlier position before the gate. Where's Rashid? asks the sena-tor who visited the residence not long ago. He hadn't noticed her standing next to him. He doesn't know any more than she does where the indignant Nigerian could be, the special unit has wiped across the image like a giant eraser, and now the thunderbolt-hurler is nowhere to be seen. I have no idea, Richard says. He's suffering from a severe cardiac condition, the senator says, I'm worried about him. Now Richard remembers that back at the assembly in the nursing home, Rashid was wearing a wristband that read *Charité*. He wondered about it, then decided that maybe there was an aid agency that shared the name of Berlin's big hospital, the Charité. Is he being treated here in Berlin? asks Richard. Yes, the woman says, he was supposed to be operated on three months ago, but then he took off in the middle of his pre-op exam, because someone in the group needed looking after. Since then he's been waiting for a new date for the surgery.

We could call him, Richard says.

The network's been down since this morning, the senator said, I tried calling him a little while ago.

Which network?

The one all the refugees' phones work on.

Today of all days, what a strange coincidence, Richard says.

Yes, strange indeed, the senator says.

And now Yussuf, the dishwasher from Richard's advanced language class—Richard hasn't seen him in quite some time—comes running out of the building, yelling in an African language, then in French, then in Italian, then even a bit of German: *leave us in peace, damn it!* and punches everyone who tries to speak with him, he even punches Richard when he goes over and tries to calm him, *I've had enough!* he shouts, spinning around his axis like a Rumpelstiltskin, and then in great agitation he starts berating the police officers, but they remain implacable, all they do is hold up their wall of shields to fend him off. Richard thinks of how proud Yussuf was when he learned the word *dishwasher*, and remembers how he said that he wanted to be an engineer. Now what he's become is a man running amok, who, if he doesn't calm down soon, will be forced into a straitjacket and taken away.

Eventually Rashid, too, appears in the courtyard. He's no longer flailing or shouting, he looks exhausted, that's all. Of course, he's allowed to leave the grounds, the security guards say, and so he joins them out front.

It's really bad, he says, really, really bad today, he shakes hands with the senator and Richard and despite everything doesn't forget to ask each of them: How are you?

Good, says Richard, dutifully.

Good, says the senator.

They treat us like criminals. But what did we do?

Richard shrugs his shoulders.

Rashid pulls out his tiny phone and presses a few buttons.

The phone still doesn't work.

Yes, we noticed that too.

Are you coming to the demonstration later? We're going to march from Oranienplatz to the Berlin Senate.

Richard and the senator nod.

Then Rashid goes over to Yussuf, who's still standing before the wall of armored officers, scolding them and poking a finger at their shields as if this row of visors concealed particularly recalcitrant pupils. Rashid claps him amiably on the shoulder a few times, it's okay, he says, it's okay. Yussuf gives the metal fence that was installed this morning a kick, curses a few times over his shoulder as he turns away, and then goes back into the building.

He's not on the list, too, is he? asks Richard when the thunderbolt-hurler starts walking back.

No, the senator says, but all of this is stressing him out. Even that refugee Rufu got sent to the psychiatric clinic over Christmas.

Oh, Lord, Richard says.

He's out now, but he's not doing well.

What's wrong with him?

He doesn't eat anymore. He can't open his mouth, or won't.

For a moment Richard feels a wave of panic wash over him. Could everything here really be beyond saving?

Where are the twelve people from the list? asks the senator.

A few left yesterday, and the others will be coming out soon, says a security guard.

They're leaving the residence voluntarily? asks Richard.

Are they supposed to start fighting again? These are people who fled from war. Then the handful of men come out, their backpacks on their backs, carrying a duffel or a couple of plastic bags. They walk past the many squad cars the police have sent, heading for the bus stop. Osarobo isn't among them, nor is Zair. Abdusalam, the singer, shakes hands with Richard and the senator and hugs Rashid before following the others. The list has been given its due.

45

In Germany, holding demonstrations is legally permitted as a matter of principle. But there are three important questions:

1. *Who is applying for the permit to hold the demonstration?*
2. *What is the route?*
3. *What is the slogan?*

The person filing the application must hold a German passport or residency papers—not so common among refugees from Libya. A German sympathizer—a tall bald-headed man from the back of the crowd—volunteers his ID for the application. Where do you want to march? Rashid says: To the Senate. Ten minutes pass, and various people show up to tell Rashid there's no point: on a Friday afternoon, none of the senators will be in their offices. The senator from before comes over and says she's heard they won't be allowed to enter the building, at most they can assemble in front. The supervising officer arrives and says: If you want to change your route and march to the Brandenburg Gate, we'll have to block off a completely different stretch. Rashid says, Who's talking about the Brandenburg Gate? And the supervisor replies: That's what the guy who filed the application says, that bald guy over there. What bald guy? I've never seen him before in my life. Another ten minutes gone. If we can't go to the Senate, Rashid says, then we'll march to the American embassy. Excuse me? says the supervisor. Yes, the American embassy. Rashid goes to the back and starts arguing with the bald man. Another ten minutes gone. The bald man walks up to the supervisor and says: I withdraw my application. If no one has an ID and address, the supervisor says, the demonstration cannot take place. Richard says, here, take my ID. Another police officer—this one so short he looks like a dwarf standing beside Rashid—asks: What's the slogan of this demonstration? Okay, time to get going! Rashid shouts above the heads of all the others. He doesn't even see or hear the dwarf asking for the demonstration's slogan. What is the slogan? the dwarf asks once more. Let's go! Is that the slogan? No, says Richard. Rashid bellows: We're done waiting! Is *that* the slogan, asks the dwarf. No, says Richard. The dwarf says: Without a slogan, a permit can't be issued, and without a permit we can't start blocking off the route. Richard: No one's started blocking off the route yet? The dwarf says: Of course not, there's no slogan. Another ten minutes gone. Without stopping to think, Richard says: The slogan is *A Time to Make Friends*. Only after uttering the words does he remember that this was the slogan of the World Festival of Youth and Students in 1973. Or was it some FIFA World Cup?

215

The supervisor comes up to Richard and says: Now you're the one who's filing for a permit to demonstrate? Yes, Richard says. You can't pass directly in front of the American embassy, do you understand? Why not? Richard asks. Because they have a buffer zone for security, that's why. Then he asks the dwarf: What's their slogan? *A Time to Make Friends*, says the dwarf. Good, the supervisor says, so now it'll be at least thirty minutes before we have the route blocked off. Rashid asks: What's he saying? And Richard translates: We can start in five minutes. Good, Rashid says, and starts gathering his people together, some of whom have started arguing with various police officers. Meanwhile the supervisor is already standing across the street beside his unmarked police car, speaking into his walkie-talkie. We start! shouts Rashid, we start! No you don't, the supervisor shouts, running back. Richard, who mistranslated his words to calm Rashid now sees that his trick has had the opposite effect. The supervisor shouts again: You stay right here! The policemen assemble in a straight line no demonstrator can slip through. Behind them the cars are still driving back and forth on a street that a hundred years ago was still a bridge. Rashid shouts at the supervisor: God will punish you! The supervisor—who apparently, thank goodness, understands no English—is grumbling to himself: I already told them the whole route has to be cleared in advance. Richard thinks it'll be practically a miracle if none of the Africans explodes in impatience. God will punish you! But perhaps the police aren't interested in a miracle. The senator says: Rashid's heart is seriously in very bad shape, I'm worried about him. Whatever you do, Rashid, don't start talking about God, Richard says. Otherwise they'll think you're a terrorist. But Rashid doesn't hear him, he's busy bellowing in the direction of the police officers: We are no criminals! We can start in a minute, Richard says, but the thunderbolt-hurler is so occupied with hurling his bolts, he doesn't hear: Change the law! He's going to collapse on us if this keeps up, the senator says. Richard sees one of the Africans raise his hands defensively and say to one of the police officers, who's trying to push him back a little: Don't touch me! A member of the police de-escalation team is now listening to an African who's berating him and nodding his head sympathetically, just as he learned in his de-escalation training. Richard sees one of the young sympathizers holding up a homemade poster on which he's written: *Long Live the Gays and Lesbians in Kenya!* At this point over ninety minutes have passed, and now the senator and Richard watch as first one, then another of the Africans suddenly start pushing and shoving and shaking their fists—Apollo for example, or Tristan, or tall Ithemba, even though they've been waiting patiently all this time. We want to stay! they shout. Or: We are no criminals! Or: Give us a place! Only after a while do Richard and the senator understand that Rashid's friends are trying to replace him at least for a few minutes. Someone has to be the leader, to shake his fists and shout to keep the demonstration under control, as the police continue to delay the start of the march. Meanwhile Rashid takes a few minutes to rest behind the front line of men. *A friend, a good friend, is the best thing in the world.*

Two and a half hours after the demonstration was supposed to start, the procession finally sets out. Richard, Professor Emeritus of Classical Languages, who has just, for the first time in his life, applied for a permit for a demonstration and given it its slogan, is very glad to see the men peacefully beginning their march and the policemen—who've been holding them in check all this time—now proceeding before them in a long line, closing ranks, to secure the street. Any passersby observing the protest can only assume that the police and the refugees have been acting in harmony from the start. Richard accompanies the procession for another couple of blocks until they reach Moritzplatz; then he goes down into the subway and returns home.

46

That evening, Richard hears on the news that since eight a.m. yesterday, the refugees from the Oranienplatz group housed in Friedrichshain have been occupying the top floor of their residence to protest their expulsion from Berlin. Several of them have gone up on the roof and are threatening to jump. According to the report, all the other floors of the building have been evacuated and cordoned off.

When Richard arrives at the residence in Spandau the next morning, only Rashid is in his room. He's lying in bed, but beckons Richard to enter: How are you? Yes, the others are in Friedrichshain to support their friends, but he's too exhausted to join them. He holds up a clear plastic bag full of medications.

Do you know the ones who went up on the roof? asks Richard.

Of course, Rashid says, we were all at Oranienplatz together. They don't have anything more to lose.

What's going to come of all this?

I don't know. Three times in the last eight weeks, I tried to speak with the Senator of the Interior. Man to man. Three times.

And?

He was in a meeting, or was away. We even requested an appointment in writing, but he never responded.

Leaving a thunderbolt-hurler to languish in your waiting room is surely the height of diplomacy, thinks Richard. A murdered father and two drowned children are nothing compared with a degree in Economics and Social Sciences, a group of refugees is not a *Volk*, and a ringleader taking a stand for his people isn't a head of state. The practical thing about a law is that no one person made it, so no one is personally responsible for it. A politician who wants to change this or that about a law can of course give it his best shot, but one with no desire to make changes will cut just as fine a figure, perhaps even a more elegant one.

Maybe there should have been some sort of protest action here in Spandau too, Richard says.

We thought about it, Rashid says, but there are children here.

I understand, Richard says. And then for a long time he says nothing more.

In the ensuing silence, Rashid's eyes fall shut, and soon he's asleep.

Richard goes on sitting beside him for a while, just as many years ago he sat beside his still breathing mother.

Eventually he gets up, goes out, and quietly closes the door behind him.

On his drive back, Anne calls him and says: Have you heard about the refugees who've gone up on the roof to protest? Yes, Richard says. One of them peed off the edge of the roof, she says, and now everyone's having a fit, did you hear that too? No, Richard says.

The smell of snow in winter is beautiful. Fresh snow blanketing rotted leaves. Open the garden gate, deeply inhale the air—he's done this the same way for twenty years now when he comes home. For twenty years, there's been winter in this garden, and it's smelled like this, and he's unlocked this garden gate just like this and then closed it behind him.

Richard knows he's one of very few people in this world who are in a position to take their pick of realities.

One day later he reads in the newspaper that the roof-occupiers have had their electricity and water shut off. Richard sees a picture of a man with outstretched arms standing on the roof, he looks like a scarecrow. The roof is slippery with frost and snow, the situation's precarious, the caption says. Richard wonders how much the speed with which a country lets people die has to do with its prestige. Why should a refugee jumping off a roof be so much worse for that country's reputation than letting him slowly expire under miserable conditions? It's probably just that there is a photographer present to capture the moment of the jump. Or is the scandal just that these men want to determine the time and manner of their own deaths, rather than continuing to let their lives—which have been made impossible—be administered by a country that doesn't want them? Is the question of power over one's own life still above all a question of power, and not a question of life? *Whether 'tis nobler in the mind to suffer / The slings and arrows of outrageous fortune, / Or to take arms against a sea of troubles, / And, by opposing, end them.*

One of the biggest German newspapers publishes on its website a tongue-in-cheek article about the refugees on the roof: *Never a dull moment in Berlin.* Richard reads: *Where does protest stop and blackmail begin?* For a brief moment he misunderstands and thinks that "blackmail" is meant to refer to the police tactic of forcing the occupiers to leave the building by turning off the electricity and water. But then he quickly realizes his mistake: it's the ones putting their own lives in jeopardy who are described here as blackmailers. The newspaper's readers praise the article in their comments, and their only complaint is why refugees should be the only ones to enjoy the privilege of standing on a roof and threatening suicide. And peeing over the edge.

Brand-new in Germany and the FIRST THING he does is pee off the roof!

The FIRST THING, eh? thinks Richard. Well, it is, after almost three years of exile and waiting.

Have you ever seen the gentlemen from the "refugee scene" or their supporters holding down a proper job or doing anything productive at all? Not me.

Denying them permission to work while at the same time reproaching them for idleness is, Richard finds, a conceptually flawed construction.

This article in this major newspaper—the ideological voice of New Germany, as it were—also describes the lives and activities of the sympathizers who've established a solidarity camp in front of the building: they sing, they dance, they deliver speeches of support. The men atop this wintry roof, the article asserts, are basically just the victims of these sympathizers, being used as tools to serve others' political goals, but unfortunately they lack the intelligence and perspective to realize this. Richard remembers the young man with the poster he saw at the demonstration: *Long Live the Gays and Lesbians of Kenya!* It's true: Richard, sitting at breakfast like the other readers of this major German newspaper, in a warm house, toast, tea, orange juice, honey, and cheese before him—Richard truly does see a bleak future looming for Germany should this supporter, helped by refugees who out of youthful exuberance and political blindness are standing on the roof and peeing, succeed in staging a coup that lands him in the Chancellor's seat.

47

Having his far-from-edifying reading experience interrupted by a message from Karon suits Richard fine.

Hi, the thin man writes, how are you?

Fine, Richard writes back, how are you?

It turns out the thin man has an appointment with the district authorities.

Richard writes: Do you have someone who can go with you?

Karon writes back: I have no body.

No body, he writes, and it occurs to Richard—it's occurred to him many times now—that all the men he's gotten to know here (these "dead men on holiday") could just as easily be lying at the bottom of the Mediterranean. And conversely all the Germans who were murdered during the so-called Third Reich still inhabit Germany as ghosts, sometimes he even imagines that all these missing people along with their unborn children and the children of their children are walking beside him on the street, on their way to work or to visit friends, they sit invisibly in the cafés, take walks, go shopping, visit parks and the theater. Go, went, gone. The line dividing ghosts and people has always seemed to him thin, he's not sure why, maybe because as an infant, he himself came so close to going astray in the mayhem of war and slipping down into the realm of the dead.

Not long afterward, as he is sitting all alone with Karon in a long hallway in the district administrative offices, waiting to be called for Room 3086, he asks: So how *do* you buy property in Ghana?

Karon waits until the footsteps of an official—who's just emerged from one of the many doors on high heels, a thick stack of files beneath her arm—have faded away.

In the village, he explains, everyone knows to whom a piece of land belongs, and sometimes also who owned it before that, because in the village everyone knows everyone from the day he is born. The king has to give his permission for the sale.

The king?

Yes, says Karon. Then you bring three witnesses who are there when you sign the contract. When the children of these witnesses grow up, they tell their children who owns this piece of land. When people die, the children still know who the owner of the property is.

So the bearing witness is a sort of inheritance?

Yes, Karon says.

And how do you know exactly how large the property is?

They just say: From that tree there to this stone, or the house, or the river. The witnesses can remember.

So ask if there's a property in your village that's the right size for your family, Richard says.

And then the door of Room 3086 opens and an official peers out and says: Anubo, Karon?

222

*

Two days later a friend of Karon's sends him a picture of a property that's overgrown, with lots of vegetation, patches of clayey earth, a couple of trees in the background. In the foreground, a sign is written in charcoal: *Plot for sale,* and the price, twelve thousand Ghanaian cedi, followed by two telephone numbers. The old deed of sale—the friend sent a photo of this as well—is less than three-quarters of a page, more or less the length of the Senate's agreement with the Oranienplatz group. *Sharing common boundaries with the properties of Kwame Boateng, Alhassan Kingsley, and Sarwo Mkambo.* Does this property really exist? Where is this village, anyhow? And how much is a cedi worth?

Three of the four signers of the previous contract pressed their fingers into violet ink and signed with their fingerprints.

Richard still remembers quite well deciding with his wife a few years after the fall of the Wall to go ahead and buy the property they'd been leasing from the government all those years. By that time, one or two of their neighbors were already embroiled in lawsuits with the so-called original owners of their properties, i.e., the families to whom the properties had belonged before they'd fled the zone occupied by the Russians in the years following the war. "Legal best practices" in united Germany—as soon was clear to former citizens of the GDR—picked up from the point in time when the East had been organized around capitalist principles, in other words 1945. Where property law was concerned, this even made sense. After all, in this part of Germany, the years between 1945 and 1990 had been nothing more than an attempt—a failed attempt, no less—to redefine ownership. Now the land titles from 1945 were lugged out again so the ledger columns could resume right where they'd broken off at the end of the war—with lawsuits filed in cases where this seemed unavoidable—in order to address those few insignificant intervening years that, alas, could not be taken into consideration. Richard remembered a useful and fascinating word from his first computer literacy class: *undo*, as if you could just turn back time that had already passed, cancel out experiences, as if you could decide what should be forgotten and what remembered, or program what would have consequences—and what would have none. Until 1989, Richard and his wife had lived their lives without hearing the words "land title" a single time. Luckily for them, the original owner of their property hadn't fled to the West before or after the construction of the Wall, he'd remained in the East and was delighted at how simple it was to sell the property to the couple who'd been leasing it for decades, contributing to the financial stability of his twilight years that he was spending in this strange land his country had suddenly become. Richard and his wife had taken out a mortgage, for which proof of income was necessary. In order for the money to change hands, they'd opened an escrow account and consulted a notary to confirm that the contract was valid. All this had taken several weeks, and even after the "transfer of property," as it was called, several more bills arrived pertaining to the sale that had to be settled before the contract could go into effect.

So now Richard is preparing to buy property for the second time in his life, this time in Ghana. Two-and-a-half acres at a price of three thousand euros, in a village in the fertile, rain-blessed region of Ashanti, at a price so cheap compared to the suburbs of Berlin that it seems practically free. How long will it be before a property this far away actually belongs to its new owner? Just as years ago Richard hoped that the bank would approve his mortgage for the requested sum, now he hopes that a Ghanaian king will approve the sale. Richard imagines him as a chieftain with a spear in his hand and jangling ankle bracelets, although he knows perfectly well that if this king is truly powerful, he's probably wearing a Barcelona soccer jersey.

*

The king says yes. And so one gray Berlin day in the middle of January, Richard takes the S-Bahn into the middle of the city with three thousand euros in hundreds stashed in the breast pocket of his winter coat—Karon said to bring cash. He walks beside Karon for a bit down the slushy sidewalk, the crosswalk light is red, turns green, cars honk their horns, it's snowing; they pass a newsstand selling lottery tickets, a shop selling cheap cell phones, a *döner kebab* place, and then around another two corners, Karon knocks on the door of a shop with the shutters rolled down. The door opens, activating a bell that no doubt dates from the time when there was a butcher's shop here or a bakery. They cross the threshold, but what counts here as inside and outside? It's foggy in the room, or smoky, so Richard is only gradually able to make out his surroundings. On stakes all around the room, braids have been tied, and he sees strange fruit piled up high in wooden bowls, some with thorns, some with transparent skin, some look like eggs, others like meat. This fruit is arranged as if around an altar, and in the middle of the room an African woman, her hair in wild disarray, sits on a three-legged stool, before her in the linoleum floor is a crevice from which vapors are rising. (Is there a bomb shelter down there that's caved in?) Young men and women lean silently against the wall, which is covered with colorfully printed fabric, fanning the seated woman with large dried palm fronds, or are they just distributing the steam rising from the crevice to make it possible to see anything at all? Karon speaks with one of the men; meanwhile the woman with the disheveled hair keeps her eyes half-shut as she rocks back and forth, then Karon translates for Richard what has just been explained to him: Richard is to give the money to the woman.

How? Richard asks.

Just like this, Karon says, put it in her lap.

Richard takes the envelope with the money out of his breast pocket and places it in the woman's lap, and the woman, her eyes still half-shut, takes the envelope and with outstretched arm drops it—just as it is, without counting the money—into the crevice in the floor.

The money! Richard shouts and tries to grab it before it's too late, but Karon holds him back and says: No problem.

Will I at least get a receipt or something?

And then the woman begins to laugh, displaying the many pointy gold-capped teeth inside her mouth. But even while laughing she keeps her eyes half-shut.

One of the young men now takes a piece of chewing gum from his pants pocket, unwraps it, puts the gum in his mouth, writes one long and one short number on the back of the crumpled paper, and hands it to Karon.

What are these numbers? asks Richard.

That's all, Karon says, we can go.

Here in this place, Karon knows his way around, and for a moment he's no longer a refugee, he's a man like any other. And then the bell tinkles again, that bell that no doubt tinkled during the first postwar years every time a German housewife left the shop with her purchases. It's still tinkling now, on this day when Richard has bought property in Ghana.

What now? asks Richard.

Now I call my mother and tell her the numbers.

And then?

Then my mother will call Tepa with the first number and say she's coming to get the money.

And then?

Then she will travel one hour to Mim and from there one hour in a share taxi to Tepa. She may have to wait until there are enough passengers for the taxi. So the whole trip takes maybe three hours.

Then in Tepa she'll get the money with the second number.

And then?

Then she'll take a share taxi from Tepa back to Mim, and from there she'll travel back to her village.

She's going to travel across Ghana with three thousand euros in her handbag?

Yes. There is no bank near our village.

I see. And then?

Then she will take three witnesses and go to the house of the man who is selling the property, and she will give him the money.

And then?

Then they will both sign the contract, and then the land belongs to us.

For three hours Richard and Karon sit in a café, waiting for an old woman in a village in Ghana to find someone who can drive her to Mim, for her to find a seat in a share taxi going to Tepa, and then to find the shop in Tepa where twelve thousand Ghanaian cedi will be paid out to her when she gives them a five-digit number. So it wasn't into a bomb cellar that the woman with the disheveled hair dropped the money through the hole in the linoleum floor, in reality she was throwing it directly to Ghana by the shortest possible path, through the Earth's curved crust. Richard remembers the article he read about the notion of the so-called *wormhole:* the idea that a worm eating its way through an apple reaches a given spot on the apple's surface much more quickly than a worm strolling across the apple's round exterior.

What would you like to order?

I don't know, Karon says, I was never in a café before.

Never in a café?

No, Karon says. Once in Italy I sat down in a restaurant at the train station because I had to wait, and they brought me a menu, but at that time I couldn't read it, so I got up and went out.

At first the shop in Tepa is closed, but then there's a different shop, and at first there's no one there, but then there is someone, and when everything has worked out after all, Karon holds his phone out to Richard, and Richard says: Hello, and an old woman in Ghana says: How are you!

That's the only sentence my mother knows in English, Karon says. She is very happy and wanted to thank you personally.

That same evening, Richard receives a photograph of the new deed of sale. It states that Karon is now the owner of a property in Ghana. His mother signed for her eldest son with her thumbprint to acknowledge the transfer of ownership. From the moment that Richard got into the S-Bahn this morning with the money in the breast pocket of his coat, until the moment when his friend Karon owns a piece of land that is now to sustain his family, no more than fourteen hours have passed.

The next morning, Karon sends a text:

Hi richard. i just want to see how are you doing, richard. I don't no how to thanks you. only God no my heart but anyway wat I can say is may God protect you. always Good morning. karon

Always good morning, Richard thinks, indeed what better thing to wish a friend?

48

And now at last Richard heads into town to see what's happening in Friedrichshain. It's been a week now since the refugees occupied the top floor and roof of the residence, and so far no aid organization has been allowed inside to bring the men food and water. Many sympathizers are gathered there, people with white skin and black, young and old, women and men. Surveying the scene before him as best he can amid the chaos, Richard sees no one dancing, singing, or delivering speeches. Many are hopping from one leg to another—not for their entertainment but because it's cold. Tristan, Yaya, Moussa, and Apollo, along with Khalil, Mohamed, Zair, and tall Ithemba stand around a fire barrel close to the blocked-off area, warming their hands. On the roof, no one is visible. The police officers are standing in front of the barricades they've used to cordon off the street, and on the narrow strip of remaining sidewalk, pedestrians pass by muttering under their breath—it's unclear whether their displeasure is aimed at the refugees responsible for this inconvenience or the disproportionate police presence. Yes, Zair says, the telephone network is back, but since yesterday all the occupiers' phone batteries are dead because they don't have electricity to charge them. So you're not in contact with them anymore? No. And soon they won't have anything left to drink because the water was turned off, says Tristan. Actually it's much like on one of the boats that brought the men from Libya, Richard thinks. But you can't drop a plastic bottle over the side of a building to at least have seawater to drink. Richard stays standing there for a while beside the fire barrel. But then he sees Rufu.

Rufu, the moon of Wismar, sits on a bench that hasn't even had the damp snow brushed off it. He too is snow-covered, flakes cling to his hair and coat. Because of this—and also because he's sitting there so quietly—he looks like a monument.

Rufu, how are you? *Come stai*, Rufu?

Rufu tries to lift his head to look at Richard but doesn't manage it.

Richard squats down in front of him, knocking some of the snow off him here and there, but Rufu just keeps staring straight ahead, murmuring something so softly Richard can't understand.

What is it? What are you saying?

Tutto é finito, Rufu says, *Tutto é finito.*

But no, Rufu, no, Richard says, everything isn't over. Sooner or later everything will work out all right, you'll see.

Rufu says something, but in a language that Richard doesn't understand.

Do you want to come with me, Rufu?

Staring straight ahead, silence.

Come read Dante, volume 2?

He is staring straight ahead, silence.

I'll cook for you—we can eat together!

Si, says Rufu at last.

There, you see, it'll all be okay.

Richard tries to help him get up. Like an old man, Rufu cautiously places one foot before the other to move forward, supporting himself by leaning on Richard, who's linked arms with him.

Look, the subway station is just up there.

Rufu makes an effort to look in front of him, but as soon as he realizes that he can't just get into Richard's car but has to take the subway, he shakes his head and stops.

Is it too much for you? Would you rather stay here?

Si.

Richard brings him back to the bench, this old man who's only twenty-four.

Rufu, are you taking some sort of medicine?

Very slowly, Rufu reaches into his pants pocket and retrieves a small slip of paper with a yellow pill wrapped up inside.

What sort of medicine is this?

Non lo so.

How don't you know?

His eyes stare straight ahead, in silence.

Rufu, stop taking these pills, do you hear me?

Si.

I'll come to the residence tomorrow morning, and you can show me the package. Do you understand?

Rufu nods.

Are your friends taking care of you?

Si.

Richard goes back to the others and asks them about Rufu.

We didn't want to leave him alone at the residence, he's really not doing well.

Will you take him back with you?

Certo.

Following the instructions issued by Dr. Richard, Rufu didn't take the yellow pill he had in his pocket. The next morning he's already looking a bit more awake and can move his head more, he can look at Richard, and say *buon giorno*. Richard notes down the name of the medication from the box, the package insert is gone.

At home, Richard looks up the side effects online: *Impairment of the vocal chords, blockage of the respiratory passages, difficulty speaking, difficulty swallowing, cough, pulmonary infection due to inhaled food in the respiratory tract.* Why is Richard suddenly remembering that Bach cantata? Maybe it was hearing Yussuf, the flipped-out future engineer, shouting *Ich habe genug!*—I've had enough!—in front of the Spandau residence. Ah! Would that from the bondage of my body / The Lord might free me. / Ah! My departure, were it here, / With joy I'd say to thee, O world: / I have now had enough. *Viral infection, ear infection, eye infection, stomach or sinus infection, bladder infection, subcutaneous infection, anomalous ventricular depolarization....* Slumber now, ye eyes so weary, / Fall in soft and calm repose! / World, I dwell no longer here, / Since I have no share in thee / Which my soul could offer comfort. *Low blood pressure, dizziness accompanying change of position, accelerated or slowed heart rate, disorientation, low energy, muscle weakness or pain, anomalous posture.* Here I must with sorrow reckon, / But yet, there, there I shall witness / Sweet repose and quiet rest.

Discomfort in the chest, skin inflammation, reduced appetite, impaired loco-motion and balance, impaired speech, chills and fever, painful sensitivity to light. My God! When comes that blessed "Now!" / When I in peace shall walk forever / In the sand of earth's own coolness / And there within thy bosom rest? / My parting is achieved, / O world, good night! *Numbness of the face, arms, or legs, stroke, ringing in the ears, loss of consciousness.* Rejoicing do I greet my death, / Ah, would that it had come already. / I'll escape then all the woe / Which doth here in the world confine me.

What had snow-covered Rufu said?

Tutto é finito.

Richard doesn't want to, but eventually he does put in a call to Jörg, the mustached husband of Monika who's a psychiatrist.

This is a drug we generally prescribe only to old people who are manic or hyperactive and might attack other residents in a nursing home or who can't settle down at night.

But he was always very calm, says Richard.

Maybe it comes in fits.

In any case this drug is pure poison.

He's still taking it, right?

Well . . .

What—you discontinued it? From one day to the next? That's not a good idea.

Richard tries to explain.

I see, Jörg says suddenly. It's a refugee. I understand.

What difference does that make?

Well, it's perfectly simple: these guys still believe in the medicine man. You dance around him in a circle a few times, and he'll be as good as new.

Jörg begins to hoot with laughter.

How many times did Richard go on vacation with Jörg and Monika? In GDR times, they always went to Hungary, and later there
were trips to France and Spain. How many times did he sit with
them drinking wine, complaining about this or that government,
or go for walks, or visit museums? A doctor can certainly aim to
serve humanity in general, but there's also nothing stopping him if
he prefers to reserve his services for a particular sector of humanity.
One Dr. Thaler, for example, two hundred years ago in Vienna, removed the skin of Soliman—a native-born Nigerian—after his de-
mise with the most illustrious permission of Kaiser Franz himself.
He flayed this man who'd saved the life of Prince von Lobkowitz in
battle, stripped the skin of this Negro named Soliman, flayed the tu-
tor to the royal house of Liechtenstein, a black man named Soliman;
he removed the skin of this Freemason of the lodge True Concord, a
moor who bore the name Soliman, he flayed the skin of the brother,
as it were, of Freemasons Mozart and Schikaneder, the sponsor of
scientist Ignaz von Born when he applied for incorporation in the
lodge; he removed the skin of an African named Soliman, skinned
a married Viennese gentleman who mastered six languages, whose
daughter later married Baron von Feuchtersleben and whose grandson Eduard rose to prominence as a poet in the early nineteenth century, in other words removed the skin of a respected member of
Viennese society who, to be sure, had once, a long time before, been
African, a child named Soliman, he skinned this person who early on
in his life had been traded for a horse at the slave market and was later
sold to someone in Messina—Soliman by name—he flayed this former slave of lowly race. He then tanned the skin, stretched it upon a
body made of wood, and, disregarding the request by the daughter
of the deceased that *the skin of her father be relinquished to her, that it might
be interred*— this daughterly request was disregarded, and her stuffed

father was placed in a display case on the fourth floor of the Imperial Cabinet of Natural Curiosities for the edification of the Viennese. Admittedly, the skirt of feathers with which the moor was adorned had been crafted by South American Indians, and so was not entirely accurate from an academic perspective, but it did nicely accentuate the exotic nature of the specimen.

For a moment Richard tries to imagine a display case in the National Museum in Cairo containing, for instance, the stuffed skin of archaeologist Heinrich Schliemann dressed in a Spanish matador's costume or a traditional Mongolian garment made of sheepskin and silk. What barbarians! one might justifiably exclaim in regard to such Egyptian museum directors. In Vienna, the "Noble Savage" was removed from display at some point, but not to be buried, instead he was placed in storage and left there—dusty and all but forgotten—until finally during the Vienna Uprising in 1848 a fire took mercy on his mortal remains.

There are black birds in the world, so why shouldn't there be black people? To Richard, this sentence from the opera *The Magic Flute* always used to adequately explain everything there was to say about differences in skin color. At the same time, it doesn't surprise him that a conversation about a patient from Niger should reveal to him whom he can still count as a friend in today's Germany and whom he cannot.

Rufu doesn't have Italian health insurance because his *permesso* has expired and for a while now he's been too sick to make the trip to Italy to get it renewed. Rufu doesn't have German health insurance either, since he isn't allowed to apply for asylum in Germany. For the treatment of acute pain, the Social Welfare Office can issue a health insurance voucher, but the patient must first submit an application and prove that something hurts. Richard doesn't ask Rufu whether he's gone to the Social Welfare Office to file an application, bringing evidence to support his claim that he's feeling poorly.

I'll pay for the exam, Richard says.

Don't worry about it, replies the young resident at the psychiatric practice around the corner from Richard's former institute.

Are you in pain? the psychiatrist then asks Rufu.

Richard translates. Rufu nods.

What exactly hurts?

Rufu points to his head, his temples, ears, and jaws.

Can you please open your mouth wide?

No.

Why not?

Rufu points between his teeth to the interior of his mouth.

May I? asks the doctor, and inserts a small mirror into Rufu's mouth. Through the gap between Rufu's teeth, he shines a light on the dark cavity and then says: There's a huge hole in a tooth on the right side.

A hole in a tooth?

Yes, a hole in a tooth.

Rufu had spent Christmas confined to a psychiatric ward of a Berlin hospital and, after his release, was prescribed medication that—as Richard sees it—nearly killed him, and now it turns out the reason for all of this may have been just a hole in a tooth.

As so often, this examination has revealed that everything depends on asking the right questions.

Rufu has most certainly never been to a dentist before. He may not even know that mankind has invented dentistry, but he obediently sits down on the chair in the dentist's office where Richard is a patient, after which it takes only a few minutes for the dentist to seal up the hole in Rufu's tooth.

Everyone I've ever seen with a hole like this, the dentist says, was going out of his mind with pain. The pain is so intense that the patient often becomes unable to situate it, which makes the anamnesis difficult.

What do I owe you? says Richard.

It's okay, don't worry about it, the dentist says.

49

Where has Osarobo gone?

Go, went, gone.

For a week now Richard has been trying to reach him by phone. *The number you are attempting to reach is temporarily unavailable.* And none of the men has been able to tell him where Osarobo is, no one's seen him since the Friday before last. So Richard calls Osarobo right back the moment he texts him: *Hi.*

Where are you staying?

With a friend.

What friend?

A man from the Ivory Coast.

Where do you know him from?

He talked to me at Oranienplatz.

Aha.

He's got papers.

Okay.

Do you have work for me?

No, Richard says. In winter he can't even have Osarobo rake leaves.

I need work, work, Osarobo says.

I know, Richard says, but it's difficult right now.

Okay.

Osarobo had learned how to get from the red-brick building to Richard's house, and then came the move to Spandau. He learned how to get to Richard's house by S-Bahn from Spandau, and now he's staying in Berlin-Reinickendorf with a friend from the Ivory Coast. They started working on the C-major scale a few months ago. When they started on the bass line for a simple blues, there was the move to Spandau. They reviewed the C-major scale and the bass line for a simple blues, it was early January, and then the first list of evictions appeared with Osarobo's name on it. Now if they go back to the music lessons, they'll be starting over, with the C-major scale and the bass line for a simple blues.

Time does something to a person, because a human being isn't a machine that can be switched on and off. The time during which a person doesn't know how his life can become a life fills a person condemned to idleness from his head down to his toes.

This morning Richard received an invitation to participate in a colloquium in Frankfurt am Main. They're asking him to lecture on the topic "Reason as Fiery Matter in the Work of the Stoic Philosopher Seneca." The colloquium is already the week after next, so he's obviously only been invited because of someone's last-minute cancellation. During his years at the Institute, Richard wrote two books about Seneca, so putting together such a talk wouldn't be hard for him. Nonetheless he sets the letter aside and goes down to the dock to have a look at the lake.

The lake has meanwhile frozen solid. Since it hasn't snowed since the last frost, the ice is as clear as black glass. Richard sees a few reeds, leaves, and blades of sea grass frozen in the ice, and beneath its surface, in the depths of the lake where the water is still liquid, he even glimpses a large fish swimming slowly past. Other years, he's often gone strolling right across the frozen lake with Detlef and Sylvia, but this year no one has proposed such an outing. What if the drowned man tried calling out to them from beneath the ice, and they saw him beneath their feet, his mouth open, hands groping around to find an opening in the frozen surface, but in the time it would take them to fetch an axe and chop it open, he'd have sunk back down to the bottom?

Do you want to come play the piano again? he asks Osarobo.

Okay, Osarobo says.

Maybe tomorrow?

No problem.

After he hangs up, Richard writes to the organizers of the colloquium in Frankfurt accepting their invitation and then for a moment imagines his former colleagues sitting in a large auditorium two weeks from now, giving papers, listening to each other, discussing—and he too will sit there, give his paper, listen to the others, and discuss, there'll be six speakers on a single day, he'll be the second one, and in the break between papers there'll be coffee from large thermos flasks in the foyer, orange juice, mineral water, and a few cookies.

Is that still his life?

Was it ever his life?

Over the past twenty-five years—in other words, ever since he was suddenly promoted to the rank of citizen of the Federal Republic of Germany—he has numbered among the professional elite. Even today he might still receive an invitation to speak when someone else cancels. But his departure from this world is attracting far less notice than his entry into it. Eventually some invitation will turn out to have been the last in his life as a scholar—but which invitation exactly is something that, fortunately, will become clear only in retrospect, when he himself is no longer in a position to notice.

He'll probably still know some of the colleagues at the symposium in Frankfurt, and maybe that Tacitus specialist will show up, the one he had an interesting talk with at a congress the January before last. But when the others go out for dinner afterward—

all these clever, eccentric, ambitious, shy, tedious, obsessed, vain scholars—he'll be on the train back to Berlin with no regrets. And when the others lay their heads on their single-room pillows in a Frankfurt hotel, he'll already be walking through the darkness between the trees in his own garden. And when the others show up for the second day of the colloquium wearing their second ironed shirts, he'll be looking at the lake.

What are you living on now? asks Richard the next day.

Osaboro shrugs his shoulders.

Sometimes, he says, I help with the packages.

At the post office?

No, packages to send to Africa.

For an aid organization?

Yes, like that.

Is it paid work?

Twenty euros per day.

For how many hours?

All day.

And how many days a week?

Last week I was there once. And maybe again in a week or two.

Oh, I see.

At Oranienplatz, people were always coming by who had work for us. But now no one can find us.

We become visible, Richard thinks.

In March I want to go to Italy.

Which city? Richard asks.

Osarobo shrugs his shoulders.

Do you have work there?

Osarobo shrugs his shoulders.

So there are only six or eight weeks left for piano lessons before Osarobo leaves, Richard thinks, and again he notes the feeling of panic rising up in him. Maybe he really can succeed in teaching

Osarobo a couple of short pieces so that he can earn some money playing the roll-up piano on the street.

When Markus, the son of Detlef and Marion, was fifteen years old, his stepfather would quiz him over dinner about the periodic table. When he was sixteen, Detlef got him an internship in an engineering firm, and when he was taking his graduating exams, Marion made him muesli with freshly grated apples to help him concentrate. Now Markus builds bridges in China.

When Osarobo was fifteen, he saw his father and friends being killed.

And he's seen for three years now that the world doesn't want him.

Do you remember C major? asks Richard.

50

Originally, Richard just planned to rework what he'd already written in his two books about Seneca, but the moment he starts flipping through Seneca's "Of Peace of Mind," new ideas come to him, and he realizes how much pleasure his work still gives him. Let his colleagues see whom they've shunted off into retirement with a fully functioning brain. If reason really is fiery matter— as Diogenes was the first to claim—this can best be seen in the way thinkers have taken up the thoughts of other thinkers over the course of centuries, each endeavoring to add something of his own as a way of keeping the thoughts alive. Just as Richard reads in Seneca—*Kindly remember that he whom you call your slave sprang from the same stock, is smiled upon by the same skies, and on equal terms with yourself breathes, lives, and dies*—Seneca in turn reads in Plato: *Every king springs from a race of slaves, and every slave has had kings among his ancestors. The flight of time, with its vicissitudes, has jumbled all such things together, and Fortune has turned them upside down.* And did not Ovid at the end of his *Metamorphoses* present the same thoughts found in Empedocles? *Thus are their figures never at a stand, / But chang'd by Nature's innovating hand; / All things are alter'd, nothing is destroy'd, / The shifted scene for some new show employ'd. / Then, to be born, is to begin to be / Some other thing we were not formerly: / And what we call to die, is not t' appear, / Or be the thing, that formerly we were.* To Richard—and also to his friends Detlef, Sylvia, and Andreas, the Hölderlin reader—the thought of everlasting flux and the ephemeral nature of all human constructs, the sense that all existing order is vulnerable to reversal, has always seemed perfectly natural, maybe because of their postwar childhoods, or else it was witnessing the fragility of the Socialist system under which they'd lived most of their lives and that collapsed within a matter of weeks.

Could these long years of peacetime be to blame for the fact that a new generation of politicians apparently believes we've now arrived at the end of history, making it possible to use violence to suppress all further movement and change? Or have the people living here under untroubled circumstances and at so great a distance from the wars of others been afflicted with a poverty of experience, a sort of emotional anemia? Must living in peace—so fervently wished for throughout human history and yet enjoyed in only a few parts of the world—inevitably result in refusing to share it with those seeking refuge, defending it instead so aggressively that it almost looks like war?

And might reason's journey also be compared to what these men have been through? How did you get to Libya? he asks tall Ithemba, who is standing beside him, warming his hands at the fire barrel. Across the Algerian border, three days on foot across a rocky desert. Some just lie down and can't go on. You leave them behind. You keep walking. What else are you supposed to do? There's nothing you can do to help them. And everything becomes heavy there, he says, you throw your shirt away (like this! he says, making a sweeping gesture with his arm), you throw your shoes away (and he mimes throwing away his one pair of shoes in the hot, rocky desert). Everything is too heavy, you have to walk for three days. The only thing you absolutely need is a canister of water. Richard looks up at the roof of the building, upon which at the moment only a single man is visible. The man leans against a chimney and just stands there. Did he too pass through the rocky desert? For thirteen days now, the men have been up there insisting on what was promised them in the Agreement: aid and assistance in pursuing vocational opportunities, among other things. Richard sees the man standing up there, high above the city, and thinks of the dead man lying beneath the lake. Suddenly this waiting seems to him like a set of parentheses bracketing off everything taking place on the ground.

And might memory too be compared to what these men have been through? How do you bury the dead in the desert? Richard asks Apollo. This is the question that went unanswered the day when the alarm suddenly went off. You push the sand apart in the middle of a dune, Apollo says, and make a furrow, and then you lay the dead man inside. You pray. How do you pray? Apollo takes Richard aside, stepping with him into a doorway that offers protection from the biting wind. Apollo crosses his hands before him, looks down, and begins to recite the prayer for the dead. Beneath his feet is a grating still marked with words left over from wartime Germany: *Mannesmann Civil Air Defense*. And then? Then you push the sand back over the dead man. Do you mark the grave? No, but you know where the spot is forever.

Maybe what these men have lived through also says something about power and powerlessness. Richard asks Khalil, who is poking around in the fire with a stick, what his crossing was like. Khalil

242

says: I was only afraid of the water, so I stayed below deck. A friend of mine who stayed up above died because the sun beat down so hard. He died of thirst. On Rashid's boat, Richard remembers, the passengers below deck had no chance at all when their boat capsized. Everything had immediately flooded, Rashid had told him on Christmas Eve. Richard observes the changing of the guard in front of the asylum seekers' residence, during which for several minutes the number of police officers in attendance isn't one hundred but two hundred.

The next morning—Richard's about to start incorporating the notes he made while standing in front of the occupied building into his paper—he learns that the Berlin Senate has retroactively declared the agreement they made with the refugees invalid. Apparently a law professor from Konstanz was called in for a consultation and discovered that a crucial signature was unfortunately—unfortunately!—missing from the document. Richard knows that various international human rights organizations have protested the actions being taken by the Berlin Senate against the refugees barricaded on the residence's top floor, and he assumes there's a direct link between these criticisms and the report solicited from the distant jurist. If a contract isn't binding, then a breach of this contract doesn't constitute legitimate grounds for a protest. A few words arriving on letterhead from Konstanz have declared the refugee's expectations—precisely at this moment when it seemed they might finally be met—to be without basis.

Later, on TV, Richard watches the police drag off Rashid and a few others who've responded to this news by demonstratively trying to construct an igloo in the snow on Oranienplatz, so as, logically, to also take back their part of the agreement. The violence with which the police go about clearing the square has its roots in the incestuous relationship between the law and its interpretation, Richard thinks, in other words, all of this is based only on a bit of ink on a bit of paper. Given this state of affairs, Richard is looking forward with particular curiosity to his first visit to Ithemba's lawyer tomorrow—he promised Ithemba to accompany him.

51

When he resigned from the papacy, Pope Benedict declared that Europe rested upon three pillars: Greek philosophy, Roman law, and the Judeo-Christian religion. Tall Ithemba's lawyer is very proud of his Roman law. When he gets up to pull Ithemba's file, Richard sees he is wearing an honest-to-goodness frock coat; the tails of this museum-worthy garment are slightly faded but nonetheless flap jauntily in a breeze of inexplicable origin in this dark, stuffy office. In Germany, we eat paper, the lawyer says and starts to giggle as he sits down again and adjusts his sleeve protectors. We eat *paper*, he says again, barely able to suppress his laughter. Paper! he sputters, the Germans eat paper! He now has tears of laughter in his eyes. He looks at Richard and Ithemba expectantly, but Ithemba doesn't laugh back, because he doesn't understand what his lawyer is saying. Richard wonders whether the lawyer is referring to what Ithemba said to Richard just a moment before in the waiting room as they sat on folding chairs among Vietnamese, Romanians, and other Africans, looking across at the innumerable file folders on the shelf beside the secretary's desk: *You can't eat paper.* But how can the lawyer have heard this sentence through the double doors leading to his office? I'm seventy-two years old, he says now, suddenly looking rather like an owl, seventy-two! and starts to giggle again, as if this were really a fantastic trick he's played on the authorities—not retiring, but instead raising objections when the Social Welfare Office pays this or that asylum seeker only 280 euros instead of the requisite 362, or when the Foreigners Office confiscates the Italian-issued IDs of African refugees so as to force them to leave the country, returning their documents to them only at the border when they present their tickets: They absolutely aren't allowed to do that! These are Italian documents! Besides which he takes serious umbrage—serious!—that the State of Berlin, the nation's capital, deviates from the practice of other German states by sending Serbian Roma and Sinti families with tiny children back to the slums of Belgrade even when the temperature is well below freezing, instead of granting them the winter stay of deportation that is customary elsewhere. Which he mentions only by the way. They send the children back! he can't help practically shouting, tiny children! The only ray of light in this entire sad world is the new pope, it's no coincidence his name is Francis: *Where compassion is and prudence is, is neither waste nor hardness of heart!* And after Francis, the lawyer soon comes to speak of the ancient Romans: *Tunc tua res agitur paries cum proximus ardet!* and is very pleased when Richard nods in assent and promptly murmurs the translation: Your own property is in peril when your neighbor's house burns.

Tall Ithemba meanwhile sits very quietly beside Richard, not understanding a word of what these two old men are saying, he doesn't know why they are laughing, he just has to sit there waiting to see whether there is something to be done or considered regarding his case. Richard can see how the sight of the innumerable files stacked on the shelves and tables has terrified Ithemba, that's why he sits there so quietly. Hundreds of brightly colored adhesive tabs are hanging out of the jaws of these files, drawing attention to hundreds of particular circumstances of life-changing import. Richard has sometimes heard Ithemba mention having an appointment with "the Social," by which he means the Social Welfare Office, or with "the Foreigners," by which he means the Foreigners Office, but it was a while before Richard understood that for Ithemba merely mentioning these appointments was already an expression of extreme horror. Ithemba, whom no military patrol on the Libyan border had dared to interrogate, who walked through the rocky desert for three days in scorching heat, who had demanded the day after his arrival in Lampedusa that he be returned to Libya—unfortunately this wasn't possible for the Italians—Ithemba, who has a glass eye and stands 6'3", is filled with terror on seeing a handful of words typed on official Berlin letterhead (the Brandenburg Gate in the upper right-hand corner and an eagle stamped on the lower left).

And maybe he should be glad he doesn't yet understand what was being communicated to him:

False statements may lead to the rejection of the application for a residence permit or stay of deportation (exceptional leave to remain), or to immediate expulsion. In accordance with the provisions governing the benefits for which you have been approved, you agree to communicate immediately any change of circumstances relevant to the receipt of your benefits. Please note that the above confirmation has no bearing on (does not extend) the legally mandated expiry date of your stay in Germany. Where conditions sufficient for deportation are found to exist, you may be deported at any time, even before the date of the interview given above. If you fail to leave the country as directed, you may be instructed to appear in person at the Foreigners Office (see Residency Law §82, para.4, p.1). If you fail to appear as instructed without adequate justification, you may be forcibly compelled to appear.

The lawyer is now flipping through the file, marking a passage here and there, adding additional yellow, green, and pink adhesive tabs, dictating letters to various agencies into his Dictaphone at frightening speed. Richard and Ithemba, sitting side by side, simply wait. A German child! the lawyer suddenly shouts at them—that's the one thing that would really make a difference. A German child! Can't he see that two men are sitting here, and one of them is moreover quite advanced in years? Then he goes on flipping, dictating: Dear colleague, allow me to draw your attention, with collegial greetings, etc.

But even an *exceptional leave to remain* would be a good thing, wouldn't it? asks Richard when the lawyer briefly puts down his Dictaphone. Then the men—at least this is what he's heard—would be able to start looking for work in nine months, no?

After nine months! the lawyer repeats, once more bursting into laughter.

Richard says, I was talking about the *exceptional leave to remain*.

Sure, the lawyer replies, continuing to flip through this file and that, giving no further response.

I mean that then they'd be able to look for work, Richard reiterates.

Of course they can look for it, the lawyer says. Flipping here, flipping there.

What do you mean? asks Richard.

Ever hear of the Preferential Employment Provision? He abruptly glances up and gives Richard a sharp look through the thick lenses of his glasses. He really does look like an owl.

No, says Richard.

Well, the Preferential Employment Provision stipulates that only in cases where no German and no European wants a job can this gentleman here, for instance—the owl glances into a folder—can Mr. Awad have a shot at it.

Even so, Richard says.

And before he's allowed to apply, the Foreigners Office has to specifically grant him permission to submit an application.

Surely permission would be granted in such a case.

Well . . . , the lawyer says.

What do you mean?

First the Foreigners Office sends his job application to the Federal Employment Agency with a request that they confirm that the employer is in compliance with the Preferential Employment Provision. This confirmation is often a long time coming, no one can say why. When the response from the Federal Employment Agency finally arrives, the Foreigners Office begins its own investigation.

247

All of this can take three months, even four. And sometimes the decision is in the negative.

Why?

You'll have to ask the ladies and gentlemen at the Foreigners Office.

Tall Ithema sits there in silence, staring straight ahead, while the two old gentlemen are conferring about his prospects. Since he has a glass eye, Richard thinks, he probably sees all the stacks of files lying around the office in two dimensions.

And even when the authorities agree, the lawyer says, the job must still be available after the entire procedure, which requires an exceptionally patient employer.

I understand, Richard says.

Richard sees that the wooden window frames in the lawyer's office have become visibly spongy in the heat and humidity of the past hundred years. The paint on the walls is yellowed all the way up to the fourteen-foot ceiling, and there's a plain linoleum floor. When Richard called to ask if he could pay Ithemba's monthly charge for two months in advance, the secretary said: Just go ahead and pay the one. A monthly installment amounts to fifty euros, and in the course of nine months, these installments add up to 450 euros, the minimum charge for an asylum case according to the Lawyers' Compensation Act. The lawyer's work ethic, as can be clearly seen by the condition of his office, has little to do with notions like cost recovery, let alone profitability.

But, Richard says, what about the category of understaffed professions? He'd promised Rashid, the metalworker, to ask the lawyer about this. On the internet he'd read that in fields in which skilled tradesmen were urgently needed in Germany, immediate employment was possible for those in possession of an *exceptional leave to remain*.

Yes, the lawyer says, but in such cases the Foreigners Office requires the applicant to prove his identity by securing a passport
his home country or at least a birth certificate.

And? asks Richard.

He might succeed in getting the passport.

In which case everything's fine?

As long as no one's playing bilateral poker.

What do you mean? asks Richard. He hears tall Ithemba pulling on his fingers under the table, making his knuckles crack.

Sometimes the government of such a country is trying to get some sort of political concession from Germany, a trade agreement, maybe even weapons. In return, they agree to take back the people whose presence in Germany is based only on an exceptional leave to remain and who hold passports issued by them.

In other words Germany is perfectly happy to get rid of the skilled workers among the refugees. Do I understand correctly? asks Richard.

You could put it that way, the lawyer says.

Ithemba asks now, What is he saying?

I'll explain later, says Richard.

You also mustn't forget, the lawyer says, that these gentlemen from Oranienplatz don't even *have* an exceptional leave to remain, and even if they did, that doesn't provide any sort of residency status.

Then what is it?

A leave to remain is just a *temporary suspension of deportation*. The lawyer draws out these words, savoring them, just the way Yussuf savored the word *dishwasher* when he first learned it.

Richard feels a headache coming on, gradually eating its way from his forehead across his temples to the back of his head. But there's still one last bullet point on his list:

And section 23? he asks, adding that he's read on the internet that if a country, a government, or a mayor so wishes, EU regulations can be disregarded and a person applying for asylum can simply be accepted, even in a country that according to the laws governing requests for asylum, is not in fact responsible.

It doesn't particularly surprise Richard that the lawyer responds with only a single word:

249

If.

I understand, says Richard, finding himself sorely overtaxed by this visit.

Haven't you read the Berlin Senate's declaration? asks the lawyer, speaking gently now, as if to an invalid who has to be encouraged to swallow a bitter pill.

What declaration?

It was in all the papers yesterday, the lawyer says, quoting from memory:

In the interest of completeness let it also be noted that granting residence permits under §23 para.1 of the Residence Act to participants in the protest movement at Oranienplatz would not serve to uphold the political interests of the Federal Republic of Germany.

No, I didn't read that, Richard says.

So listen, the owl says now: The more highly developed a society is, the more its written laws come to replace common sense. In Germany, I estimate that only two-thirds of our laws are still anchored in the emotional lives of the people, as it were. The other third are laws pure and simple, formulated with such a high level of precision and abstraction that all basis in human emotion has become superfluous and thus ceases to exist. Two thousand years ago, no one was more hospitable than the Teutons. Surely you are acquainted with the lovely section in Tacitus's *Germania* devoted to our ancestors' hospitality?

Yes, Richard says, nodding.

May I recall the passage in question for you?

You may.

The lawyer gets up, goes over to the bookshelf, his coattails flapping in the inexplicable office breeze, pulls his Tacitus off the shelf, and opens the small book at a page marked by a slip of paper.

Ithemba, who can see that the conversation with the lawyer is nearing its end, carefully gathers up his papers, stacking them neatly, and puts them back in the folder he brought with him expressly for this purpose. Richard nods to him, and now the lawyer begins his recital: *It is accounted a sin to turn any man away from your door. The host welcomes his guest with the best meal that his means allow. When he has finished entertaining him, the host undertakes a fresh role: he accompanies the guest to the nearest house where further hospitality can be had. It makes no difference that they come uninvited; they are welcomed just as warmly. No distinction is ever made between acquaintance and stranger as far as the right to hospitality is concerned. As the guest takes his leave, it is customary to let him have anything he asks for; and the host, with as little hesitation, will ask for a gift in return.* The lawyer claps the book shut and asks Richard: And nowadays?

And nowadays? asks Richard in return, feeling a faint sense of hope.

Now, two thousand years later, we're left with section 23, paragraph 1 of the Residence Act.

The lawyer places one hand over his heart and bows as if he's just completed a little theatrical performance. Then he opens the double doors and says: If you'll be so kind, thus indicating that their appointment is over. Richard knows perfectly well how many Romanians, Vietnamese, and Africans are still waiting outside. As he passes the coat rack on his way out with Ithemba—there really is a top hat on the shelf above—he finds himself almost entirely convinced that this lawyer, who reminds him of an owl, must have flapped his way from some previous century into the twenty-first, this new and yet already so old century with its endless streams of people who, having survived the passage across a real-life sea, are now drowning in rivers and oceans of paper.

52

And then comes the day Richard leaves for Frankfurt am Main. In the morning, while Osarobo is practicing the piano, he prints out

251

his lecture, proofreads it, and shows Osarobo the manuscript even though he obviously can't read it in the German.

This is for a newspaper?

No, it's a lecture, I'll read it aloud.

People are coming here?

No, I'm going to take a train to Frankfurt am Main tonight. I was invited to visit and read this lecture.

And then?

Then we'll talk about it.

Aha.

Do you know Frankfurt am Main?

No. Only Würzburg.

Würzburg, Richard remembers, is where the first Oranienplatz refugees arrived from two years ago. Even before they set out on their march, they'd made headlines, since several of them had sewn their mouths shut to draw attention to their precarious situation. Involuntarily he looks to see whether Osarobo has scars, but his mouth looks normal.

I'll be back the day after tomorrow, Richard says.

Okay, Osarobo says.

Shall we have a cup of tea before you leave?

Okay.

And so for the first time they sit together in the kitchen drinking tea.

One day later, Richard stands before the podium in a lecture hall in Frankfurt, giving his paper on "Reason as Fiery Matter in the Work of Seneca the Stoic" before an audience of classical philologists. He speaks not only about reason, but also about memory, power, and powerlessness. He isn't sure if this is the same sort of talk he used to give during his years at the Institute. During the break, there's coffee in big thermos flasks, and also orange juice, mineral water, and a few cookies.

Unfortunately the Tacitus specialist isn't there this time, but there are a few others Richard knows, and they come over to say hello and clap him on the shoulder: So, how's retirement treating you? What, you're no longer at the Institute? Haven't seen you in a while—how long has it been? Well, I'm flying over to Boston next week. So-and-so is extremely interesting. Have you heard about the retranslation of.

No one says a word about his paper. Richard doesn't know if this is a good or a bad sign. There are three women among the scholars, including one with insanely high heels, but he doesn't wind up speaking with her. As for the rest, the people here are like people always are at this sort of symposium: clever, stupid, eccentric, ambitious, shy, obsessed with their fields. When the others go back to the hotel to rest for a while before meeting for dinner, he's already carrying his overnight bag to the station and getting on a train. And when the others are just laying their heads on their single-room hotel pillows in Frankfurt, he's already found his car in the garage under Berlin's Hauptbahnhof, driven back to the suburbs, and now he is walking in the dark between the trees to his house. When he goes inside, it's very cold. Did he leave a window open somewhere—now, in the middle of winter?

The drawers of his desk have been pulled out and are stacked this way and that on the floor. Documents and photographs are strewn everywhere. The wooden housing of an old music box was splintered when it was pried open. Richard goes from one room to the next. Some English money is scattered on the rug, the wallet lying beside it, and over here a cabinet door stands wide open. Upstairs in the bedroom his wife's costume jewelry is strewn on the floor, in the bathroom the cardboard box he keeps his medicine in has been dumped out into the sink, and finally, when he comes downstairs again, wondering what the source of all the cold air is, he sees the window pried from its frame in the music room. He closes the door to the music room behind him, then goes down to the basement and through all the rooms of the lower floor to reassure himself that he's alone in the house. The computer—which would have been easy enough to take—and the TV are still there at least. Richard leaves everything the way it is and goes upstairs. In bed, after he's turned out the light, he tries for a moment to imagine what the rooms in his house would look like when illuminated only by a flashlight. It would probably be like picking one's way through an impenetrable landscape in which everything concealed in darkness appeared hostile, even just a couple of chairs, a pile of books, a houseplant, a jacket on a hanger. Didn't he himself go wandering through the dark house at night not long ago?

The next morning, two investigators come by to collect evidence, coating everything the thief must have touched with a black powder. Do you have any suspicions who it might be? No. Well, it could have been much worse, you got lucky. Really? Oh, yes. Sometimes the burglars pull every last thing off the shelves, clothes, books, you name it. Apparently he had no use for the British pounds. And he didn't take the computer! True, the other policeman says, this was a respectful burglary. It shows. Respectful? asks Richard. Well, so to speak. Take a few days to look through everything carefully and see what's missing. Here's the claim form, you'll need it for the insurance.

A little later, a repairman comes by to screw the unbroken window firmly back into its frame. That'll hold for now, you don't have to worry. I'm not worried, says Richard.

Not until early afternoon does Richard call Detlef and Sylvia to tell them what happened. That's really awful, Detlef says, but I'm glad you happened to be out of town. What did they steal? Richard had seen at a glance what was missing when he gathered up the inexpensive jewelry left behind on the floor: his mother's ring, the only piece of jewelry she'd brought with her when she fled from Silesia to Berlin. As a child, he'd sometimes held the black opal up to the light to make the red and green lines in the depths of the stone flash. When he and Christel got married, his mother gave the ring to his new wife as an heirloom, but Christel never wore it, she said it was impractical and got caught on everything. Also gone is the gold bangle bracelet he'd once brought back for Christel from Uzbekistan, and a ring she was once given by Krause the dentist, her lover before his time: a sapphire in the middle, surrounded by small diamonds.

Krause died late last year.

The envelope in which Richard always keeps a few hundred-euro bills, so as not to have to drive to the bank all the time, is still lying amid the socks in his dresser drawer, the thief didn't find it.

Want to come over? says Detlef.

Did anyone know you were going to be away that night? Yes, Richard says. One of your Africans? asks Sylvia. Yes, says Richard. Which one? The piano player. That would be a real shame, says Sylvia. But that definitely doesn't mean it was him, says Detlef, there've been so many burglaries around here. Do you remember last year when all the tools were stolen out of the neighbors' shed across the way—and who was it? Ralf's nephew. Ralf is the president of the Anglers' Club. That's right, says Sylvia, and there was a break-in at Claudia's too—the pharmacist—when they were away over Christmas. She was just telling me about it. Richard nods a few times, says yes and no a few times, drinks two glasses of whiskey, and then goes home.

The next morning he calls Anne, whom he hasn't been in touch with since New Year's.

Sylvia told me what happened, she says. Listen, she says, when Ali was living here, he could have stolen all sorts of things. He could have done anything to me or my mother. But, when it was over, he didn't even want to let me pay him any more than we'd agreed on.

Was there something going on between the two of you?

Anne bursts out laughing: He's twenty-three!

Richard has actually forgotten for a moment that Anne's as old as he is, for a moment he's forgotten his own age. Was it really fifty years ago that he lay beside a buck-naked Anne on the floor of some farmhouse, her hair in such disarray that she said: Now I have a bird's nest on my head!

Just try to find out whether or not it was your piano player.

He's always asking me for work, Richard says. He probably doesn't have anything else to live on.

So you do think it was him. You're judging him without giving him a chance to defend himself. That isn't nice.

What would be nice?

Ask him if he did it.

And if he did?

You said the thief took your mother's ring.

Yes.

That's terrible.

I guess so. But it's not as if I had any plans for it in the end.

Seriously, Richard, you know what you can do with your excuses.

Richard can hear that Anne, as always, is doing her dishes while she's on the phone. She's no doubt wedged the phone between her ear and shoulder, and from time to time she blows a strand of hair out of her face (her hands are wet) to keep it from falling into her mouth as she speaks. He can hear her blowing her hair aside, and also the sound of the streaming water.

If it really was him who stole your ring, you have to yell at him! Tell him that you want your goddamn ring back. Make a scene!

Why would I do that?

Because you have to take him seriously. If you make excuses for his betrayal, then you're basically just putting on airs, playing the morally superior European.

Why exactly hadn't Anne or he thought about becoming a couple fifty years ago?

You're saying that I should file a police report if it was him?

Why no, Anne says, speaking patiently as if to a slow child, this has nothing to do with the police. The point is that you care what he does.

I understand.

Then there's silence for a while.

Richard, are you still there?

Hey, Richard says, how come the two of us never got together?

Are you drunk?

After he hangs up, Richard sends Osarobo a message of the sort he's sent him several times before:

Tomorrow?

Okay, Osarobo writes back.

At two p.m.?

Okay.

Now Richard puts on rubber gloves and wipes down all the surfaces blackened by the police, he puts everything back in its place, pushes the drawers back into their slots, and lowers the blind in the music room so you can't see the missing bits in the window frame.

He spends the rest of the day at his computer, typing whatever comes to his mind in the box for search terms:

Probability

Probability is the measure of the likelihood that an event will occur. Probability is quantified as a number between zero and one (where zero indicates impossibility and one indicates certainty).

The higher the probability of an event, the greater our certainty that the event will occur.

Certainty

Certainty is perfect knowledge that is entirely safe from error, or the mental state of being without doubt. Objectively defined, certainty is the total continuity and validity of all foundational inquiry, to the highest degree of precision. Subjective certainty is the absence of doubt regarding convictions felt to be sufficiently grounded in fact, often with reference to natural or moral states of affairs. Factors contributing to a sense of certainty may include evidence, the reliability of expert opinions, as well as external circumstances like widely held beliefs, and internal modalities like emotional stability.

Schrödinger's Cat

A cat is penned up in a steel chamber. In a Geiger counter, secured against direct interference by the cat, is a tiny bit of radioactive substance, so small, that perhaps in the course of the hour one of the atoms decays, but also, with equal probability, perhaps none. If an atom decays, the counter tube discharges and through a relay releases a hammer that shatters a small flask of hydrocyanic acid. If one leaves this entire system to itself for an hour, one could say that the cat still lives if meanwhile no atom has decayed. The first decay of an atom would poison it.

Cat State

In quantum mechanics, physicists view the cat state as composed of two simultaneous and diametrically opposed conditions resembling classical states. To produce such a state, it is necessary to isolate the system from its surroundings.

Quantum Suicide

The experimenter sits before a firearm that deploys when a particular radioactive atom decays. In this case, the experimenter dies.

Quantum Immortality

According to the many-worlds hypothesis, the firing of a weapon occurs at different times in different parallel universes, with the result that the possibility of the experimenter's survival is a more common outcome than his death. Viewed over the totality of systems, the experimenter does not die during the experiment. The probability of his survival is never equal to zero, meaning that he invariably survives in some universe. Seen in this way, the experimenter is immortal.

The next morning, a worker from a window company arrives to take the measurements for a new window.

Around two p.m. Richard waits for the doorbell, but it doesn't ring.

At two thirty, he looks at his phone and sees that he has a new message:

I can't make it today.

He sees something else as well: Osarobo has changed his profile picture. Instead of his picture, he now has a watercolor in light blue, pink, and pale green, depicting Jesus blessing a sinner who kneels before him, the sinner's head tilted to one side to receive his absolution. Or is the man on his knees merely praying?

I can't make it today.

That evening at seven, Andreas, the Hölderlin reader, finally back from the spa, stops by for a visit. The plan had been to watch a movie together. Now they sit in the kitchen, drinking beer.

The problem is there's no way of knowing if it was him, says Richard.

So too grow the woodland oaks:/Each knows nothing of the other trees, despite their years, says Andreas by way of reply.

Do you know Schrödinger's cat?

The one locked up in purgatory?

Exactly. There's a fifty percent probability that it's dead. Do you think it was my piano player?

I can't say.

Two days ago I was sitting right here with him, just like I'm sitting with you. For the first time, we had tea together.

Andreas nods. Richard takes a sip out of his bottle, and Andreas also takes a sip.

We drank tea. I was thinking how it was the first time, and maybe he was thinking it was the last time.

Andreas nods.

Maybe, says Richard. But maybe not.

Yesterday I rode a bicycle again, Andreas says. I didn't think I'd ever do that again.

Richard nods: It's always back and forth, back and forth, and then at a certain point it's only back and never forth, but you don't know when that's going to be. Now I understand, he says, why they call it a *wave function*. And why they call death a *wave function collapse*.

Wave function collapse, Andreas says. That's practically Hölderlin.

The cat no doubt knows whether it's alive or dead.

You'd think, Andreas says.

But Schrödinger says that until you open the box, the cat is both: alive *and* dead. Does that make sense to you?

Andreas takes another sip of beer.

Richard thinks of the music box whose wooden case the burglar —whoever it was—broke open looking for money. Was he disappointed when all he saw inside was the metal plate with the turned-up prongs that, when the thing is set in motion by turning the crank, play the Duke's aria from *Rigoletto: La donna é mobile*?

Things exist independently of whether you open the box, says Richard.

Maybe, says Andreas, I mean how do you know?

Richard is looking very dissatisfied. I understand, he says, taking a sip. At the end of her life, his wife had always drunk Chantré because it was cheaper.

At the spa, says Andreas, I took walks beside the sea. There was never a wave function collapse.

Richard tries twice more to get together with Osarobo.

Once he suggests they visit the bakery where they tried to converse the first time they met. Osarobo says yes; but then Richard sits there alone over his peppermint tea, reading: Sorry, I can't make it today. The woman from behind the counter looks down at him from above and says: That'll be 2.80 euros.

In the evening he sees that Osarobo has changed his profile picture again: a painting that shows Daniel in the lions' den, with bound hands, he stands before the lions, who are afraid to attack him. *If God is for us who can be against us?*

The last time Richard tries, he writes:

If you have something to tell me I'll wait for you tomorrow at Alexanderplatz by the World Time Clock at three p.m.

Okay—see you tomorrow.

Richard takes the S-Bahn into the city and hopes that his effort will lead to something. But at 3:05 p.m., Osarobo writes:

Home now, is snowing.

Yes, it is indeed snowing. Richard stands holding his cell phone beneath the World Time Clock, a popular meeting spot among his friends when he was a teenager. Magadan, Dubai, Honolulu. What time was it in Niamey, the capital of Niger?

By the time he gets home, he's managed to pull himself together, but then he sits at his desk in front of the dark screen of his computer. The soul of Osarobo, he knows, is now flying out into the universe, flying somewhere where there are no longer any rules, where you don't have to take anyone else into consideration, but in return you are left forever, completely and irrevocably alone. But Richard remains on Earth with people like Monika and mustache-wearing

Jörg. He can already see them baring their teeth like the lions in Osarobo's profile picture: What did we tell you?

Richard weeps as he hasn't wept since his wife's death.

Or maybe it wasn't Osarobo after all?

53

The ghosts, Karon says, only come as far as the Italian coast. They don't cross over into Europe. Immediately after his arrival in Lampedusa, he had three more dreams and he hasn't had a single one since. The ghosts also demand their tribute on the crossing, he says. For this reason, it makes no sense to stop a person who loses his mind during the crossing and jumps into the water. One single time, Karon says, a miracle occurred. A man had fallen from the boat into the water, and the captain didn't want to lose time turning the boat around, but he at least turned off the motor for a minute. A few men called out the man's name, all of them looked to see whether he might still be keeping his head above water somewhere, but you couldn't see him anywhere. Then everything became quiet for a moment. The sea grew calm and looked as smooth as a mirror, and suddenly two dolphins came swimming up close together, and between them they were carrying the unconscious man and brought him back to the boat so that the other passengers could lift him up, and then the man regained consciousness. A miracle. Not long afterward, the motor suddenly stopped working. It turned out that the survivor was the only one who knew about boats and was able to repair the motor.

Otherwise all of us would have died, Karon says.

Karon suddenly appeared from nowhere in a heavy snowstorm right in front of Richard's study window, and a moment later he'd knocked on the terrace door. Now the two of them are sitting drinking hot lemon in water at the living room table.

Richard says: I almost forgot—your friend sent me a picture of your family.

Earlier the pictures of the property and the deed of sale had arrived in Richard's phone, and yesterday he received a picture of Karon's mother, his two younger brothers, and his half-grown sister. The two women are wearing brightly colored dresses, in the mother's case a dark purple one that reaches to the ground; she looks solemn and thin. The sister isn't looking at the camera—out of shame? Or pride? What a sister, Richard thinks.

What's her name? he asks, pointing at the young woman.

Salá Matú, says Karon.

Compared to the two women, Karon's brothers, standing between them, make a shabby impression. They're wearing t-shirts and pants with holes in them. The older brother's left shoulder is higher than his right, he looks misshapen. The younger boy's t-shirt says *Kalahari*, and since the Kalahari Desert is about as far away from where Karon's family lives as Barcelona is from Minsk, Richard deems it unlikely that the t-shirt made its way into Karon's brother's possession by crossing the African continent. Rather, he assumes, it must have come from some charity collection bin and taken a detour, say, by way of Hannover, Freiburg, or Berlin-Charlottenburg. Karon's mother and his three siblings are standing beneath the eaves of a cinderblock house that has two doors hanging crooked on their hinges and no windows.

Karon sits in the living room on the sofa, holding Richard's phone in his hand, and for a long, long time looks at the photo, while outside the snowflakes fall. In those globes you have to shake to produce a snowstorm, it's exactly the opposite, Richard thinks, with winter beneath the bell jar.

See that post there in the picture, says Karon, pointing at one of the posts propping up the eaves of the house. I repaired it, I still remember.

It's true, Richard sees it too—there's a spot where the post was broken and has been stabilized with a splint. It's not much of a job as repairs go, but it was completed in a time that remains the present for Karon's family and only for him has become inaccessible.

Karon points to the high threshold under the eaves: In the rainy season, there's so much water, that's why the houses are raised up. The house has three rooms, but in the rainy season only one of them is habitable, the other two don't have a roof, so they get flooded ... My father didn't manage to finish building the house before he died.

How were houses made before?

They were made of mud. But when the mud got cracks in it, snakes came in, and that's dangerous. And when you filled in the cracks with more mud, it didn't hold for long. The roofs used to be made of reeds or palm fronds, but all it took was for someone to hold a match to them and the whole house would burn down.

Why would someone do that?

You never know.

So now it's roofing tiles on top?

No, the roof is made of metal. But it's so lightweight that sometimes during the rainy season when the big storms would start, we would all stand in the living room and use ropes to hold the roof in place. All five of us had to use all our weight. When the storms started, all of us were afraid all the time. Outside, because everything was flying around. And inside, because the roof might fly off and take us with it.

54

In early February, the letters from the Foreigners Office arrive for all the men from the Oranienplatz group who haven't filed an application for asylum in Germany. Case after case has been individually reviewed and decided. It turns out—as was already clear in the fall of the previous year when the Oranienplatz camp was dismantled—that the legal responsibility for the men who landed in Italy is borne by Italy alone.

Ali from Chad, who's worked as a home health-care aide for Anne's mother, has to go.

Khalil, who doesn't know where his parents are, or even if they're still alive, has to go.

Zani, the one with the bad eye who collected articles about the massacre in his hometown, has to go.

Yussuf from Mali, the dishwasher who wants to become an engineer, has to go.

Hermes, the one with the golden shoes, has to go.

Abdusalam, the singer with the squint, has to go.

Mohamed, who for reasons of fashion lets his pants slip down below his buttocks, has to go.

Yaya, who cut through the wire for the alarm bell to end the fire drill, has to go.

And even Rufu with the new filling in his tooth.

Apollo has to go, Apollo who is at home in the deserts of Niger, in the region where France is prospecting for uranium.

Tristan has to go.

And Karon, the thin man, has to go.

Even tall Ithemba, who cooks so well. When they order him to leave his room, he slits his wrists before the eyes of the police officers and is brought to the psychiatric ward.

And even Rashid has to go. On the Monday when he receives the letter, he pours a can of gasoline over himself on Oranienplatz and tries to light himself on fire.

Where can a person go when he doesn't know where to go?

Where can a person go when he doesn't know where to go?

The church gives seven men a small apartment to share in the north of Berlin, donated by a member of the congregation. The main room is furnished with seven mattresses on the floor, and a tiny bedroom is reserved for backpacks, suitcases, and shopping bags. Since it's a ground-floor apartment, the people from the church advise the men to keep the blinds lowered so no one can see in, because you never know.

The church places fifteen men on a boat that in summer is used for pleasure cruises. In winter, it docks along the bank of the Spree River outside Treptow. A few of the men are given semi-private cabins, while the others sleep in donated bunks set up in a common room in which all of them also cook and eat. To be sure, it's difficult to heat a pleasure boat in winter.

Eleven men are permitted to occupy a makeshift shelter run by a foundation in Berlin-Mitte: there's one large room with a cooking area and table in the middle, surrounded by a ring of mattresses at its edges.

Twelve find beds in the community room of a church in Berlin-Kreuzberg.

Sixteen find beds in the community room of a church in Berlin-Adlershof, but only until March at the latest.

Fourteen are taken in by ministers and congregation members in their own homes, and on the internet, the ministers and congregation members are reviled as *lowlifes* and *smugglers*.

Twenty-seven are taken in by African friends legally residing in Berlin.

One man is permitted to spend the night on the floor of a Nigerian restaurant in Berlin-Neukölln.

One sleeps on the sofa of an insurance agent.

One is given temporary quarters in an apartment share, sleeping in the room of a student who's spending half a semester in Cambridge.

One is staying in the apartment of a theater director who's touring abroad.

*

Various people when asked to help say: We keep hearing that these men are completely traumatized. How do we know they won't trash our apartment?

They say: Even if we help them, the problem still won't be solved.

They say: If we take them in, we won't be doing them any favors since there are so many Nazis in the neighborhood.

And also: Even if we let them sleep here, what will they live on?

Say: We could help out if it were just for a short period of time, but it doesn't look as if things will be getting better any time soon.

They say: One person could possibly stay here, but is that even worth it? There are so many of them.

The Berliners as a whole, represented by the Minister of the Interior, say what they said two years ago when the men first came to Germany from Italy to live in tents on Oranienplatz. They repeat what they said half a year ago when the men dissolved the camp: What's the point of having a law like Dublin II to determine jurisdiction if we don't abide by it? They say, we're allowed to invoke section 23 at our discretion, but since we have the choice whether or not to do so, we choose not to.

Only twelve exceptions are made out of the total 476 cases, including three of Richard's friends:

Tristan is issued a medical certificate by his psychologist and granted a six-month exceptional stay, which entitles him to a placement in a residence. Places in residences are difficult to come by, so he has to consider himself fortunate when they find a bed for him in a homeless shelter in Berlin-Lichtenberg, a former school, where he's the only dark-skinned resident and has to share a room with two German alcoholics and a bathroom with thirty others. It's not easy, he says, it's not easy. The room for three has three beds, one table, one cupboard, one TV. Richard sees two-thirds of the table belongs to Tristan's two roommates: it's crammed with food scraps, crumbs, and bottles. The third of the table that is Tristan's territory is empty and wiped clean. He's my buddy, one of the roommates says, pounding Tristan on the shoulder. Yes, yes, says Tristan, he's my friend. It's only difficult at night, he says. There's a lot of shouting, and people argue and even fight. On his way out, Richard sees a basket filled with *Berliner Pfannkuchen* beside the porter's lodge. Someone wants the homeless to have a good time when carnival arrives. But Tristan doesn't know what a *Berliner Pfannkuchen* is. So much sugar! he says, pointing to the glaze atop the donuts....Take care, he says to Richard, his customary words of parting, and returns to the shelter space allocated to him because of the serious trauma he's suffered, space he shares with the desperate, the addicted, the insane and extremely poor.

Tall Ithemba, whom Richard accompanied to the lawyer's office, spends several days in a psychiatric ward, where he keeps saying they should bring him back to Africa right away. On the basis of the medical certificate issued by his psychiatrist, he is issued a four-week exceptional stay that possibly—they can't promise in advance—can be renewed another few times. He is assigned a bed on the pleasure boat. No good people, he says, speaking of the people with whom he is forced to share quarters there. And the toilet doesn't work right, he says. It stinks.

Rashid the thunderbolt-hurler is granted a six-month exceptional stay because of his heart condition and general psychological state. He is assigned a room in a Workers' Welfare Association dormitory.

Meanwhile, Sylvia and Detlef help Richard push the large round table in the library to the edge of the room. Four men can sleep here now on the burgundy-colored Persian rug. In the music room, one man can sleep under the piano, and another to the side of it: that's two more spots. (Richard found two air mattresses in the shed, and

for the other men he's piled several layers of blankets on the floor.)
Two men can fit at right angles to each other on the living room
sofa, one more on two upholstered chairs pushed together. Richard has Apollo and Ithemba help him carry his wife's half of the
bed from the bedroom to the guest room, which now sleeps three.

Detlef and Sylvia say that the guest house in their garden has a
small wood stove, so if the men don't mind having to keep the fire
going ... The three pool players don't mind in the least.

Detlef's ex-wife, the one with the tea shop in Potsdam, says:
The shop isn't open at night, so it doesn't matter to me if there's
someone sleeping in the back room. He just can't go in and out all
the time during the day. Her husband says: But then you risk losing
your business. There was a time, Detlef's ex-wife says, when you
could get the death sentence for hiding people. You have a point
there, her husband says. So Hermes of the golden shoes moves into
the tea shop in Potsdam.

It makes perfect sense that Ali should move in with Anne: He
feels at home with us, she says. And if he wants to bring his friend
Yussuf with him, that's not such a big deal.

Even the Hölderlin reader offers: I don't have any extra space in
my room, but it'd be fine for someone to come by during the day
to use my computer.

Thomas, the professor of economics, says: Three can move into
our studio apartment in Prenzlauer Berg, we almost never use it.
I'll tell my wife later.

The archaeologist has been in Egypt as a guest professor since
February and will stay until May. He tells Richard: Ask the neighbors for the key.

Marie, Peter's twenty-year-old girlfriend, says: Hey, I bet it
would be fun to have one of them sleeping on the kitchen sofa.

But somehow no one thinks of asking Monika and mustached
Jörg.

In this way, 147 of the 476 men now have a place to sleep.

Richard doesn't know what has become of the 329 others.

The church pays the men in their shelters five euros a day from donations, but it isn't enough to, say, travel to Italy when your *permesso* runs out. If Richard wanted to give each of the men living in his apartment five euros a day, it would add up to 1800 euros per month.

One of the men is hired to clean a friend's apartment, another can paint a wall or two at a construction site. The third can dig out the driveway of an elderly neighbor when it snows, and the fourth can chop wood. But most of the time when Richard asks, what he hears is: Off the books? Unfortunately that doesn't work for us. When Richard, Andreas, and Detlef's ex start organizing weekly film screenings followed by an African meal at the tea shop in Potsdam— the idea being to collect donations—many of the people who come to watch a film, eat a meal, and drink cola, beer, or wine often donate no more than five euros. That means that fifteen visitors add up to seventy-five euros. Subtracting the cost of the beverages and rice, couscous, vegetables, beef, and lamb, there's often no more than ten or fifteen euros left over for Ithemba and his sous-chef.

Finally, Thomas, the economics professor, helps Richard open a bank account for donations. The thing is, he says, that the Money-Laundering Law can be a problem if you can't prove where the money is going. Yes I realize, Richard says. Richard starts telling certain people: I've opened a bank account for donations, and most respond: Aha, interesting. Some ask: Can you give me a receipt for my taxes? Most people aren't willing to donate if they can't take it off their taxes, but there are exceptions, and the money that trickles in is better than nothing.

The only thing the Berlin Senate will still pay for in the case of the men who now aren't supposed to be here at all is the German classes.

Barely five months have passed since they first started lessons back when they were still living in the nursing home:

Gehen, ging, gegangen.

Four months ago they moved to Spandau and missed a number of classes when the individual interviews were being held, and then they had to start over again from the beginning: *gehen, ging, gegangen.*

When their friends went up on the roof approximately a month ago, they stood around the fire barrel with its view of the roof instead of going to German class, and after that, since they'd forgotten almost everything, they had to start over again from the beginning: *gehen, ging, gegangen.*

Now only a few of them make their way from their various mattress barracks to the language school twice a week to go on learning: *gehen, ging, gegangen.*

Rufu, the Dante reader, sits at Richard's Biedermeier desk in front of his open notebook and says: *Ich gehen.*

Looking over his shoulder, Richard corrects him: No, it's *ich gehe.*

Rufu: *Ich gehen.*

No, *ich gehe*!

I want to smash all the German verbs, Rufu says.

Smash is a really beautiful verb, Richard replies.

Richard has now made a bed for Rufu in the library and also one for Abdusalam the singer, who was on the very first list and now is happy to move from the Nigerian restaurant to Richard's house. Also Yaya—who can sleep here without worrying about an alarm going off—and his friend Moussa with the blue tattoo on his face.

Khalil (who still doesn't know if his parents are still alive), his friend Mohamed (who likes to wear his pants down low), and tall Ithemba, whom Richard summoned from the foul-smelling boat with instructions to cook for everyone, are living in the guest room.

Apollo and Karon sleep in the music room. The sofa in the living room is now the sleeping place of Zair, who was on the same boat as Rashid and put on his best shirt in honor of moving to Richard's house; and as for Tristan (Awad)—after something like twenty-five phone calls to the Social Welfare Office, Richard succeeded in having his house recognized as a home shelter, and so Tristan is allowed to leave the homeless shelter and move in. Finally, the two upholstered chairs pushed together are now the bed of Zani, who often flips through his folder of photocopied articles about the massacre in his hometown.

When there are no odd jobs or meetings to attend, the Africans sleep late, and even during the day when they're awake, they often lie on their mattresses dozing, playing with their phones, or watching internet videos on the two old computers Richard has given them. Sometimes they pray, sometimes they go into town to meet their friends. When someone asks Ithemba how he's doing, he says: a little bit good. Once, Khalil and Mohamed take Richard to a club where sixty-year-old women in hot pants dance with twenty-year-old black men. One time Karon takes Richard to a funeral ceremony for a Berliner of Ghanaian descent. As a refugee and non-family member, Karon has to sit in the last row.

It's possible, he says, that the people who grow up here soon won't remember what culture is.

Culture? Richard asks.

Good behavior.

And otherwise? In the evening, everyone reassembles in Richard's kitchen when the meal Ithemba has cooked is on the table. He gratefully accepted Richard's offer of food money, saying he can manage the shopping on fifty euros a week. At first Richard was always given a separate plate, knife, and fork, while the others stood around the kitchen table eating together from a baking sheet. Now he eats as they do, tearing off a piece of the cooked rice-flour or yam dough Ithemba has heaped on the baking sheet and dunking it in the "soup," a thin stew made with vegetables and sometimes with meat, sometimes with fish. It tastes not terribly different from his mother's goulash, maybe better. If there's some soup left over at the end, you can always scoop up the last bit with your hand. Has he ever eaten soup with his hands before?

After the meal, Abdusalam sometimes goes out on the chilly terrace with a few of the others and starts to sing. The Brandenburg night then resounds with a song of the emigrants in foreign lands called "Aburokiye Abrabo," and it goes like this:

> *Mother, oh Mother, your son*
> *has made a terrible journey.*
> *I am stranded on foreign shores.*
> *Darkness surrounds me.*
> *No one knows what I must endure in my loneliness.*
>
> *A mission without success brings disgrace.*
> *How can I ever return?*
> *When you fail, no child will be named for you.*
> *Then it is better to die*
> *than to feel this shame forever.*
>
> *Ghosts of our ancestors,*
> *gods of our ancestors,*
> *watch over our brothers in foreign lands.*
> *Grant them a safe journey home.*
> *All who live in Europe understand their laments.*

55

Now the first warmer days arrive, and it's time to burn the branches left behind by fall and winter storms. Richard hasn't celebrated his birthday since his wife's death. But today he buys veal and lamb sausages at the African supermarket in Wedding and makes the potato salad himself, now that he's learned how best to slice the onions. Ithemba's in the kitchen too, along with Tristan and Yaya; the others went shopping the day before for couscous, flatbread, and a large sack of rice. Rashid is invited, of course, as is Andreas, the Hölderlin reader, Thomas, the economics expert, and Marie, the girlfriend of Peter, who himself is unfortunately still in Cairo. Naturally, Detlef's ex-wife Marion is invited, along with Hermes, Anne along with Ali and Yussuf, and Detlef and Sylvia with their three pool players. (Might any of the men have the Ethiopian language teacher's phone number? Richard is too embarrassed to ask.) Osarobo suddenly wrote out of the blue a few days ago: *Hi! How are you?* and his profile picture is now a kitchen table with four empty chairs. Might he be intending to leave for Italy without Richard's being able to clear up with him what really happened? *Fine—how are you?* he writes back right away, but the only answer he receives is: *I am good.*

Won't some disappearances leave no trace?

Only now does it occur to Richard that his view of the lake has become inextricably linked to his memory of the fact that a man drowned in it last summer. The lake will forever remain the lake in which someone has died, but it will nonetheless remain forever very beautiful: a lake with fog above it in the mornings, in whose waters a pair of ducks with a few ducklings behind them carve a path each spring, a lake in which fresh reeds crowd out the previous year's brown stalks year after year, on whose banks dragonflies hatch, on whose sandy bottom lie shells, a lake full of seaweed between which fish promenade as though the vegetation were framing a woodland path; it's a lake that gleams in the sun and looks black when it storms, and winter after winter it freezes, sometimes with snow on it, as white as a sheet of paper. Maybe Richard will swim here again next summer—but in any case, as in each of the last twenty years—he will sit on the bank and feel happy to be looking at the water. Rashid said to Richard in one of their conversations that not even his memories of his wonderful life with his family could console him, since these memories were bound up with the pain of his loss and that's all there was. Rashid said he wished he could cut off his memory. Cut it away. Cut. A life in which an empty present is occupied by a memory that one cannot endure, in which the future refuses to show itself, must be extremely taxing, Richard thinks, since this is a life without a shoreline, as it were.

Richard covers the potato salad with plastic wrap and brings it outside.

There's still a lot to do before the guests arrive: Moussa mows the lawn, Mohamed and Khalil rake the leaves, Karon sweeps the terrace, Rufu and Abdusalam together place the heavy bench on the dock, Richard retrieves the garden furniture from the shed with Apollo while the potato salad is cooling, the spiderwebs and dry leaves from the previous summer have to be swept from the tables and benches, their covers shaken out and folded. Richard finds some torches at the back of the shed that he now sticks in the ground, he bought them on a shopping trip with his wife and never had occasion to use them after her death. He turns the water in the garden back on for the first time this year, in case the campfire has to be extinguished in a hurry, where does the hose get screwed in again? And the little rolling frame for the hose is missing a screw, the metal brush for the grill has to be cleaned of rust; dishes, flatware and garbage bags have to be carried down to the fire pit. They'll chill the beverages in the lake, which has only been entirely free of ice for a few days now. Are there enough napkins? Ketchup and candles? Bread, chips, pretzel sticks, and fruit? Karon runs down to sweep the dock. Richard pours alcohol in some lamps and places them on the table just as the first guests are walking across the garden.

And now the coals are lit and the grill "fired up," as they say out in the suburbs, and yes, Richard says to one or the other of the arrivals, the meat is *halal*, because he's meanwhile learned: *Forbidden unto you are carrion and blood and swine flesh, and the strangled, and the dead through beating, and the dead through falling from a height, and that which hath been killed by the goring of horns, and the devoured of wild beasts.*

There is eating and drinking, napkins and glasses are distributed, two are playing badminton, a few are playing bocce, here there's a conversation about how none of the African men drink alcohol, here one about the fear of swimming, and over there one about what exactly is celebrated on Easter and what on Pentecost. When twilight arrives and Richard lights the lamps, Rashid exclaims: Like in Africa! He picks up a lantern and starts waving it around enthusiastically. Time for a group photo! cries Anne, the photographer. Before it gets dark! And now Rashid crouches down with the lantern in his hand before the large yew trees, and all the others form a semicircle around him, the thunderbolt-hurler holds in his hand the ship's lantern from the German home-improvement store, lighting up the black and white faces all around him, feeling just as much at home as in distant Kaduna in Nigeria. Only now, when Richard turns around for a moment to inspect the arrangement for the group photo, does he notice that Sylvia isn't standing next to Detlef. Where is she? Only now does he realize that he hasn't seen her at the party at all. And Detlef? Richard sees that Detlef can't manage a smile even for the photograph.

After the picture, they all sit down again before the fire, which has already burned down almost all the way. One says: it's getting nippy after all, another: I'll lend you my jacket, a third: any wine left? A fourth: I'll put a bit more wood on. After the group photo, Richard sits down next to Detlef and quietly asks amid the general background murmur: What's happening with Sylvia? Detlef watches someone put more wood on the fire and pushes a log into the embers; he doesn't respond until the flames blaze up again. She went in for her exam today. And? They kept her there, he says, it doesn't look good. And even though he says these words in a very low voice and in German, everyone instantly falls silent, as if it's obvious to all that one of the most difficult sentences in the life of a human being has just been uttered.

For God's sake, Richard says.
  What's going on? asks Rashid.
  His wife is very ill, says Richard.
  I'm very sorry for you, Rashid says to Detlef.
  Thank you, says Detlef, poking around in the fire.

One man now thinks about how his wife always kissed him on his eyes.
  One thinks how well the woman he loves always fit in his embrace.
  One man thinks about her running her hand through his hair, and another how good her breath smelled when her face was beside his.
  One thinks how his wife stuck her tongue in his ear.
  Another how his woman's body gleamed when she lay down beside him.
  One man thinks about how her lips felt.
  Another how she looked when she was asleep.
  One man thinks about her clinging to his hand, and another about how his wife smiled sometimes.
  All of them think for a moment about women they have loved, who once loved them.

From Italy I called the woman I wasn't allowed to marry in Ghana two more times, Karon says, but then I threw her number away.

I would so love to have a child again before I have to die, says Rashid.

Once, Tristan says, I met a woman on the subway. We made a date and went for a walk and talked. We made a second date, went for a walk and talked. On the third date she asked me if I wanted to sleep with her. I told her: not yet, maybe later. My mind wasn't there. She didn't come to our next date. It's not easy, says Tristan. Not easy.

When things get serious, Khalil says, we have no chance here. I've seen it with my friends. The girlfriends always break up with them sooner or later. Their parents are against it. Or else there's a German boyfriend after all.

Ithemba says: Yes, it's true. Nobody loves a refugee.

No one? asks Peter's girlfriend Marie. I don't believe it.

It's true. Nobody loves a refugee.

Detlef sits bent over, a wineglass in his hand, and listens to everybody else talking about love.

Apollo says: I have a girlfriend. But I wouldn't marry her.

Marion asks: Why not?

If I married a German woman now, she'd think I was marrying her only to get papers.

You would really refuse to marry a woman you love and who loves you because it might look as if you were doing it to get papers?

Yes, Apollo says.

At borders, things sometimes turn into their own opposites, Richard remembers, thinking of his first impressions when he visited Oranienplatz. Neediness displaces and distorts even what little might be simple. For the refugees, preserving their dignity is an arduous task that is demanded of them every day, pursuing them even when they lie in bed.

Even if you did do it to get papers, would that be so terrible? asks Richard.

He can still hear the lawyer saying: A German child! A German child is the one thing that really helps.

Look, Apollo says, there has to be some order. First I have to have work, then an apartment, then I can get married and after that have children.

Besides, Tristan says, a woman can get pregnant by anyone, and even if the man is worthless, the child still stays with her. If you're a man, you have to find a good woman, someone to stay with when she has your child. But where do I find a good woman?

Maybe if you go dancing, Richard says half-heartedly, thinking of his outing to the bar with the sixty-year-olds in shorts.

I won't go to a bar, says Tristan.

Never?

Never.

Rashid, who fell asleep for a moment, perks up again and says: In Nigeria the mothers pick out wives for their sons. A mother knows how to recognize a good wife. But here? I don't even know how to start talking to a woman. I'll never do that.

Do you still think about Christel a lot? says Detlef out of the blue, addressing his friend Richard five years after his wife's death. They've never spoken about anything like this before.

Of course, says Richard.

And what exactly do you think about?

The way she stood when she was smoking. The way she put her hair up with a clip when it was hot. I think about her feet.

Do you miss her?

Sometimes I used to think I might not miss her at all if she were gone.

Richard tries to remember the time when he thought it might be possible not to miss Christel.

As you know, we often got into arguments in the evening, pointless ones.

Why did you argue?

She was a drinker. The alcohol always made her a completely different person, especially late in the day.

But why did she drink? Ithemba now asks.

Probably, I suppose ... well, probably because she was unhappy.

And why was she unhappy? asks Ithemba.

The orchestra she played in was disbanded, says Thomas and takes a drag on his cigarette.

And Richard had a mistress, says Anne.

She wanted to have children, says Marion.

She said that to you? asks Richard.

Yes, says Marion.

But you told me that you and she decided that together, didn't you? asks Zair, apparently still remembering the conversation they had so many months ago in Spandau.

She got pregnant once, says Richard, but it was too soon for me. I hadn't even finished my studies. I talked her into getting rid of the child.

I see, Zair says.

I didn't want it just then.

I understand.

But in those days it wasn't legal yet. She went to see this woman, who did it right on her kitchen table. I waited in the courtyard downstairs.

Richard still has clear memories of the back courtyard where he'd waited. Eighty-five degrees, the hot shade in which he stood beside large garbage containers made of metal, with covers bent out of shape.

When she came out, she nearly collapsed, I had to hold her up, and all at once she was so heavy. It took a long time to reach the S-Bahn station. And only after we were sitting in the S-Bahn did I see the blood dripping down her legs. I felt ashamed of her. I had to take care of her, but I found it terribly embarrassing.

Richard shakes his head as if even he can hardly believe what he's saying.

Why were you ashamed of your wife? asks Ali.

I think actually I was afraid.

What were you afraid of?

That she might die, says Richard. Yes, he says, at that moment I hated her because she might die.

I can understand that, says Detlef.

I think that's when I realized, says Richard, that the things I can endure are only just the surface of what I can't possibly endure.

Like the surface of the sea? asks Khalil.

Actually, yes, exactly like the surface of the sea.

ACKNOWLEDGMENTS

I am deeply grateful for many good conversations with
  Hassan Abubakar
  Hassan Adam
  Stephen Amakwa
  Malu Austen
  Ibrahim Idrissu Babangida
  Saleh Bacha
  Yaya Fatty
  Udu Haruna
  Nasir Khalid
  Adam Koné
  Sani Ashiru Mohammed
  Fatao Awudu Yaya
  Bashir Zaccharya

I would like to express my heartfelt thanks for various forms of support, assistance, and cooperation to Katharina Behling, Ingrid Anna Kade, Cornelia Laufer, Malve Lippmann and Can Sungu, Marion Victor, and Wolfgang Wengenroth.

For giving me time and space to write, I owe great thanks to Professor Paul Michael Lützeler, as well as to Kerstin, Nils, and Pascal Helbig.

For insights, consultations, and information, I would like to thank Akinda, Taina Gärtner, Liya Siltan-Grüner, Hans Georg Odenthal, and Bernward Ostrop.

For their practical assistance, I thank Viola Förster v. d. Lühe, Frauke Gutberlet-König, Bedriye and Felix Hansen, Miriam Kaiser, Dr. Eva Krause, Sandra Missal, Dr. Riesenberg, Rainer Sbrzesny, Tabea Schmelzer, Jule Seidel, René Thiedtke, and Rui Wigand.

For advice and inspiration I thank my father John Erpenbeck.

And for always supporting and encouraging me to write this book with his curiosity, critiques, openness, and his own actions, I thank my husband and first reader Wolfgang Bozic.

This book has been selected to receive financial assistance from English PEN's Writers in Translation programme supported by Bloomberg and Arts Council England. English PEN exists to promote literature and its understanding, uphold writers' freedoms around the world, campaign against the persecution and imprisonment of writers for stating their views, and promote the friendly co-operation of writers and free exchange of ideas.

Each year, a dedicated committee of professionals selects books that are translated into English from a wide variety of foreign languages. We award grants to UK publishers to help translate, promote, market and champion these titles. Our aim is to celebrate books of outstanding literary quality, which have a clear link to the PEN charter and promote free speech and intercultural understanding.

In 2011, Writers in Translation's outstanding work and contribution to diversity in the UK literary scene was recognised by Arts Council England. English PEN was awarded a threefold increase in funding to develop its support for world writing in translation.

www.englishpen.org

Keep in touch with
Portobello Books:

Visit portobellobooks.com to discover more.

Portobello
Books

THE OLD CHILD

and

THE BOOK OF WORDS

Jenny Erpenbeck

Translated by Susan Bernofsky

'Eerily brilliant' *Independent*

A child is found standing on the street, with an empty bucket in her hand, and no memory of her name, her family or her past. Elsewhere, a girl grows up surrounded by familiar faces – a wet nurse, a piano teacher, gardener, a best friend and a distant mother – but soon finds them slipping mysteriously from her life. In the company of these girls, we are compelled to tread the uncertain terrain of memory, where words are dropped like clues to reveal what has been hidden, forgotten or erased.

'With the detached spare prose and mysterious internal logic of a fairy tale, the writing has a dark, transformative power . . . it gets into the bloodstream and refuses to leave. Beguiling and original' *The Times*

'Erpenbeck excels as a miniaturist, examining the psychology of her blank-eyed outsider with language as sharp as a scalpel' *Guardian*

'Intense and beautifully written' *Time Out*

'A haunting, offbeat novella of real possibility' Lionel Shriver

'I haven't read anything this good – this bracing, unflinching and alive – for a long time' Nicole Krauss

Also available from Portobello Books
www.portobellobooks.com

VISITATION

Jenny Erpenbeck

Translated by Susan Bernofsky

Also available from Portobello Books
www.portobellobooks.com

THE END OF DAYS

Jenny Erpenbeck

Translated by Susan Bernofsky

'Hypnotically involving' *Independent*

'Exhilarating' *Guardian*

'Concise and moving' *Daily Telegraph*

WINNER OF THE INDEPENDENT FOREIGN FICTION PRIZE

A dazzling story of the last century told through the various lives of one woman: an intoxicating masterpiece that pulls apart the threads of destiny and allows us to see the present and the past anew.

'*The End of Days* prises open the troubled box that is 20th-century European history and entrenches Erpenbeck's position as the most brilliant European writer of my generation' Neel Mukherjee, 'Book of the Year', *Irish Times*

'So powerful and so poetic . . . Erpenbeck has important things to tell us; and she tells them beautifully. Masterful' *Independent on Sunday*

'Startling and profound' 'Books of the Year', *Guardian*

'Astonishing and deeply humane' BBC Radio 4, *Saturday Review*

SELECTED AS A BOOK OF THE YEAR IN THE GUARDIAN, IRISH TIMES, INDEPENDENT AND DAILY TELEGRAPH